‘

KC cried.

"I think you and I should have a little talk," Pierce said, yanking the door from her grasp and shutting it firmly behind him.

"Apparently being sheriff has gone to your head," she snapped. "For your information, forced entry is as illegal for you as it is for anyone else."

"This has nothing to do with my job," Pierce said gruffly. "This has to do with us. There's chemistry between us, honey. And I think it's time we acknowledged that."

He brought her forward and molded her against him.

"Don't be ridiculous," she whispered. "Let me go."

"You're not fighting very hard."

A flame ignited in Pierce's eyes. His mouth came down, not too roughly, not too gently. He possessed her lips, claiming them. He gathered her in a more intimate embrace, holding her closer. Her mouth opened beneath his; her tongue met and mated with his. A need for air interrupted the kiss briefly.

Then, wildly, their lips united again . . . and again. . . .

Dear Reader:

Welcome to Silhouette! What better way to celebrate St. Valentine's Day and all the romance that goes with it than to indulge yourself with a Silhouette Desire?

If this is your first Desire, let me extend an invitation for you to sit back, kick off your shoes and enjoy. If you are a regular reader, you already know what awaits you.

A Silhouette Desire can encompass many varying moods and tones. The books can be deeply emotional and dramatic, or charming and lighthearted. But no matter what, each and every one is a sensual, compelling love story written by and for today's women.

I know you'll enjoy February's *Man of the Month*, *A Loving Spirit* by Annette Broadrick. But I think *all* of the February books are terrific. Give in to Desire . . . you'll be glad you did!

All the best,

Lucia Macro
Senior Editor

JACKIE MERRITT

HEARTBREAK HOTEL

SILHOUETTE *Desire*

Published by Silhouette Books New York

America's Publisher of Contemporary Romance

SILHOUETTE BOOKS
300 East 42nd St., New York, N.Y. 10017

ISBN: 0-373-05551-X

First Silhouette Books printing February 1990

Printed in the U.S.A.

Books by Jackie Merritt

Silhouette Desire

Big Sky Country #466
Heartbreak Hotel #551

JACKIE MERRITT

and her husband live in Nevada. An accountant for many years, Jackie has happily traded numbers for words. Next to family, books are her greatest joy, both for reading and writing.

One

The road was one sharp curve after another, following the configuration of the aptly named Snake River. A steep embankment on KC Logan's right, the river on her left and a narrow two-lane bit of asphalt kept her tense and clutching the steering wheel of her compact red sedan, especially when she drew near to yet another huge diesel truck loaded with logs. She was in western Montana, traveling an unfamiliar and sometimes frightening highway, making her way to a town she hadn't even known existed a month ago.

Almost a month had passed since her grandfather, Dallas Logan, had called from Harmony, Montana, with his big news, and KC was still flabbergasted over the elderly man's eccentric behavior. The Logans had always lived in San Francisco, and Dallas had taken a senior citizens' bus tour of the northwestern states in June. KC had expected him to return at the end of July, but she'd received a long-distance call just before the Fourth of July holiday.

"I won't be coming back, KC. I bought a saloon and eight-unit motel here in Harmony, Montana, honey."

"You what?"

Dallas had gone on to explain, and KC had been aghast to learn that her seventy-two-year-old grandfather had plunked down most of his life savings for a business with which he had absolutely no experience. A saloon . . . and an eight-unit motel. KC had cringed every time she'd thought of it, then had stewed over the only conclusion she could reach: someone had taken advantage of Dallas Logan. The elderly man had no doubt been an easy mark. He'd been unhappy and lost since KC's grandmother passed away, which had been the main reason KC had urged the bus tour on Dallas. She'd thought a change of scene would do him good, but she had certainly never dreamed he wouldn't return to San Francisco.

KC had been contemplating a change of scene herself. But she'd been thinking along the lines of a new job rather than anything so drastic as leaving San Francisco. She'd been discontent with her position as assistant to a pompous advertising executive for some time, and had even made a few discreet inquiries about possible openings within the advertising community. Dallas's news had brought everything to a head, however, and after worrying for a week, KC had decided she could do nothing else until she rescued her grandfather.

After giving two-weeks notice to her employer, KC packed her car and headed north. For her own peace of mind she had to see Harmony, Montana and the business Dallas had become enmeshed in with her own eyes. She left San Francisco with definite goals: to get her grandfather's money back, if that was possible, and to bring him home where he belonged.

KC's worries never stopped during the three-day trip. Dallas Logan had arthritis in his shoulders, a sensitive stomach and was sometimes laid up for days with a migraine headache. Other than a daily walk, Dallas had been doing very little, and he'd complained incessantly about his aches and pains. KC couldn't even imagine him running a business when a four- or five-block walk had been bothering him. Also, on top of her concern for her grandfather's physical well-being, she actually wondered if his normal good sense had deserted him. Perhaps that worry was what had really prompted her trip, KC unhappily mused again as she followed the winding highway on the last leg of the journey.

Ahead, placed just before another abrupt curve in the road, KC spotted a sign: Welcome to Harmony, Montana. Population 2,216.

"Good," she said with a sigh, very glad to finally be there. KC had never made such an extensive car trip by herself, and while she'd seen some breathtaking scenery, she'd had a few harrowing experiences—a flat tire in Oregon, a wrong turn in Idaho.

But she'd made it. And she wasn't sorry she'd driven her own car, even if everything hadn't gone as smoothly as she would have preferred. Now the minute she got Dallas to see reason, they could leave. It also made good sense to have transportation in Harmony, and with the town such a complete unknown, KC hadn't had the slightest idea if there was a car-rental agency in the area.

She could have asked Dallas, of course. But she hadn't told him she was coming. After debating the issue, KC had decided it would be best to just arrive, to take her grandfather by surprise so she could see things as they really were.

Rounding the final curve before town, KC got her first look at Harmony. It was tucked into the same narrow canyon she'd been traveling through for some miles, with buildings on both sides of the river and creeping up the rugged, densely treed mountainsides. The same road she was on appeared to be the main street of the town and contained the usual mixture of businesses: gas stations, a drugstore, a grocery store, several restaurants and taverns, a rather impressive brick bank building and numerous other small enterprises.

KC drove slowly as she watched for the Harmony Saloon and Motel, her grandfather's recent purchase. Logging trucks, both loaded and unloaded, were amassed around a truck stop; dozens of pickups and a smattering of cars lined the street; and it surprised KC that the little town appeared quite active. She'd had a vague expectation of sluggishness in Harmony, but it was apparent that the town relied heavily on the area's timber industry and was anything but sleepy.

The possible prosperity of the town was neither here nor there, though, KC decided. It was her grandfather she was worried about, not whether the business he'd bought had the possibility of making a profit.

Peering through the windshield, KC kept watching for the Harmony Saloon and Motel. She had driven clear through the business district and was approaching the opposite end of town, and still she'd seen no sign of the place. Frowning, KC proceeded at an even slower speed, and at a pullout just beyond the last house she could see, she stopped the car.

Craning her neck, she looked out the car's rear window back to the town, wondering if she'd missed the motel's sign. Strange little worries flitted through her mind, worries about her grandfather. Was he even really in Harmony? Had the whole preposterous story of buying a saloon and motel been a figment of a failing mind? Her heart sinking, KC opened the door and got out. With one hand shading her eyes, she carefully scanned the signs behind her on both sides of the road.

She noticed a brown car slowing down, but she didn't see the sheriff's insignia on its door until it made a U-turn and pulled up in front of her car. She had turned around by then, glad of a chance to ask directions. A tall, dark-haired man in jeans and a tan shirt got out and called, "Having trouble, ma'am?"

"Thanks for stopping," KC called back. Oddly, despite the fact that her thoughts were so taken up by Dallas, she was immediately struck by a surprising awareness. The sheriff was wearing dark aviator sunglasses, so KC couldn't see his eyes very well. But she didn't need to clearly see the man's eyes to realize that he was a striking example of rugged good looks. His shoulders filled the tan shirt, his denim-clad legs were long and sinewy, his nearly black hair was thick and just barely controlled, and his mouth was a notable mixture of sensuality and strength, pleasingly tempered by a hint of humor.

"What's the problem?"

KC offered a faint, tentative smile, somewhat taken aback by the attractiveness of the lawman. "I'm looking for my grandfather. And the Harmony Saloon and Motel."

"You must be talking about Dallas Logan."

Relief flooded KC to the point of weakening her knees. One worry had been laid to rest—Dallas was at least known in Harmony. At once she breathed more freely. "Yes. I'm KC Logan."

"Pierce Wheeler."

"Nice meeting you, Mr. Wheeler."

"Just get into town?" From behind his sunglasses Pierce was studying KC Logan. Dallas had mentioned his only living relative, a granddaughter with the nickname of KC, a much smaller mouthful than Katherine Carol. But even Dallas's description— "prettiest little gal you ever saw"— hadn't prepared the sheriff for the woman in front of him. She was slightly built and exceptionally pretty, with smooth, shoulder-length hair the color of taffy and wide green eyes. An oversize, off-white T-shirt shrouded her top half, except for her well-shaped breasts, and matching off-white shorts revealed tanned, extremely attractive legs. From the open toes of her brown leather sandals peeked peach-polished toenails that coordinated with the peach paint on her fingernails, Pierce noted in a once-over that was traveling upward again, and he privately acknowledged that KC Logan was one neatly packaged, well-put-together young woman.

"Not more than five minutes ago," KC replied, and attempting to disregard the persistent and thorough scrutiny she was still getting, she glanced back down the road toward town. "I must have missed the Harmony Saloon and Motel."

Pierce stopped staring and shook his head. "You haven't come to it yet. It's about a half mile ahead of you."

KC raised an eyebrow. "Out of town?"

"Just on the edge of town. Around that curve." Pierce jerked his thumb in the direction KC's car was pointed. "There are two more houses, then the motel. You can't miss it."

KC nodded appreciatively and dared a peek into the dark sunglasses. "Apparently you know my grandfather."

"Sure do. He's a great old guy."

"Yes, he is." KC finally smiled freely at the handsome sheriff. He rated at least one genuine smile for his helpfulness, she felt. "Well, thank you for the information." She began to sidle toward her car.

Pierce followed, too interested in Harmony's latest addition to let her go without some kind of personal note. Her smile had been surprisingly sweet, lighting up her face with an appealing little-girl quality and diminishing the almost stern expression of capable independence she was wearing again. "How long are you in town for?"

KC shrugged offhandedly, although she had caught on that the sheriff wanted to prolong this accidental meeting. "I don't have the slightest idea. It depends on . . . well, several things." KC's thoughts surpassed the reticent comment: the length of her stay depended precisely on how quickly she could light a fire under her grandfather.

Pierce acknowledged KC's vague answer with a nod and a glance at his watch. It was almost noon and he had no pressing business. KC Logan was much too interesting to turn loose without a little more conversation. "Tell you what. I can eat lunch at the saloon as well as anywhere else. Just follow me."

KC's eyes widened. With the saloon and motel just around the next curve in the road, it was certain she didn't need a guide to get there. But Sheriff Pierce Wheeler looked rather determined. So, after only a brief hesitation, she gave in gracefully. "All right. Thank you."

"My pleasure," Pierce returned with a warm smile that gave KC a funny little sinking sensation in her midsection. The last thing she wanted in Harmony, Montana, was a personal involvement. It would suit her purpose to a T if Dallas would agree to leave Montana tomorrow morning. By quitting her job, she'd cut her most significant tie with San Francisco, but it was only a temporary measure, and getting back and finding a new position was of high priority.

Relaying her cautious feelings with a restrained nod of her head, KC turned and went back to her car. The short drive behind the official vehicle gave her a few minutes to think, and she knew she hadn't been overly friendly with her first acquaintance in Harmony. But the sheriff's detailed visual inspection left no room to doubt his immediate personal interest, and there was no point in encouraging the man, she reasoned. Hopefully, she and Dallas would be gone before Pierce Wheeler could blink twice anyway.

KC spotted the two houses the sheriff had mentioned, then saw a large sign ahead. Harmony Saloon and Motel shone in tall yellow letters on a black background, and below that eye-catcher KC read Hot Dogs, Ice Cream, Clean Motel Units. The sign was bright and new-looking, but the rest of the place?

"Oh, Lord," KC mumbled, deeply and instantly shaken. The buildings had once been barn-red, but the paint had faded and cracked and the rough lumber siding showed through the drab remnants of the ancient color. The windows and doors all sagged, and the parking area was dirt covered by a thin layer of gravel.

Stunned, realizing she hadn't expected anything quite this bad, KC pulled into a parking space and turned off the ignition. She sat motionless, staring, until her car door opened and Pierce Wheeler peered in. "Coming?" he asked.

KC turned forlorn eyes on him. "It's terrible," she breathed huskily.

"Terrible?" Pierce straightened up and tried to see the place through KC Logan's eyes. He was so accustomed to the old paint and run-down buildings that he'd never given them much thought, but, yes, the place could look pretty bad to a newcomer. He ducked his head to see into the car again. "It's a lot better inside, KC. Dallas is fixing it up, too. That new sign is his doing. And this parking lot used to be a mess. He had all the debris picked up and the gravel hauled in."

"It's still a mess," KC sighed gloomily, then added, almost to herself, "I can't believe Granddad put all his money into something like this."

Pierce heard the morose lament and it surprised him. But bending over the way he was, he was close enough to be affected by KC's scent. Then, when she turned her big green eyes on him again, he felt their impact right in his solar plexus. There was something vulnerable in that radiant green, something soft and defenseless. It socked Pierce with the impact of a fist, and he had to remind himself that he and KC were strangers to stop himself from gathering her up in a protective embrace.

Frowning, Pierce studied the small woman behind the wheel. "Do you know the person who sold Granddad this . . . this atrocity?" he heard.

Pierce hesitated a moment, wondering what KC was getting at. "Yes, I know the man. He doesn't live around here anymore, though."

"It figures. He unloaded this dump on an elderly man, then skipped the country."

The vulnerability was gone from KC's eyes and demeanor, replaced by indignation, and Pierce felt almost relieved as his empathetic tension relaxed. "Hey, it wasn't like that. Besides, your grandfather doesn't feel that way."

KC's frustration was getting the best of her. She felt on the verge of a tearful explosion, and an acquaintance of five minutes telling her how her own grandfather felt about something an elderly man shouldn't even be involved with wasn't calming her nerves any. "How would you know how my grandfather feels?" she asked sharply.

Pierce could deal with anger, which he could see KC was leaning toward, much easier than that disturbing vulnerability he'd caught a glimpse of, and his answer was quick and to the point. "Anyone with half a brain can see how he feels. Before you pass judgment, don't you think you should go inside and see for yourself?''

"That's·what I drove a thousand miles for," KC retorted, and she swung her legs around abruptly. Pierce stepped back and offered his hand. Ignoring it, KC got out of the car on her own. A niggling resentment for this man's intrusion into a family matter was mingling with all her worries, leaving her momentarily unconcerned about good manners. She should have known the place would be this bad, she thought angrily. While Dallas's life savings had been a nice sum of money, it certainly hadn't been enough to purchase a *successful* saloon and eight-unit motel. Why, this place was the worst-looking establishment she'd seen in Harmony so far.

Reading the taut, belligerent look on KC's face as trouble and fearing she was going to march inside and lambaste her elderly grandfather, Pierce took her arm. "Look, KC, I try not to interfere in people's personal lives, but—"

KC broke in. "Where were you . . . where was the law when that . . . that crook foisted this white elephant off on a seventy-two-year-old man?''

Pierce felt his muscles tensing with responsive anger. KC wasn't making it easy to maintain professional detachment. For one thing, she smelled sexier than any woman he'd ever been around. She exuded a perturbing mixture of soap, a musky, compelling perfume and just plain femaleness. She wasn't a kid, she was a mature woman and she was appealing enough to be giving him some rather erotic ideas. Yet she was behaving rather irrationally, angry at something she'd predetermined, lashing out at him simply because he was handy.

"Take a look around this parking lot," Pierce demanded gruffly. "Tell me what you see."

"I beg your pardon!"

"What do you see?"

KC's glance flicked over the area. "Pickups and cars," she drawled sarcastically. "Am I missing your point, Sheriff?"

"No, you got my point exactly. There are eight pickups and four cars to be exact. That constitutes business, KC. There are at least a dozen customers inside right now, laying their money down for a beer or a hot dog. Those motel units bring in money, too. Your grandfather made a darned good deal here, and I don't want you going in there and jumping on the old guy for something you obviously know nothing about."

KC's mouth had dropped open, and she gave her arm an abrupt jerk to shake off the big hand she was finding presumptuously familiar. "You're the one who knows nothing about the situation! My grandfather is seventy-two—"

"Sweet Jesus! Why do you keep harping on his age? The man's doing fine. Leave him alone!"

Had she actually heard him right? KC wondered, stung that a virtual stranger was practically ordering her to leave *her* grandfather alone. A desire to set this man straight, to tell him to mind his own business, nearly erupted in bitter words that were on the tip of her tongue and hard to suppress. It took a moment and several deep breaths to cool her flaring emotions, but KC finally managed to regain enough composure to walk away from a confrontation that would do nothing but get her off on the wrong foot in Harmony.

She heard boot steps crunching in the gravel behind her, but she didn't look back. And she yanked the front door of the saloon open before Sheriff Pierce Wheeler could open it for her.

Inside was a small foyer, then the main room. KC stopped within the ample archway between the two and looked around. She felt the tall sheriff right behind her, standing close enough to bump into if she should back up a step. But she was determined to ignore Pierce Wheeler. It wasn't often she met a man who appealed to her physical side as noticeably as Sheriff Wheeler had on sight, but he was otherwise just too damned overbearing for her tastes.

Several people seated at the bar looked over their shoulders at the new arrivals, and it was evident to KC that there was some curiosity about the stranger walking in with the sheriff. Quickly, wanting to immediately and pointedly disassociate herself from Pierce Wheeler, she started across the room.

"Hi ya, Pierce."

"Hey, Wheeler."

KC approached the bar from one end and saw Pierce walk to about midcenter and perch on a stool while he greeted friends. Just then Dallas came through a door located behind the bar, which, to KC, appeared to lead to a storage room. Dallas spotted the sheriff and stopped with a broad grin. "Well, howdy, Pierce. What can I get you?"

Pierce's hands were on the bar. Without speaking he lifted his right forefinger and motioned to the other end of the long bar.

Dallas turned to see what the sheriff was indicating and looked first disbelieving, then elated. "KC! Well, for crying out loud!"

KC smiled in spite of her sour mood. She dearly loved her grandfather, and just seeing him went a long way in satisfying that unsettled part of herself that had made this trip mandatory. "Granddad," she murmured as Dallas came around the end of the bar for a big hug. They held each other a moment, then Dallas stepped back.

"How'd you get here?"

Studying the elderly man intently, worriedly looking for signs of exhaustion or illness, KC answered, "I drove. How are you, Granddad?"

"Just fine. You drove all that way by yourself?"

KC noted that Dallas's white hair was neatly combed and his clothing clean and tidy. He had a large white towel tied around his waist, and his blue eyes, behind gold-rimmed glasses, were brimming with curiosity and concern. "Don't worry. I made it just fine," she said quietly, suddenly aware that everyone in the room, including Pierce Wheeler, was watching.

But Dallas wasn't a bit put off by the audience. "How come you just up and came without any warning?"

A hasty glance at the sheriff evidenced his interest in her answer, too, and KC took her grandfather's arm and urged him away from the bar. In a low voice she asked, "Can you leave so we can talk in private?"

Dallas shook his head. "Not until six, honey. That's when Katie Seberg relieves me. I'll get you one of the motel keys and you can get settled."

"Don't you have a house?"

"Heck, no. What would I want a house for?" Dallas went back behind the bar, plucked a key from a board containing key pegs and returned to KC, who'd been having a little trouble digesting the housing situation.

"You mean you're living in one of the motel units?" she inquired in an anxious undertone.

"It suits my needs just fine, honey. I'm over here most of the time anyway. Here, take the key. It's to room five. Get yourself comfortable and then come back and have a sandwich. After lunch, when the place clears out a little, we can talk some."

Reluctantly, KC accepted the motel key.

"Before you go, though, come and meet my good friend."

Dallas was drawing KC behind the bar. "What friend?"

"The sheriff."

"But..."

"KC, this is Pierce Wheeler. Pierce, this is KC, that pretty little granddaughter I told you about."

The sheriff was obviously fighting back laughter, and KC stiffened, noting that the dark glasses Pierce had been wearing had concealed startling, gray eyes. Right this minute, without the barrier of tinted glass, they were looking much too amused, even while the admiration she'd previously sensed still hovered within their smoky depths.

"We've already met, Granddad," KC said coolly, sending Pierce the most distant look she could drum up. "The sheriff gave me directions here."

"Well, now, ain't that nice?" Dallas beamed. "The three of us will have to get together one evening for dinner. All right with you, Pierce?"

"Perfectly all right," Pierce replied smoothly. "Just let me know when, Dallas."

KC swallowed a sharp refusal and pointedly turned away from the sheriff. "I'll go and get settled, Granddad. See you later." On tiptoe, KC planted a kiss on Dallas's leathery cheek and retreated from behind the bar.

"Nice meeting you, KC," Pierce called.

Darting a glare over her shoulder, KC managed a reluctant, "Thanks," and hurried across the saloon and out the door. "Damned man," she muttered. Attractive or not, doling out unwanted advice made Sheriff Pierce Wheeler nobody but a busybody in her book.

"Was she having trouble finding the place?" Dallas was asking Pierce at the bar.

"I think she thought it was in the middle of town," Pierce answered. "Give me a couple of hot dogs and a lemonade, Dallas."

Dallas kept grinning while he filled Pierce's order. He set the plate and frosty glass of lemonade on the bar. "Could have knocked me over with a feather when I saw KC standing there."

Pierce picked up one of the hot dogs and took a big bite. "You had no idea she was coming?"

"Not a hint." Dallas stopped for a beat. "Wonder what she did about her job. I didn't think she had any vacation time coming."

"What does she do in San Francisco?" Pierce asked casually.

Dallas smiled proudly. "KC's got a good job with a big advertising company."

Another customer called for a beer and Dallas ambled away. Absently watching the elderly man behind the bar laughing and joking with his customers while he filled their orders, Pierce ate and pondered KC Logan. The sheriff had a strong feeling that KC's arrival in Harmony boded no good for her grandfather. She hadn't driven all that way for just a visit; there was something cooking behind those green eyes, and it had to do with Dallas and this business.

While he wished he hadn't antagonized her, Pierce still felt the same protectiveness toward Dallas that had prompted the hard line with KC. Something about the gentle old guy had reached Pierce at their first hello, maybe because he'd never known either of his own grandfathers and because his father had been a loudmouthed, drunken bully who'd abused anyone within reach. Pierce had stood it until he turned sixteen; then, just before Thanksgiving that year, he had left Brooklyn and hitched his way west.

He'd been an ignorant kid. Streetwise, but so dumb he hadn't even known how far west he'd come when he found himself in Harmony during a killer blizzard. The sheriff at the time, a man named Russell Dobrinsky, had spotted the half-frozen, half-starved boy and picked him off the streets. Pierce had been positive he was headed for jail, but instead Russ Dobrinsky had taken him home with him. That had been a milestone in Pierce's life.

Russ and Rose Dobrinsky had had four kids of their own, but their house had been big and their hearts bigger. It was several years before Pierce confessed that he wasn't an orphan, as he'd initially led them to believe out of fear they would send him back to Brooklyn. In the meantime, they made him go to school, they gave him a home and they made him a part of their family. He owed everything he was and had accomplished to the Dobrinskys. Russ was dead now, but Rose still lived in Harmony and Pierce saw her often.

Maybe Dallas reminded him of Russ, Pierce mused. Despite being the law in the area for many years, Russ Dobrinsky had been a gentle man. Dallas Logan, with his twinkling blue eyes and ready smile, exhibited the same gentle and kindly nature that had marked Russ as special. At any rate, Pierce saw something in the elderly man that didn't deserve a granddaughter or anyone else railing at him over spending his own money.

With the hint of a wry grin Pierce admitted that while Dallas struck him as special, so did his granddaughter. In completely unrelated ways, of course. KC was special in a very female way—unusually pretty, sexually exciting. And there was that one moment when he'd sensed her soft interior. She wasn't as controlled and independent as she wanted the world to believe, was she? She'd sure been shook at seeing this place, and nothing but negative about Dallas's ownership. She really thought Dallas was over the hill, didn't she?

True, Dallas was no spring chicken. But age didn't automatically destroy a man's ambition. So what if he wanted to spend his waning years doing something he enjoyed?

After checking the time, Pierce tossed some bills on the bar and slid off the stool. "See you later, Dallas," he called.

"Stop in again soon, Pierce," Dallas called back.

Outside, Pierce walked to his car, then paused and glanced at room five. KC's red car was parked in front of the unit, but there was no sign of her.

Grinning, Pierce got into his car. Harmony was a small town, and if KC stayed around he'd see her in spite of her obvious preference to ignore the local sheriff. For his part, he'd like nothing better than to see more of Miss KC Logan. She was a bit of an enigma, but she was also the prettiest, most exciting thing to have hit Harmony in quite a spell.

Two

KC got busy unpacking her suitcases. The motel unit was small and old-fashioned, which she'd expected, and decorated in varying shades of fading blue. All in all, blandly unremarkable. But it *was* scrupulously clean. It astounded KC that her aged grandfather was living in a motel room, but even viewing her unit with an extra-critical eye, she had to admit the place wasn't that uncomfortable. An inquisitive glance out the window revealed a white pickup truck parked in front of unit number two and a blue sedan in front of number seven. As Dallas didn't own a vehicle, KC concluded that her grandfather occupied one of the other units.

The whole situation gnawed at KC like a mouse nibbling at cheese. Dallas didn't look any less healthy than before he'd boarded the tour bus. In fact, in all fairness, there was a bit of zing in his step. But how long could that last? Undoubtedly he was still enthused about his recent purchase. At his age, especially when his aches and pains began acting up, he could easily slide back into the doldrums he'd been in for the past two years. Then he'd be stuck with a demanding business and no energy to run it.

Almost two years had gone by since KC's grandmother, Harriet, had passed away. Without Harriet, Dallas had slumped into a saddened state, which KC had understood very well. Her grandparents had been a devoted couple, happily content with a quiet, retired life-style. Without his other half, Dallas had been totally lost.

KC had known for some time that her grandfather should find something of interest to occupy his time. But not this. Not a taxing business a thousand miles from home. She was deeply, achingly worried about the elderly man. And Pierce Wheeler's input in the matter was interference from a man who couldn't possibly know or understand how seriously she viewed Dallas's strange behavior. The sheriff had no right to intrude, no right at all.

While KC emptied her suitcases, she realized intuitively that hoping for an immediate return to San Francisco was futile. She would have to exercise patience with her grandfather. Based on the few minutes she'd seen him, he appeared to be still having fun with the business. What she should try to make him see was how trapped he would be when serving beer and hot dogs was no longer fun.

Rather tense over the situation, KC freshened up, changing into white slacks and a blue blouse and took a little care with her makeup and hair. Not because she might see that interfering Pierce Wheeler again, either, she told herself. Actually, all it did was annoy her that she could find the man attractive in spite of his overbearing intrusiveness. As far as brawn went, Harmony's sheriff was an outstanding specimen; few women would dispute that obvious fact. But that's as far as his appeal went. She, for one, wanted nothing to do with such a presumptuous know-it-all.

When KC exited room number five, the sheriff's brown car was gone. Several common pickups and cars were in the parking lot, which made one car stand out like a sore thumb. It was a large, sparkling-clean, silver-gray Mercedes, an ordinary sight around San Francisco, but, KC suspected from what she'd seen so far in Harmony, unusual in this part of the world. However, a Montana license plate made her realize she shouldn't be too quick to judge what was typical in Harmony.

When KC walked into the saloon, she saw that two tables were occupied and three men sat at the bar, one of whom was at the far end talking to Dallas. Instantly KC knew he was the patron who'd arrived in the Mercedes. The man was splendidly dressed, wearing a beautifully tailored gray suit and accessories that would have been notable in San Francisco's financial district; in the logging community of Harmony, Montana, the fine clothing was like a beacon of good taste.

Not only that, but the man himself was notable. Even when seated, he appeared to be tall and slender. He had gleaming, golden hair, an aristocratic, handsome face and a self-assured manner, all of which favorably impressed KC.

She saw Dallas look up and spot her. "KC! Come on over, honey."

The man turned on the stool, and an immediate look of surprise altered his expression. KC went behind the bar and walked its length to reach her grandfather, aware, with every step, that the man's interested gaze never left her.

"Honey, I'd like you to meet the local bank manager, Kyle Rudman. Kyle, this is my granddaughter, KC Logan."

Smiling, KC extended her hand over the bar. "Very nice meeting you, Mr. Rudman."

Kyle's larger hand closed around hers. "The pleasure is all mine, and please call me Kyle. Dallas mentioned his granddaughter was paying him a visit, but I hadn't expected anyone so lovely."

The hand holding hers was warm and pleasant, the compliment not that surprising after the admiring look she'd received the past few moments. "Thank you," KC replied without coyness and withdrew her hand. "I saw an imposing brick bank building on my way through town. Is that your bank?"

Kyle laughed easily. "It's where I work, yes."

He had remarkably white teeth, KC noted, and a very nice laugh. Kyle Rudman was an exceptionally attractive man, and it struck KC as odd that she should meet two appealing men in the same day.

Instantly she amended the thought. As handsome as he was, Pierce Wheeler should hardly be categorized with this man. It was apparent that Kyle Rudman was a man of breeding and good taste, while Pierce had an air of rugged individualism. Pierce fit the surroundings of mountains and pickup trucks and blue jeans in and around Harmony; Kyle Rudman didn't. It was completely obvious—even without knowing either of them very well—that the two men were as different as night and day.

"I didn't mean to intrude," KC said apologetically.

Kyle's smile was warmly aggressive and polished. "You're very welcome in this discussion, as far as I'm concerned, KC."

"Heck, yes, honey," Dallas chimed in. "We weren't talking about anything you can't hear. Kyle wants to buy me out."

KC froze. Was it going to be this easy? Just walk up, meet a wonderfully appealing man and hear that he *wanted* the saloon and motel? Her eyes darted to Kyle Rudman. *Why* would he want it? Why would a man who exuded good taste right along with his expensive cologne want this run-down, dilapidated chunk of real estate?

It took a moment for her to tell herself that the man's reasons were his own and that she should only be thankful, and another moment to produce a smile and murmur, "Why, that's wonderful."

Kyle's reply was boyishly wry. "I'm afraid your grandfather doesn't agree with you. He turned me down again."

"Again?" KC turned startled eyes to Dallas. "You mean Mr. Rudman made you a previous offer, Granddad?"

Dallas was chuckling like an elderly elf. "The day after I bought it, honey. I kind of slipped in and made a deal on a place Kyle had had his eye on for quite a spell. Ain't that right, Kyle?"

"Very right, Dallas. Jack Walters knew I was interested in this property, but for some reason of his own he decided to sell it to you." Kyle spoke to KC. "I offered your grandfather five thousand more than he paid for the place."

KC's heart had begun beating a mile a minute. An excellent offer, even a nice profit, and Dallas had turned it down. Why? What had gotten into Dallas Logan to even buy the business in the first place?

She felt sick to her stomach as the full impact of the situation struck her. If Dallas wouldn't accept Kyle Rudman's generous offer, what chance did she have of convincing her grandfather to sell at all? Would she ever get him back to San Francisco?

How could she ever go back home and leave him here alone? She wouldn't have a moment's peace worrying about him. What would happen when he had one of those horrible migraines? Who would take care of him? Who would make him mild chicken broth, the only thing he could keep down at those times? And what about the arthritis that nearly debilitated him during cold weather? What would he do in a cold, northern climate in the winter?

For that matter, uncomfortable as Dallas's physical infirmities were, they weren't life-threatening. At his age, anything could befall a person. What would happen to the elderly man if a serious medical problem should arise?

Something of her frightening thoughts must have shown on her face, KC realized, because she saw a sudden understanding in Kyle Rudman's golden-hazel eyes. For a moment she felt as if he were actually reading her mind, and a glance of pure communion passed between them. It unnerved KC, because she'd always felt that such communication was uncommon between people without a longer acquaintanceship. And yet it was too strong a sensation to deny.

With a congenial smile Kyle slid off the stool. "I have to get back to the bank, Dallas. KC, I hope you won't think me forward, but I'd appreciate it if you'd walk out to my car with me."

KC knew why immediately, but Dallas gave first Kyle, then her, an inquisitive look. Then a cute twinkle appeared in his eyes. Clearly, he was pleased that Harmony's bank manager found his granddaughter attractive.

Allowing the misconception, KC nodded. "I'd be glad to walk out with you, Kyle. I'll be back in a minute, Granddad."

"No hurry, honey. Take your time."

Gritting her teeth, KC walked around the bar and preceded Kyle Rudman out the front door. The minute they were outside, she stopped and faced him. "You understand why I'm here, don't you?"

Kyle nodded somberly. "I certainly do, KC. And I couldn't agree with you more. This is no place for a man of your grandfather's mature years."

"I'm worried sick about him," she admitted gravely.

"Of course you are. I would be, too, if it were my grandfather on his feet for ten, twelve hours a day."

KC's spirit deflated even more. "Has he really been putting in that kind of time?"

"As far as I can tell, yes. I know he opens the place up very early in the morning and stays until about six. A local woman handles the bar in the evening, but think of the behind-the-scenes responsibility, KC. The beverage and food ordering, overseeing the motel units, the book work. Why, I've actually wondered if the old gentleman sleeps at all.

"I'm extremely glad you showed up, KC. And please believe me, it's not only because I'd like to buy this property. I've been genuinely concerned about your grandfather. He's an exceptionally personable man and I liked him from our first meeting."

KC met Kyle Rudman's distressed gaze with mounting fear. "He means the world to me. Granddad is my only living relative."

Kyle put a hand on her shoulder in a tender gesture. "I deeply sympathize with you. You've got to somehow convince him to give up this foolish venture. For his own good."

"I know," KC agreed huskily, close to tears. "I was hoping I'd have to be here only a short time, but now...?"

Kyle smiled. "Well, I can't say I'll be sorry if you have to stay a while. I meant it when I said you're a lovely woman. I'd like very much to see you again."

His hand was still on her shoulder, and it felt pleasant and almost brotherly. Of course, there was nothing brotherly about the light in Kyle Rudman's eyes. He was as admiring as...as Pierce Wheeler had been earlier.

Only, with Pierce Wheeler, *she'd* felt differently.

With Pierce Wheeler, she'd felt too warm and much too aware of his masculinity. Why would she respond like that to a man she *knew* she was going to have nothing to do with, when a man she respected on sight, a man who had sensitivity and understanding, did nothing for her libido?

Foolish woman, KC chided herself in self-castigation. And to prove how determined she was to ignore Pierce Wheeler, she gave Kyle Rudman an inviting smile. "I'd like to see you again, too, Kyle."

"Wonderful," he murmured, and allowed his hand to slide down her arm to her hand. KC realized how personal the contact was, but she was neither drawn nor repelled by it. Kyle's gesture felt only...nice. "I have a previous engagement for tonight, KC. But how about dinner together tomorrow night?"

"That would be best anyway, Kyle. I haven't had five minutes alone with Granddad yet, and I have a dozen questions I need answers to." KC sighed. "I keep hoping that I'm misinterpreting his involvement here."

Kyle shook his head. "I don't think you're misinterpreting anything, KC. I firmly believe you have a genuine reason for concern." He squeezed her hand lightly. "I'll see you tomorrow night around seven, all right?"

"Seven will be fine."

When Kyle headed for the Mercedes, KC went back into the saloon. Dallas was busy with a customer and called. "Help yourself to a hot dog, KC."

"Thanks, I will." After putting together a hot dog and pouring a soft drink, KC sat on the stool Kyle had vacated and ate. Unobtrusively, she watched her grandfather at work. While the place was never rushed, a steady stream of customers, one and two at a time, kept the elderly man filling orders and engaging in friendly conversations. Apparently, Dallas Logan was already well liked, which didn't surprise KC in the least. Like Kyle Rudman had pointed out, Dallas was a very likable person.

Likable or not, he was doing entirely too much to suit KC. He cleared and wiped tables, and served beer, soft drinks, hot dogs and ice cream. He rented two of the motel units for the night; he washed glasses behind the bar; he accepted money and made change.

He sat down very few times.

Finally, getting more perturbed by the minute, KC got up. "Granddad, let me help out. I can't sit by and watch you work like this."

Dallas looked surprised. "Help if you want to, honey. But you sure don't have to."

"Oh, yes, I do," KC mumbled under her breath. And she dipped her hands into the sink of soapy water to wash some glasses. By six, when the relief bartender arrived, KC was ready to call it quits. She was tired from her long trip and anxious to speak to Dallas alone, and she was unhappily realizing that Dallas was pretty firmly entrenched here. Getting him to leave Harmony was going to be far from easy.

After Dallas turned the place over to a woman he introduced as Mrs. Katie Seberg, he preceded KC out the backdoor. "I'm in unit number two, honey. Give me a minute to shower and change and we'll go have dinner."

KC frowned at the white pickup parked in front of unit two. "I thought, with that truck there—"

"It's mine," Dallas proudly announced.

"Yours! Granddad, you haven't driven in years!"

"Well, I'm driving now. How would I get around if I didn't drive? Harmony doesn't have buses and taxis on every corner like San Francisco does, honey." Chuckling, Dallas left KC at number five and headed for his own room.

Sputtering, KC went in and slammed the door. This was getting worse by the minute. Driving, indeed! Why, Dallas Logan had given up driving after two potentially serious accidents, both of which had been his fault. Grandma Harriet had demanded he give up driving for the sake of the general public, if not for himself. Dallas was behaving like someone who'd just been set free from a long, unjust imprisonment. What was wrong with him? Why had he stopped acting his age?

Pacing, KC wielded the hairbrush. What arguments could she possibly use to make a seventy-two-year-old man realize again that he *was* seventy-two and worrying his granddaughter into premature gray hair?

KC insisted on doing the driving to the restaurant, but it didn't seem to faze Dallas in the least. He sat in the little sedan's passenger seat with his hair all slicked down and wearing clean, dark pants and a white shirt, and asked KC about her trip as though she really had come for just an ordinary visit.

Biting her tongue to keep from blurting out what was really on her mind, KC narrated her trials on the open road. It wasn't until they were seated in the restaurant and had placed their dinner orders that KC dared to open *the* subject.

"Your call floored me, Granddad. What happened? You left on a bus tour and the next thing I knew, you were here in Harmony."

Dallas looked pleased as punch, as though he'd heard only admiration in his granddaughter's words. "It's a long story, honey."

"Well, I'm certainly ready to hear it," KC drawled dryly.

Hear it she did. All through the salad the entrée and into the dessert. In great detail, down to almost daily weather reports, KC learned that Dallas had stayed with the tour for only two weeks.

"I couldn't take that bus load of old people any longer, honey," he declared, astounding KC once again. "Every morning, every danged one of them went through every creak in their old bones. Then they discussed how they'd slept, and what they could and couldn't eat at every meal. It was depressing.''

"Granddad, they were all people your age," KC pointed out.

Dallas looked hurt. "Well, I don't have to like people just because they're my age, do I?"

"Of course not. But I honestly thought you'd enjoy a tour with people your own age."

"Well, I didn't," Dallas said stubbornly. "Do you want to hear the rest of the story, or do you want to sit here and discuss why I should have liked people I *didn't* like?"

Sighing, KC slumped back against the booth. "Tell me how you got to Harmony."

Dallas's face brightened. "I got off the tour bus in Seattle and rented a car."

KC felt herself go pale. She cleared her throat. "Then what?"

"I toured the Olympic Peninsula and . . ."

Through three cups of decaffeinated coffee, KC got another detailed accounting, this one sounding like a travelogue of Washington, northern Idaho and Montana. In the back of her mind, she kept thinking, *And I thought you were safe on a bus with a professional driver! Good Lord.*

For several weeks Dallas had gone where he'd wanted to and seen what he'd wanted to see. The postcards she'd received from a half dozen different places had only recounted the good times he'd been having, not that he'd been having them solo. Too stunned to even comment, KC listened silently.

Until Dallas said, "Then, I met this very nice lady."

"Lady?" KC echoed weakly.

"Mary Collier. She lives here in Harmony, but she'd been doing some traveling, too. Mary told me what a great little town Harmony is, and that I shouldn't miss it."

"I see. So you came to Harmony. Apparently you liked it."

"Sure did. I checked into the motel, the same unit I'm still using, by the way. Jack Walters, the owner, and me hit it off real well. One night he looked real sad, and after we talked a while, he told me some bad news. He's only sixty-three, KC, and he's got cancer."

"Oh." Immediately affected by the dreadful word, KC softened. "And he wanted to sell his business," she said quietly.

"He calls every so often, honey. He moved back east to be with a sister. He's getting treatments and there's a good chance of recovery."

"I'm glad," KC said in all sincerity. "But…did you buy this business just to help him, Granddad? I mean, with Kyle Rudman wanting the place, Mr. Walters already had a buyer, didn't he?"

"Heck, no, I didn't buy it because Jack needed to sell," Dallas rebutted spiritedly. "I bought it because I wanted it. Jack was having a great time running it. It got me thinking. Why should I just wither up like an old prune?" Dallas leaned forward, deadly serious. "Can you tell me why I should just sit back and wither up like an old prune?"

A close-to-hysterical giggle nearly choked KC. Hiding it by grabbing her glass and gulping some water, she managed to croak, "You're not an old prune, Granddad."

Dallas snorted. "I was getting close."

During the narration, KC had been developing a strange loss of the familiar. Dallas was still Dallas, but with a disturbing difference. It was that difference that alarmed KC. What did a burst of independence mean in a person who was more than seventy? How should she convey her concerns so she wouldn't damage her grandfather *and* the very good relationship she and Dallas had always had? She didn't look on this wonderful old man as an ordinary grandparent; he was as dear to her as any father could ever have been.

Sick at heart, KC realized she had to walk on eggs at this point. Despite his newly found independence, Dallas was still elderly, still physically fragile. She had to make him understand that he belonged back in San Francisco with her, not in Harmony, Montana with a demanding business and cold, harsh winters.

"Granddad," she said softly, reaching across the table to take his hand. "I can't go back home and leave you here alone. Who will look after you when you get a migraine? Who will see that you eat properly and—"

"You don't understand, do you?" Dallas interrupted sadly. "I hoped you would, honey."

"Hello, Dallas. KC."

For a moment KC couldn't focus on the man standing by the booth. She and Dallas had talked so long, and so intently, she had almost forgotten where they were. Pierce Wheeler had come into the restaurant and she hadn't noticed, no more than she'd noticed anything else for hours.

Dallas grinned up at the tall sheriff. "Pierce! Glad to see you. Sit down. Have a cup of coffee with us." He slid over in the booth to give Pierce some room. While Pierce settled down, Dallas beamed across the table at his granddaughter. "This young fella sure gave me a lot of support when I was getting started in the business, honey."

KC's gaze tangled with Pierce's for a moment. "I don't doubt it," she said evenly.

"Yep, I just don't know if I could have done it on my own," Dallas continued. "Business licenses, enough paperwork to choke a horse...the sheriff was there anytime I needed advice."

"I'm sure you would have managed just fine." Pierce was talking to Dallas, but he was looking into KC's icy-green eyes. "But I'm here anytime you need me, Dallas."

A slow flush developed right along with KC's anger. The damned man was declaring his loyalty and daring her to challenge it. What did he think she was—a threat to her own grandfather?

She was getting a brand-new perspective on Dallas's misadventure, one in which Pierce Wheeler played an irritatingly starring role. On top of that, the man had the nerve to sit there and stare at her like a cat at a mouse hole!

Dallas liked him, but that didn't mean she had to. With a murderous look at the sheriff, KC got out of the booth. "Please excuse me," she said sharply, and with her purse, headed for the ladies' room.

Pierce watched KC cross the dining room. "I don't think she likes me very much, Dallas," he said with a small laugh.

"KC? Heck, why wouldn't she like you? KC's just worried about me, Pierce."

Pierce gave the older man an in-depth look, then nodded. "Yes, I think she is. She doesn't like you running that business, Dallas."

Dallas rubbed his jaw thoughtfully. "I guess it's understandable. I haven't done much of anything for quite a few years now."

Pierce smiled. "Well, you're doing something now. How's Mary?"

"Just fine. Had dinner with her last night."

"Does KC know you're keeping company with a lady?"

"I mentioned Mary, but I don't know if KC caught on. I didn't tell her right out. Maybe I should."

"Only if you think it best, Dallas."

Dallas nodded, then changed the subject. "Are you still on duty?"

"I'm just now through for the day. There was another highway accident this afternoon, about five miles out of town."

"Aw, hell, that's too bad. Anyone hurt?"

"Two people. That road's a real menace, Dallas. I'll sure be glad if and when the state ever makes a decision on that new highway."

KC returned in time to catch the last part of Pierce Wheeler's remark. She'd been gone only a few minutes, but she'd used the time to calm herself and decide again that patience was the only thing that was going to separate Dallas from Harmony. "What new highway?" she asked as she slid into the booth.

Pierce gave her a direct look, and behind his reply he was again absorbing KC's magnetic good looks. His gaze roamed her face, her throat, her hair and the blue blouse while he spoke. "The canyon highway. You had to come in on it. It extends another ten miles on the other side of town, too. We average about an accident a week on it during the summer, more when it's icy. The state's been going to put in another highway for years now, but the cost estimates are astronomical because of the terrain, and the delays go on."

"That's easy to understand," KC responded, able to speak civilly to the sheriff on this impersonal topic. "The canyon's incredibly narrow, with a solid wall of granite on one side of the road and the river on the other side. Construction costs are bound to be sky-high."

"I've heard that the state keeps changing the exact route," Dallas put in.

"That's true," Pierce agreed, then grinned. "Well, one of these days they'll make up their minds. Can't be too soon for me."

Dallas glanced at his watch. "KC, do you realize we've been sitting here for almost three hours?"

KC had been inwardly squirming over the intense scrutiny she'd been getting from the sheriff. He had the most disconcerting way of looking at her, as if she were a tasty morsel and he'd been without food for a long, long time. Which she doubted. Pierce Wheeler didn't strike her as a man who would go without "tasty morsels" for *any* length of time. Gladly, she picked up her purse. "We better be going, Granddad."

"Come on back to the place with us, Pierce," Dallas invited. "Unless you've got something better to do," he added with a man-to-man grin.

"Nothing better," Pierce said softly with a pointed look at KC.

KC took a quick, startled breath. If the sheriff thought he was coming back to the saloon to spend time with her, he had another thought coming. "Well, I, for one, am going straight to bed," she announced. "I'm exhausted."

They all got out of the booth. "How about a game of cribbage?" Dallas asked the sheriff.

"Sounds good," Pierce answered with another smoldering look at KC.

She turned her face away. They could play cribbage all night, as far as she was concerned.

Wait a darned minute! Dallas had worked all day. "I think Granddad should get to bed, too," she said coldly.

The two men looked at each other and burst out laughing.

"What's so funny?" KC demanded with renewed anger flashing in her eyes.

"You are," Pierce replied with another laugh. "Who do you think this man is, your kid?"

KC's face flushed three shades of red. "I *know* who this man is, you...you arrogant fool. Do *you* know that he's been on his feet for twelve hours today?" Spinning, KC stormed out of the restaurant.

Pierce turned to Dallas and grinned. "Told you she didn't like me."

Three

—

KC's anger diminished as she stared at the display of lights and shadows on the motel ceiling. She hated losing her temper the way she had, and letting Pierce Wheeler drive her up the wall had accomplished nothing. In retrospect, she felt rather foolish.

As difficult as it was to accept, Dallas was blissfully going his own way, exasperatingly unmoved by KC's opinion. Along with a startling new independence, the elderly man had expanded a streak of stubbornness that KC knew he'd always had, but had been much less noticeable in his previous life-style.

Patience was the watchword here, KC realized again. If she were going to succeed with her grandfather, she would have to be less emotional and more patient. Another thing she might as well make her mind up to—she was going to be in Harmony a lot longer than she'd planned.

It couldn't be helped. She absolutely could not leave her grandfather here alone. After all, looking at the situation reasonably, she'd only been in town half a day. Surely, with a little time and Kyle Rudman's excellent offer in the wings, she'd come up with a way to convince Dallas that this whole thing was some kind of bad joke.

Pierce Wheeler was a particular thorn, though. Damn the man! He acted as if Dallas was *his* grandfather and needed protection from KC. No matter how KC looked at it, Pierce Wheeler was galling. She would try very hard to maintain self-control around him, but it wasn't going to be easy to do.

Restless, unable to find a comfortable position no matter how she tried, KC got out of bed at eleven, switched on some lights and padded barefoot to the bathroom. She took two aspirins, noted from her mirrored reflection that in her earlier fury she hadn't removed her makeup and decided to wash her face.

She had the warm water running in the sink when she heard a loud knocking at her door. Why it hadn't occurred to her that it might be Pierce Wheeler making all that noise amazed her when she opened the door and saw him. Ducking behind the door, she whispered, "What do *you* want?"

"I saw your lights on."

"I happen to be in bed for the night."

Pierce had seen the soft-rose, ankle-length, satiny night gown, and realized that KC must have anticipated that it would be Dallas at the door. Her taffy-colored hair was tousled and the bed behind her all torn up. She *had* been in bed, but she sure hadn't been sleeping. Maybe she was as sorry for that foolish little episode at the café as he was and hadn't been able to sleep.

"I'd like to apologize, KC. May I come in for a minute?"

"Absolutely not," she snapped.

Pierce hesitated a moment, then came in anyway, pushing the door and KC back at the same time. "What do you think you're doing?" she cried.

"I think you and I should have a little talk," Pierce said, and tore the door from her grasp and shut it firmly. KC dove for her bathrobe and yanked it on.

"Apparently being sheriff has gone to your head," she raged, forgetting that she'd just been regretting her earlier show of temper with this man. "For your information, forced entry is as illegal for you as it is for anyone else."

"This has nothing to do with my job." Pierce was staring. The bathrobe matched the nightgown—old rose and satin, slippery-looking, sensuously draping around female curves. His body was reacting to the sight. He really had come to apologize and attempt to make KC see that Dallas's contentment was no threat to her. Now, those intentions were oddly draining, away while others were gaining strength. What he'd like to do was move closer, take this sexy woman in his arms and make slow, delicious love to her. It was impossible, he knew, and too soon for such antics, but damn, she was something!

Anyway, from the sharp glint in her green eyes, she'd probably bat him one if he tried anything. Shaking his head, Pierce walked around the little room.

"Say what you came to say and leave," KC demanded, following his prowl with as much anger as she'd squelched in the past two hours.

He glanced back at her. Her beautiful face was framed with wildly disarrayed, sun-streaked hair, and despite common sense, it was all he could do to stop himself from taking the few steps to reach her so he could tangle his hands into the inviting mass.

Pierce turned fully to face her and and drew a deep breath. "All right. Since you're so nervous, I'll make this short. I'm sorry I rubbed you the wrong way today, but—"

"No buts, Wheeler. You stuck your nose in something you had no business getting into," KC declared sharply. She hadn't been looking for a fight, but this was a damned good chance to tell this overbearing man what she really thought of his interference. "You're encouraging Granddad in this fiasco, and what I'd like to know is, what are you going to do when I leave and something happens to him? Are *you* going to take care of him? Are you going to accept the responsibility for an elderly man's well-being?"

A frown furrowed Pierce's forehead. "What the hell are you talking about? There isn't anything wrong with Dallas. Any one of us—you, me, anyone—could get sick. Are we supposed to live in fear or in a glass bubble because of it?"

KC sneered. "Of course anyone could get sick. But you're not seventy-two. And don't tell me again to stop harping on Granddad's age. If he was fifty, do you think I'd be here worrying about him?"

"Give the man a break," Pierce groaned. "He's not senile, KC. His mind's as sharp as a tack. He just beat me in a two-out-of-three-cribbage match."

KC narrowed her eyes. "Where is he now?"

"Gone to bed."

"He should have been in bed two hours ago."

"That's *your* opinion, little lady, not his. Not mine, either."

"I don't give a damn about your opinion. I'm beginning to believe that without your misguided encouragement, Granddad wouldn't be in this mess. Why don't you mind your own damned business! He's not your grandfather, he's mine!"

The look in Pierce's gray eyes became steely hard. "You're right. But I wish to God he *was* my grandfather. I can tell you one thing—I sure wouldn't be doing my level best to make the old guy's last years as miserable as I could possibly manage."

KC sucked in an outraged breath. "I'm not doing that, you . . . you jerk! I only want him home where I can take care of him. He gets migraine headaches, he has arthritis in his shoulders, his stomach acts up something terrible sometimes. Who else is going to take care of him when he gets sick—you?"

"Damned right," Pierce growled. "I'd do it in a minute. But I'm not his only friend in Harmony."

"Oh?" KC returned sarcastically. "Who else would care if he got sick?"

Mary Collier was in Pierce's mind, but the very nice widow lady was Dallas's business, not his. "Just take my word for it. Dallas has other friends here besides me."

"Kyle Rudman?" KC persisted, and saw Pierce's eyes become two tense slits.

"You've met our fancy-pants local banker?" he drawled in a cynical tone that surprised KC.

"Yes, I have. He's an exceptionally fine man."

"Oh, is he really? And what do you base that blatantly female observation on—the cut of his clothes?"

KC flushed. "He's a man of quality," she hurled defensively.

"More quality than me?" With a grim expression, Pierce advanced. "Do you think he's more man than me, KC Logan?" he asked softly.

KC's blood began pounding in her ears as she saw what the argument had unleashed in the sheriff. He was big, his broad shoulders and height overpowering the tiny room. He could break her in two with one hand, if he chose. His body looked rock hard, his belly board flat, his arms and legs long and muscular.

But he didn't look violent. Any anger in the man was directed at what he'd seen as a slur against his manhood. Which was silly. She'd meant no such thing. Quality had nothing to do with virility. Quality meant breeding, taste, manners. Dammit, didn't this irritating man know anything?

"What are you doing?" she asked suspiciously as Pierce moved closer.

"Proving something, honey," Pierce drawled, and snaked a hand out. It curled around the back of her neck, big, hard, making KC's spine tingle and her mouth go dry.

"You have no right to touch me," she croaked shakily.

His fingers worked beneath her hair, and his palm found the skin of her neck. His smoky eyes bored into her while one corner of his mouth turned up in a bemused half smile. "No right? Did I ask for permission?"

In the next instant she was brought forward, molded against him, and still he stared down into her startled eyes. "There's a lot of chemistry between us, honey. Is that quality?"

"Don't be . . . ridiculous," she whispered tremulously. "Let me go."

"You're not fighting this very hard. I think you *want* me to kiss you."

KC wet her lips. "You're not only overbearing, you're conceited."

A flame had ignited in Pierce's eyes, and twin bonfires seared KC as she looked and looked at him, questioningly, astonished again that she could dislike him and still be mesmerized by whatever magic he exuded. Her breasts were pushed into his chest by his hold—one arm around her back, the other hand still under her hair. She found a weak voice. "What will this prove, other than you're stronger than me?"

Maybe he'd been looking for an excuse to do this, Pierce had to question. And then again, maybe he'd known it was going to happen, excuse or not. "Tell me about quality," he commanded in a low, intense voice.

KC blinked. "Let me go."

"No." Pierce moved his fingers on the back of her neck, sending a radiating thrill through her system. "You're a nice armful, honey."

"And you're—"

"A jerk? Isn't that what you called me a few minutes ago? And what was it at the restaurant? An arrogant fool? You've got quite a penchant for name-calling, haven't you?"

"You...you make me so angry," she whispered. "Pierce, let me go."

Pierce smiled lazily. "I like the way you say my name."

"This isn't funny," she rasped.

"No, it's not, is it?" Sobering, Pierce brought his head down slowly, steadying the jerk of her head with the hand on her neck. "Easy, honey," he cautioned softly. "Let's find out about that quality bit."

"It has nothing to do with kissing, you . . ."

His expression darkened. "Call me one more name and I'll turn you over my knee," he threatened. At the disbelief in her eyes, he added, "And don't doubt that I'd do it, KC."

"You wouldn't dare," she mocked.

"Try me." While their gazes locked in silent combat, Pierce took a second to wonder why KC mentioning Kyle Rudman had hit him so hard. The bank manager was an odd duck; people meeting him for the first time either couldn't stand him on sight or took to him with more affection than Pierce thought normal. For his part, he wasn't comfortable around the man. Rudman was too smooth, too urbane, too much of everything for Harmony.

But it was apparent, from KC's immediate defense, that she wasn't one of the people who had disliked Kyle Rudman on sight. And that disturbed Pierce. He didn't want to get into a competition with the banker for a woman's attention, and if KC Logan stuck around for a while, he knew he wanted her attention.

She felt right in his arms, too damned right. When had a woman felt more right?

And he knew full well what she'd meant about "quality," too, despite his veering off of the exact definition. Her being impressed with expensive, tailor-made clothes and fancy manners had hit him wrong. Labeling Kyle Rudman "quality" because he preferred suits over jeans and was a first-class bootlicker riled the hell out of Pierce.

What he intended proving to Miss KC Logan was that quality came in a lot of styles. He was holding a woman, not licking her hand.

And he'd delayed making his point long enough!

His mouth came down, not too roughly, not too gently. He *possessed* her lips, claiming them as his own, and the gasp KC emitted at the initial contact was lost in the swirl of a swift and immediate passion between them. Who was possessing whom rapidly became a moot point, Pierce realized dizzily, because whether KC wanted to or not, she was kissing him back with a fire that rocked him.

He reacted naturally, gathering her up in a more intimate embrace, holding her closer. On tiptoe, stretching to reach her goal, her arms went up around his neck. Her mouth opened beneath his, her tongue met and mated with his. A need for air interrupted the kiss briefly, only enough time to catch harsh breaths. Then, wildly, their lips united again . . . then again.

This wasn't happening, KC thought frantically. She wasn't clinging to and kissing Pierce Wheeler like a wild thing. But her body and senses weren't hers any longer; they were his! This was what she'd felt at their first meeting. She'd heard about such intense physical attraction, but she certainly had never experienced it before.

His kisses were searing storms of emotion, and it was as if she'd been in limbo all of her life and parched for the sensation. Surges of intense appetite, of desperate wanting, shook her wave upon wave, until her legs trembled with the effort of supporting her. Then it wasn't necessary. Pierce was standing straighter, bringing her up with him, lifting her feet off the floor.

Dazed, KC felt movement . . . they were moving across the room. She was being carried. To the bed! Her body cried yes while her brain rebelled. This was too fast, too unexpected. She couldn't. . . . Yet when Pierce brought them both down on the rumpled bed, her lips were parted for another kiss, *eager* for another kiss.

Hungrily his hands slid over her satin nightclothes, searching out the secrets of her body. His lips left hers to travel her face, to drop kisses on her temple, her cheeks, beneath her chin, burrowing into the sensitive curve of her throat.

The robe was opened, drawn back, the nightgown moved and rearranged to expose ivory skin and rose-crested breasts. A hot mouth closed around a pert, upright nipple, and KC moaned deep in her throat, stunned by the shooting, explosive pleasure this man's mouth was giving her. She was shocked by Pierce Wheeler's gall, by her own response, but nothing—no other man, no other kisses—had ever affected her this way.

Something still sane in the back of her mind was looking for a way out of this. This morning she hadn't known Pierce Wheeler even existed, and tonight she was on a bed with him, writhing under knowing, hot hands and a much-too-wise mouth. His tongue circled the nipple he was lavishing such ardent attention on, and then, as if he had a perfect right to such boldness, he began working up the skirt of her nightgown. His hand reached her inner thighs and lingered, softly caressing the satin of the skin it had encountered.

KC struggled with old standards, waging a battle between morality and the incredible sensations his slowly moving fingertips were creating. In a moment he would move higher, she knew. If she was going to stop him, it had to be now.

She grabbed for his hand and whispered raggedly, "No, Pierce."

He was so aroused he hurt. And yet he understood. She wasn't the kind of woman to engage in sex with a man she barely knew. He hadn't thought she was. He hadn't thought at all. Nothing in his past had prepared him for the effect they'd had on each other. A kiss had never become so uncontrolled so fast before. Another few minutes without a brake on their passion and nothing could have stopped them.

Understanding or not, Pierce felt the first seeds of the agony that cooling down unfulfilled would give him, and he raised his head to study her face with a forlorn, needful expression and labored breaths. Her lips were wet and swollen, her hair a tangle of taffy on the pillow. She was so beautiful that just looking at her added to the distress in his loins. "What happened?" he whispered gruffly.

"You want too much," she breathed hoarsely.

"No, I don't mean why did you stop me. I know why you did that. What I don't understand is what happened before that."

She was becoming more calm, and her green eyes searched his. "Didn't you expect—"

"Fireworks? I always expect fireworks when I kiss a beautiful woman. And I knew there was chemistry between us. But kissing you is like catching the tail of a comet."

Suddenly embarrassed, KC turned her face away. Then she realized she was half-naked. Her breasts were bare and pointed at him, and the hem of her nightgown was bunched up around her thighs. Pierce was supported on an elbow, his upper body above her, his lower body pressed into her hip. Behind the denim of his jeans, he was hard and ready for action. He was a big man, big and so sexually exciting, she was still in a daze.

She worked the top of her nightgown back in place, aware that his eyes followed every flutter of her hands. But he didn't move over nor make an attempt to get off the bed. Instead, when she was covered again, he touched her cheek gently. "There's something very special between you and me," he said hoarsely. "Do you understand it?"

"No," she whispered, too shaken to even speak normally, let alone deny the obvious.

His eyes were dark gray and serious. "I want you, you know."

She nodded her head once. "I know."

"You want me, too."

"It . . . that doesn't matter."

"What do you mean, it doesn't matter?"

KC swallowed nervously, at a loss for a reasonable answer. "We can't keep lying here like this."

"Why not? You're as safe as you want to be. It's really up to you, you know. If you say the word—"

"I'm not going to say it."

"I know you're not. Not tonight."

She evaded the knowing, confident light in his eyes by looking over his shoulder. "I think you should go."

"Look at me," he commanded, drawing in a harsh, uneven breath.

She closed her eyes. "Please go," she whispered brokenly.

He took her chin and held it, and quite tenderly—considering the still painfully vibrant beat of his heart—slowly caressed her mouth with the tip of his thumb. "You're very beautiful."

"Please. You shouldn't even be in this room, let alone in my bed."

Pierce considered her renunciation soberly, but he knew that this was far from being the end of it with them. "Will you go out with me tomorrow night?" he asked quietly.

Her head moved back and forth on the pillow negatively. "I can't."

"Why not?"

"Because—" an inner voice warned her, yet she had no ready reply but the truth "—because I'm having dinner with Kyle Rudman." She felt Pierce tense, go totally stiff beside her, and the hand that had been on her face abruptly left it. "You have no right to object," she cried.

"Are you going to kiss him like you kissed me?"

"I doubt that he'd force his way into my room the way you did."

Pierce's mouth twisted grimly. "I suppose quality folks don't do things like that, right?" Climbing over her, he got off the bed. KC sat up and swung her feet to the floor.

"Please don't start another argument," she said wearily.

"Me? Honey, everything you say starts another argument." Without modesty, Pierce adjusted his shirt and jeans, tautening the fit of his shirt by tucking it deeper into the belt around his trim waist. "This is a weird situation, isn't it?"

KC ignored the question and sighed.

"Isn't it?" Pierce repeated, bending over so his face was almost level with hers.

"Yes, it's weird," she agreed waspishly.

"You don't want to like me, do you?"

She raised her eyes to his. "No, I don't. As a matter of fact, I *don't* like you."

Pierce slowly grinned. "That would be pretty hard to prove to anyone who'd witnessed the two of us a few minutes ago, honey."

"Stop calling me honey like that," she demanded irately. "I'm not your honey."

Pierce looked at her intently, then took her by the shoulders and lifted her to her feet. His gaze probed hers. "Are you Kyle Rudman's honey?"

"Damn you! I'm no man's honey! I've just met the two of you today, if you'd care to remember."

"Yeah, I guess it was just today, wasn't it? It seems like a lot longer, somehow." Releasing what sounded like a troubled breath, Pierce stepped back. Turning, he walked to the door. He stopped and gave her a small grin, apparently recovered from any thoughts that might have been troubling him. "Don't do anything I wouldn't do," he quipped.

"Which, I suspect, is very little," KC retorted immediately.

Laughing softly, Pierce opened the door and left. KC stared after him for a long time, then turned off the lights and crawled back into bed. The blankets were a mess, and she kicked and clawed them into place, muttering curses while she did it.

Never, never, had she run into anyone like Pierce Wheeler.

And, Lord help her, may she never, ever run into anyone else with his irritating habits again.

Nor with his alarming ability to turn her on.

KC saw dark circles under her eyes in the morning, which only made her disgustedly shake her head. The long trip, the sleepless nights, the worry—what else could she expect?

After a long, somewhat reviving shower, she pulled on a pair of jeans and a clean white T-shirt, fixed her hair and makeup and spent fifteen minutes tidying the motel unit. Then she went over to the saloon.

Dallas was serving coffee and sweet rolls to early customers, which explained to KC why a saloon would open its doors before noon. A steady stream of "coffee and roll" customers kept Dallas busy. KC washed cups, made fresh pots of coffee and watched the activity. It was apparent that even with the several restaurants in town, the saloon had a horde of loyal followers.

Why, if one put in a small kitchen and served bacon and eggs, the breakfast business would be amazing, KC realized. One could grill hamburgers the rest of the day, maybe add fried or broasted chicken to the simple menu....

Realizing the direction of her thoughts, KC stopped stock-still. What was she doing? Expanding the business wasn't her goal: getting Dallas away from this place was!

Still, while KC busied herself refilling coffee cups, wiping tables and ringing up sales on the cash register, she took a closer look at the saloon. The public area was one large room. A divider could easily separate a restaurant area from the tavern. The walls were rough dark barn wood. One could play that up with rustic decorations.

What if one cleared a space for a small dance floor?

Frowning thoughtfully, KC eyed the setup. The saloon's potential hadn't even been partially tapped, and Kyle Rudman must have seen that, too. It was the only thing that accounted for his interest in the place, KC decided.

She was walking around with the coffeepot, stopping to refill cups, when she saw the sheriff walking in, larger than life, immediately the most impressive person in the place. Turning her back on him didn't prevent a rush of color to her cheeks, nor an immediate barrage of intimate memories. Hot, wet kisses, his mouth on her breasts, his big hands . . .

"Morning, KC."

He was right behind her. "Good morning," she responded without looking at him. Escaping, she hurried behind the bar to put the coffeepot back on the warmer.

"Morning, Dallas," she heard, and a quick glance over her shoulder placed Pierce at the end of the bar with Dallas going over for a word.

Pierce had another tan shirt on, and today KC understood that it must be his one concession to the normal uniform of his office. His handsome face was bright and refreshed-looking, as though he'd slept very well, and it annoyed her that he might have gotten a solid night's sleep while she had tossed and turned.

"I see you've got a new waitress," KC heard from Pierce, and she shot him a dark glower. Dallas's responsive chuckle grated on her nerves, too, so she included him in the dirty look.

Pierce's aggravating teasing went on. "But she seems to be in a bad mood, Dallas. Is that good for business?"

Without a word, KC stalked from behind the bar and out the door. No way was she going to put up with Pierce Wheeler this morning. She was in a bad mood, but it was all his doing. *He* was the strength behind Dallas's crazy behavior, she saw that very clearly now. If that wasn't enough interference to send her over the brink, he'd had the audacity to invade her room *and* her person.

After going to her room for her purse and car keys, KC jumped into her car and headed for town. She drove around aimlessly for the better part of an hour, then stopped at the drugstore and prowled up and down the aisles, finally purchasing a bottle of hand lotion and two magazines. Feeling somewhat more controlled, she started back to the motel.

Then, for some irritating reason, she spotted a beige brick building with the sign, Levine County Sheriff's Office, and at the same time noted two brown cars bearing the official insignia parked outside the structure.

She had thought that she'd driven Pierce from her mind, but at sight of the county building, KC realized that she'd been kidding herself. His big, handsome, sexy and infuriating image was almost real enough to touch as she drove back to the saloon. Why had she lost her head with him last night? That had never happened to her before. It wasn't because men were a big mystery, either. There had been two relationships in her twenty-nine years that could be tagged serious, both of which had nearly concluded in marriage.

That they hadn't had been her doing. Something had always stopped her from making that final commitment. What had she been looking for, a Pierce Wheeler? A man who could turn her inside out with a touch?

"Lord, I hope not," KC whispered, positive that the only charms Pierce Wheeler had were purely sexual. What woman in her right mind would hope for a domineering, insolent, egotistical, pushy mate?

Four

Pierce occupied the only private office in the building. Four deputies, a jailer, a radio dispatcher and a secretary all made do with open architecture and a few waist-high room dividers. Levine County covered twelve thousand square miles, running approximately one hundred miles north and south, and one hundred and twenty miles east and west. Harmony was the most centrally located town and it was the county seat, making it the logical location for the county's main law-enforcement agency.

Harmony was growing, spreading up and down the canyon—the only directions it could spread—more each year. Tucked along the river between immense mountains, the town was terrain-locked into a narrow, elongated pattern. The people of Harmony saw only beauty in the scenic setting. Up to a point Pierce couldn't disagree with their opinion. That point stopped at the road system around Harmony, a twisting, winding stretch of highway twenty miles east and ten miles west of the town's site. Lives were lost every year because of that road, and it was the sheriff's fondest wish that the state would get off its duff and put in the new highway the county had been promised for at least five years.

Thus, when the mayor called with news about the proposed highway, Pierce sat up and took notice. "You mean that they've finally made a decision?" he exulted.

George Lester concurred. "I was just told by the head engineer in Helena that the surveying would begin in a few weeks."

"Well, I couldn't be happier, George. It sure took them long enough."

"Actually, Pierce, it seems that the decision was made some months ago."

"Why weren't we notified?"

"Good question. Guess it doesn't really matter, though. We know now. The engineer said we could count on construction starting next spring, as soon as the weather permits."

"How about the route through town? Any information on that?"

"No. I got the impression the whole thing isn't completely settled yet."

"Another delay," Pierce said with a groan.

"Maybe, but I'm happy with this much progress, Pierce. Eventually, we're going to have a fine new highway."

"And a safe one," Pierce added. "Is this for publication, George?"

"Sure is. I'm having a piece put in the newspaper about it."

"Good. Everyone will be glad of the news."

After Pierce put the receiver down, he sat back in his oversize brown leather chair and digested the conversation. He felt a twinge of uneasiness that wouldn't quite disappear. Why hadn't the state's decision reached Harmony before this if it had been made several months ago? And why wasn't the route through town settled? There could only be one route, right through the middle of Harmony, just like the existing road. Where was the problem in that?

Of course, once beyond the town proper, the route could and no doubt would deviate from the old road. As a matter of fact . . .

Pierce got up and went over to a large, detailed map on the wall. The engineers had to concentrate on getting rid of the dangerous curves.

"Well, I'll be damned!" He was suddenly seeing something that had completely gone over his head before. The Harmony Saloon and Motel was sitting right square in the middle of the only sensible route up the canyon!

With his forefinger Pierce traced a relatively straight line from Dallas's property back to town. Who owned *that* property? he wondered. He knew who used to own it, but those families didn't live out there any longer. And what about the raw land out that way? Who owned that now?

Too curious to let the questions go unanswered, Pierce walked out of his office to the main room. "Millie," he said to the secretary. "I've got a little job for you."

"Sure, Pierce. What is it?"

"Some research. I want to know who owns some particular parcels of land just east of town."

"No problem. I can check them out with the assessor's office."

A little later, alone in his office again, Pierce had to laugh, even if it did come out sounding cynical. KC was in such a dither about Dallas running that business, and it could all be for nothing. There was a darned good chance the state would be buying it, and poor old Dallas would be right where KC wanted him, with nothing but a bigger bank account.

It was really too bad. Dallas was having a ball in that saloon. Why couldn't KC see that when it was so obvious to others?

Pierce knew he had a suspicious nature. It wasn't that he automatically mistrusted people's motives, but when things didn't add up, he seldom failed to wonder why, like the ownership of the land he was having Millie check on. Why KC was so all-fired hot to get Dallas away from that business was yet another puzzle, though it was completely unrelated.

Sitting back in his chair with a frown of concentration, Pierce mulled over the possibilities. *"I can't believe Granddad put all of his money into something like this."* Yes, that had been part of KC's initial response to seeing the saloon and motel. Damn, could her true concern be as basic as the money Dallas had invested?

The speculation made Pierce uncomfortable. He didn't want to think of KC as mercenary, but she'd planted those seeds herself. KC was an exciting, beautiful, passionate woman, even if she was as jumpy as a mare with a burr under her saddle. But was her particular burr the fact that her grandfather had spent money she'd had other plans for?

Maybe she had a real fondness for money. Maybe that's why she'd taken to Kyle Rudman. Whether Rudman had any real money or not was only conjecture, but the man lived as if he did. If KC's head had been turned by his expensive clothes and his big car, she wouldn't be the first person who'd been influenced by the appearance of wealth.

And she and the banker had a dinner date tonight.

"Damn," Pierce growled, the thought surprisingly painful. He didn't like where his skepticism had taken him. He didn't like tainting KC's image with avarice, and yet she was the one who'd brought up money. Unhappily, Pierce had to admit a touch of greed would explain a lot of things, notably KC's interest in Kyle Rudman.

"Quality, hell," the sheriff muttered, finding that the more he thought of KC with Kyle, the more he disliked the bank manager. And picturing her *kissing* him made Pierce's blood boil.

She was a sexy armful, despite any less than noble traits she may or may not have. Did she turn on like that for any man? Would she let Rudman bare her breasts and kiss them as he had? Her skin was like silk, especially between her thighs. Would Rudman discover that sensuous spot, too?

Pierce released a harsh breath. He was torturing himself, and a fat lot of good it would do him. He'd teased KC this morning, and he shouldn't have. *Why* had he teased her? He wasn't usually a guy who tripped over his own dumb words. KC was bothering him more than any woman ever had, but that was his problem. He didn't know how to deal with it, especially when she didn't even like him.

At least, that's what she'd said. And other than that little scene in her room, that's the way she acted, too. Pierce's eyes narrowed in thought. Was KC afraid to get too friendly with him because he was the one person who might catch on to the real reason she was here hounding her grandfather? On the other hand, if that were really true, why had she kissed him back as if there were no tomorrow?

Well, the best course was to find out, Pierce finally decided. He wasn't going to suspect KC of something underhanded without giving her a chance to prove him wrong. And his high-mindedness wasn't only because she was a woman he wanted.

Or, was it?

KC hadn't packed with "dates" in mind, and most of her wardrobe consisted of casual clothing. But luckily, or perhaps because she knew better than to go anywhere without at least one dress, she'd tucked in two: one black, the other off-white. They were both simple designs; the black, simply because of its color was a little more formal. She decided on the white for dinner with Kyle Rudman.

She took pains with her hair. It swung loose on her shoulders, slightly curled at the ends and fell smoothly away from her forehead in a shimmering cascade. Care with her makeup came next, then dressing in sheer hosiery and lacy lingerie, and finally the dress and high-heeled black-and-white pumps. A spritz of her favorite perfume, and KC stood back from the mirror for a head-to-toe inspection. She would do.

Kyle appeared at the door promptly at seven, which KC had somehow expected. If it had been Pierce Wheeler coming, she wouldn't have known what to expect, she thought with dry humor as she opened the door. "Good evening," she said, her smile pleasant.

"KC, you look enchanting."

"Thank you. You look very nice, too." He did. Kyle Rudman was immaculately pressed and combed to perfection; every golden hair was in place, not a wrinkle or particle of lint anywhere in sight. He was wearing pale blue—suit, shirt and tie. Only the gleaming tips of black shoes varied the monochromic drama of his apparel. "I'm all ready," KC announced, and tucking a black-and-white clutch bag under her arm, she stepped out of the room and pulled the door closed behind her.

Kyle escorted her to his car, seated her in the passenger's seat and walked around the front of the Mercedes to the driver's side. The motor purred to life. "Perhaps I should explain something before we go, KC."

She smiled expectantly.

"There isn't a decent restaurant in the entire area."

"Granddad and I had a very nice meal at Layton's Café last night."

"Mediocre at best, I'm sure. Anyway, I rarely eat out. I have an excellent cook, a lady I brought from Philadelphia with me. I hope you don't object to dining at my home."

"Well . . . I hadn't expected . . ."

"I know. I should have mentioned it yesterday. You don't really mind, though, do you? Mrs. McCollum is a wonderful cook, and certainly enough of a chaperone."

KC gave a self-conscious laugh. She was being silly, rather prudish. Dinner at Kyle's home wasn't any worse than being in this car with him. "Your house is fine, Kyle."

"Thank you." Turning the car around, Kyle pulled out onto the highway.

"So, you're from Philadelphia?" KC said brightly, deciding that was as good a place as any to begin a conversation.

"No, but I lived there for three years. Actually, my family ties are in Boston."

"Well, how in the world did you end up in Harmony?"

Kyle smiled at her. "I've lived quite a few different places, KC. How about you?"

"Only San Francisco."

"Great city, just great."

KC was watching the road and realizing that Kyle was heading toward the river. The ride through town was brief, and he pulled into the driveway of a very striking home with an impressive lawn that swept right down to the water's edge. "This is lovely, Kyle."

"Thank you. I like it."

The interior of the sprawling house was delightfully elegant. Kyle introduced Mrs. McCollum, then brought KC to a massive, off-white and mauve living room. He prepared drinks, which he poured into crystal glasses, turned on an excellent stereo system and joined KC on an eight-foot sofa.

KC sipped her cocktail and glanced around the posh, perfectly decorated room. "Your home is outstanding, Kyle."

"As you are. You're an amazingly beautiful woman, KC. What does KC stand for, by the way?"

"Katherine Carol. My father dubbed me KC as a toddler."

"Is your father still living?"

KC recounted the tragic boating accident that had taken her parents' lives when she was only seven years old. "Granddad and Grandma Harriet, my father's parents, took me after that. They gave me a wonderful home."

"Which is why you care about Dallas so much."

"Yes, of course. After Grandma Harriet died, Granddad was like a lost soul. He'd retired at sixty-two, and I always assumed he was completely content with retirement. He's acting so strangely lately, though, I don't know what to think. For example, he's driving again. He hasn't driven in years, and he has that big pickup truck now. Just the thought of it is terrifying."

Kyle smiled with solicitous understanding. KC set her glass on the coaster Kyle had placed on the coffee table and turned to him. "I can only guess at your reason for wanting that business, Kyle, but I'm grateful you do. I wish I knew how to convince Granddad to sell it to you."

"So do I. For his sake, more than mine, I might add." Kyle sipped, then stared down at the liquid in his glass. "KC, I'm going to confide in you."

"Confide?" Did they know each other well enough for confidences? She had spoken rather freely about her grandfather, but she'd mentioned nothing she wouldn't say to Dallas's face.

"Yes. There's a reason, which I'm not at liberty to talk about at the present, that puts a time limit on my offer."

KC's spirit instantly flagged. "Granddad doesn't know about that, does he?" she asked quietly.

"No one does. I'm only telling you because of your deep concern for Dallas. I'd like a positive answer within a week. After that, well, the situation is a bit iffy, but there's every chance that I'll have to withdraw my offer."

"A week," KC parroted hollowly. Could she accomplish anything in a week? It seemed ages ago that she'd thought she could slip in and back out of Harmony in a day with Dallas in tow. Now, a week looked like an impossibly short amount of time.

Reaching for her glass, KC sipped slowly. But the delay didn't relieve the situation nor the tenor of her thoughts. Kyle was a businessman, a banker. This probably had something to do with bank business. And if he said a week, then a week was all she had.

"Kyle, if you withdraw your offer, is there much chance of anyone else being interested in the place?"

Kyle shook his head. "I sincerely doubt it. Of course, who can say for sure? A buyer could pop up from out of nowhere."

"Yes, but on the other hand, there might not be another buyer for years," KC added glumly. "I've simply got to make Granddad see reason. Kyle, may I tell him about the time limit? It could make him see the offer differently."

"I'd rather you didn't. That's what I meant about confiding in you, KC. I really shouldn't have said anything about it to anyone. If I didn't share your concern for Dallas, I would have said nothing. I hope you understand."

KC sighed. "To be perfectly honest, I don't. But I realize that discretion is important in business transactions. I won't mention the time limit. You have my word on it."

"Thank you." Kyle smiled broadly. "Well, that's enough about business. Let's enjoy the evening. Do you like classical music?"

Kyle Rudman was the perfect host. Dinner was excellent; the wine extraordinary; the silver, china and table linens of the best quality; the banker's manners impeccable.

But it perplexed KC that she wasn't really enjoying herself. It was all so... perfect. So even-keeled. Not a bump, a misstep, a word out of place occurred. The hot food was hot, the cold food cold and each course was served by the dignified Mrs. McCollum without the tiniest slipup. The unseen stereo speakers generated soft, exquisitely beautiful classical music. By the end of the meal, KC had the feeling she was part of a magazine layout on the perfect dinner for two.

It was all very lovely, but she was finding it dull. Which was surprising because she truly liked classical music and fine manners. It was because of *Kyle*, she finally admitted. He certainly knew how to wine and dine a lady, but he had as much pizzazz as a limp dishrag. His conversation was intelligent, but a yawn. He had very little wit, and if he gave off any sexual sparks, KC wasn't picking them up.

With sardonic self-analysis KC asked herself if she would prefer an evening with Pierce Wheeler. While she had no proof of a sense of humor in his case, she'd certainly had firsthand experience with his "sparks."

She'd also had firsthand experience with his meddling, she reminded herself when a tide of warmth began at her toes and worked its way up at the thought of last night's bedroom scene.

This wasn't fair. Kyle Rudman was the man she'd prefer feeling sparks for, not an overbearing brute who'd threatened to turn her over his knee. Would he have done it if she had dared call him another name? Actually, she'd been rather kind with her name-calling. There were a few far less polite labels she could have laid on the sheriff, and still felt like doing. Especially now, when she knew she had only one week to convince her grandfather to go home with her. Without Pierce's influence, she knew she'd stand a much better chance.

"Shall we have brandy and coffee in the living room?" Kyle asked.

KC cleared her throat. "Kyle, this has been lovely. But I'm still exhausted from my trip. Would you be terribly upset if I asked you to just take me back to the motel?"

He frowned for a moment, but ending up smiling. "Of course not. I know how tiring long car trips can be."

"I thought you might understand," KC murmured, despising her disdain of a considerate man like Kyle. She should have stuck to her guns about not getting involved with *any* man in Harmony. Still, it was too bad that one couldn't somehow mesh Pierce Wheeler and Kyle Rudman into one perfect male. With Kyle's manners and sensitivity and Pierce's fire. . . .

KC shook off the impossible fantasy. Before leaving she stopped to thank Mrs. McCollum for the delicious meal. Then she walked out of Kyle Rudman's flawless, immaculate house and got into his flawless, immaculate car. The evening had been dull, dull, dull, and without wanting to be unkind, KC could hardly wait to get back to her drab little room and relax.

Kyle drove directly to the motel and parked next to KC's car. He left the Mercedes's motor running, but got out to escort KC to the door. With her key out and ready, she turned. "Thank you, Kyle. It was a pleasant evening."

He reached for her hand and brought it to his lips. "More than pleasant, KC. I enjoyed myself immensely. I hope we can do it again soon."

She smiled weakly. "Perhaps."

"KC . . ."

"Yes?"

"May I kiss you good-night?"

A little startled and having not the slightest inclination to kiss Kyle Rudman in anything other than friendship, KC quickly rose on tiptoe and brushed his cheek with her lips. "Good night, Kyle," she said firmly and turned away.

Inside, KC leaned against the door with her head back, breathing a long sigh of relief. The "date" had been a mistake, one she wouldn't repeat. It was all too apparent that Kyle was much more impressed with her than she was with him, and he was too nice a man to lead on when nothing could come of the relationship. If he asked for another evening together, she would refuse tactfully. As understanding as he was, one refusal should get her message of disinterest across.

KC pushed away from the door, tossed her purse onto the dresser and started for the bathroom. A soft rapping at her door stopped her, and she frowned over her shoulder, immediately curious, a little wary. Kyle? Granddad? Surely, not Pierce. His knock last night had been forceful and demanding. The rapping tonight was of knuckles barely grazing the door.

KC moved back to the door. "Who is it?"

"Pierce."

Her heart began to pump harder.

"Please open the door."

He sounded subdued, unlike his normally aggressive self. "Why, Pierce?" she asked quietly.

"Please open the door," he repeated.

In a flash of utter reality, several things popped into KC's mind: the time limit, Pierce's interference, her urgent desire to separate Dallas from the saloon and Harmony. Would it help to really explain her worries to the sheriff? To plead for his cooperation? His influence on Dallas was monumental, she felt. If Pierce told Dallas he should consider Kyle's offer, Dallas would listen.

She made up her mind fast, simply because there was no time to do otherwise. It seemed like a common-sense approach to the problem, and certainly, arguing with the sheriff had gained her nothing.

Hesitating just long enough to let him know she was in command, KC unlocked the door and pulled it open. Pierce's dark eyes washed over. He was wearing gray slacks and a white shirt, and looked so totally male, KC's breath caught. Why couldn't she have felt so breathless around Kyle Rudman?

"I've been waiting for you," Pierce said low.

"Waiting for me! Why? Where? Were you outside when Kyle brought me back?"

"Yes."

"Spying?" KC's green eyes were charged with emotional disbelief.

"Not spying, just waiting. May I come in?"

Was it possible to talk to Pierce about Dallas without the wild flow of electricity shaking her right this second causing problems? Maybe, but not here, not in a motel room where a bed was the most obvious piece of furniture. KC shook her head. "No, you can't come in. But I'll go for a ride with you."

"You will? All right, let's go."

KC ducked back into the room for the motel key, then returned to the door. Pierce hadn't even stepped over the threshold, and it relieved some of her tension to realize he didn't seem in a mood to grab her as he'd done last night. Maybe they *could* talk like two normal people.

Pierce wasn't driving his on-duty car; he led KC to a silvergray and navy-blue van, an attractive, gleaming vehicle with tinted windows. She smiled wryly. No wonder she hadn't noticed him waiting for her. Without the familiar brown sheriff's car in the parking lot, she couldn't possibly have anticipated such a thing.

Settled behind the wheel, Pierce started the van's motor. "Buckle your seat belt," he said quietly. "Anyplace in particular you'd like to go?"

"No. I just wanted to talk to you."

Pierce pulled the van out onto the highway, turning away from town. "I want to talk to you, too. Did you enjoy dinner with Rudman?"

KC sucked in a quick breath. "That's really none of your business, Pierce."

"I want to make it my business. I thought about you all day."

KC turned her face to the side window. There was nothing outside the van but blackness—black trees, black brush, a black night. Pierce's admission shook her. She'd thought of him, too. With melting memories, then with resentment for his interference.

"You're beautiful in that dress."

She still didn't answer.

"I'm sorry I teased you this morning."

KC brought her eyes to him, seeing him as a shadowy form in the dash lights. "I'm not normally so sensitive."

"But I rile you."

"Yes."

"And you don't like me."

She stared. "I do and I don't."

He laughed softly. "That's what I thought."

"Don't read more into that than you should," she warned.

"What *should* I read into it?"

KC turned away again, pronounced unsteadiness in her voice. "I don't know. I never expected you, or Kyle Rudman, or the degree of Granddad's involvement here. If I sound confused, it's because I *am* confused."

"What's confusing you, KC?" Behind the question was Pierce's speculation earlier in the day. His wish that KC would clarify her position and negate his suspicious was as fervent as a prayer. Every human being had some faults and frailties, but he didn't like the possibility of KC following Dallas to Montana because she might have an eye on his money.

"What happened last night, for one thing."

"You and me, you mean. Well, if it makes you feel any better, I'm not completely clearheaded about that, either."

KC was watching him. "Is that why you came back tonight?"

His glance found her in the semidarkness of the van. "Probably. You've been on my mind all day."

"But you had no idea how long I'd be...out with..."

One of Pierce's eyebrows went up. "It was a rather short date, wasn't it? Didn't you and Rudman hit it off?"

If he'd been waiting and watching for her, he had to have seen the chaste little peck she'd given Kyle as a good-night kiss. Yet a strange rebellion kept her from baring her soul. Whatever she had or hadn't felt for Kyle, she wasn't going to discuss it with Pierce. "He's a very nice person," she said with a hint of defensiveness.

Pierce prevented a derisive snort. But he couldn't prevent himself saying, "Maybe he's so nice he's boring. If that goodnight kiss was any measure, he hardly did much for you."

"He's a gentleman," KC retorted sharply. "He doesn't grab like—"

"Like me?"

KC hesitated. The tone of their conversation was changing, and an accusation would change it more. She'd suggested the drive so she could appeal to Pierce's better side, if he had one. All she wanted to do was take her grandfather home with her. It was why she'd braved a long car trip alone, the only reason why she was even in Harmony. Given her plans, it was crazy to have gone out with Kyle Rudman, crazier still that she was so drawn to Pierce Wheeler. Her life had suddenly erupted into channels she couldn't even have imagined only a few days ago.

She had one purpose, one goal, and she kept losing her hold on it.

"I don't want to fight with you, and if I answer that question, that's what will happen. Another argument," she said wearily. "Pierce, I want to talk about Granddad with you."

Pierce's pulse took a wild leap. Maybe they could clear his suspicions up right now. There was something rare going on between him and KC, something that had never touched him before. Right this minute, driving down the road in the shared intimacy of the van, he wanted her. She was as beautiful and desirable as any woman he'd ever seen. And more important, he *wanted* her more than any woman he'd ever seen. But they hardly knew one another, and there was a lot of ground to cover before he could advance his thoughts beyond a strong sexual attraction.

"Shoot," Pierce invited gruffly. "I'm listening."

KC took a breath. "Thank you. I don't think you really understand why I came here."

"I think you came with the idea of taking Dallas back to San Francisco," he said quietly, hoping ardently that that was the extent of KC's objective.

"Yes, but that's a rather simplified portrayal of the situation. He's not a strong man, Pierce. True, his health problems aren't life-threatening. But they're still serious. Apparently, from what I've been able to gather, he hasn't had any bad spells lately. For that, I'm very thankful. But . . ."

"KC, before you manage to convince me that Dallas is on his last legs, let me ask you something. Your grandfather has as much life and desire to do something productive as I do. Why do you want to take that away from him?"

KC couldn't answer right away. Pierce was going at this all wrong. Taking something away from Dallas wasn't her goal; seeing to his health and well-being was. Couldn't Pierce see the difference?

"You're twisting my words," she accused. "I wouldn't hurt Granddad for anything in the world. But he's all I have, don't you understand? And I'm all he has."

Pierce frowned. If KC had an ulterior motive with her grandfather, she was awfully good at concealing it. "You might be all the family he has, but he has friends. Some very good friends."

"You?"

"And a few other people."

"Well, I have friends, too," KC returned with mounting irritation. She should have known Pierce wouldn't discuss the problem rationally. "But I'm talking about family. Getting back to Granddad..."

"KC, I respect and like Dallas. I admire his spunk, and I only hope that when I'm seventy-two, I'll have half as much."

Every drop of KC's hope was seeping away. Slumping back against the seat, she couldn't even muster up any degree of anger. All she could see was going back to San Francisco alone, leaving her grandfather here, then worrying the rest of his life how he was feeling, what he was doing, how he was getting along.

Tears suddenly scalded her eyes, and she blinked fast in an attempt to elude the good cry she felt was imminent. She'd come to Montana with only good intentions, the *best* of intentions, and she was getting nowhere. And who should she blame? Dallas? This man? Herself, for being just a little overprotective?

Thinking about it, Pierce's stand on the matter looked much worse than Dallas's. Pierce wasn't a part of the Logan family. He was only a month-long friend. It was fruitless to lament again that he had no right to interfere, but it was true. He didn't.

Well, the "talk" was over, wasn't it?

"Take me back to the motel," KC whispered huskily.

Pierce shot her a sharp look, realizing she was crying. He looked for a place to pull over. The dark road was narrow and uncooperative for another mile, then Pierce spotted a turnoff. Without preliminaries, he veered off the highway and stopped the van.

There was a center aisle between the two bucket seats, and Pierce slid to his knees and put his arms around KC. She tried to push him away, but at his show of sympathy the tears flowed in earnest, and she ended up crying on his shoulder.

"Why do you feel so bad about this?" he questioned softly, soothing her by caressing her back and hair.

"Why won't you at least try to understand?" she sobbed. "Without you telling Granddad what a great job he's doing, he'd listen to me."

"Honey, I can't compromise my principles on this thing. Your granddad *is* doing a great job. You should be proud of him."

"I'm not proud. I'm worried."

Pierce hesitated, knowing he was beginning to really believe KC's sincerity. Hell, he wanted to believe her. Holding her like this, he might believe anything she said. But if a genuine concern for Dallas was really all this was about, then it was pretty damned silly. Dallas was a mature, capable man. Why couldn't KC see that? "I wish I could make you see how foolish your attitude is."

Stung, KC sat up and away from him. He hadn't grasped a word she'd said. "My attitude is *not* foolish! Oh, take me back. I wish there was a way to never set eyes on you again. This whole thing is your fault."

"You don't really mean that," Pierce said quietly.

"The hell I don't! Take me back to the motel right this minute, or so help me, I'll get out and walk!"

Five

Pierce peered at KC in the dark. It was very dark, the kind of velvety blackness canyon dwellers were accustomed to. The steep, heavily treed mountains blocked the heavens' natural night lights, and unless the moon was directly overhead, it offered little visual aid to night travelers. Surely KC wouldn't jump out of the van into the almost pitch-blackness and start walking!

Suddenly Pierce realized that he didn't know her well enough to predict what she might do, and there was no doubting how upset she was. He understood her frame of mind...and he didn't. A part of him thought she was overreacting, a more tender part of him ached for her unhappiness.

"KC," he said softly, giving in to the ache. "What do you want me to do, lie to Dallas?"

Was he beginning to understand her point of view? KC wasn't ordinarily a weeper, and this emotional eruption had been the result of too much tension for too long a time. She should have wept in San Francisco when she'd first gotten Dallas's call. Then her emotions might not have built to this point. But in San Francisco she'd been positive she could right the sudden upheaval of her and her grandfather's lives. She hadn't realized how *settled* Dallas would have become in only a month.

She also couldn't have anticipated that Dallas had an ally like Pierce Wheeler. "I only wish you wouldn't pump Granddad up so much."

Pierce was sitting back on his heels, squinting at KC in the dark. The new highway and its possible ramifications to the Logan family came to mind. Should he tell KC that she might win simply by waiting for the state's decision on the route for the new road? Yet what if he were wrong, and the saloon and motel were completely bypassed in the final announcement? Was there any point in getting KC's hopes up over mere conjecture? Besides, if there was still a chance that her concern for Dallas was based on monetary gains for herself, the information would only be one more piece of ammunition for her to use on Dallas.

No, it was best he keep that speculation to himself, Pierce decided. Consoling KC would have to come from something else, not from blabbing a premise that was completely unfounded at this point.

Still, turning his back on Dallas, even to console KC, rubbed him the wrong way. "He's my friend," Pierce said quietly. "And you're asking me to be less than a friend in return. Do you realize how hurt he'd be if I started ignoring accomplishments I've done nothing but praise since he bought that business?"

"Hurt?" KC sat back, jarred by the word. Everywhere she turned, she was stopped by something. Dallas *would* be hurt if Pierce suddenly turned off on him. The elderly man valued friends and friendship, although he'd had little enough of friendship lately. In his grief, he had cut himself off from old friends. And look what had happened on the tour. Instead of making some new friends from the group, he'd found fault with them.

Well, she was stymied again, wasn't she? Pressing Pierce to withdraw his support would only hurt Dallas, and the thought of deliberately hurting her grandfather was intolerable. "All right," she said with painful resignation. "I see your point."

"KC, I'm not trying to cause you a problem; that was never my intention. What I wish more than anything else is that you could see Dallas as I do."

Her voice was dull. "And I wish you could see him as *I* do. At home, a daily walk was a chore. How do I stop worrying about him? I can't. He's the most important person in my life."

"He knows you're worried," Pierce said cautiously, wondering again if there was a valid reason for suspecting KC's motives. She seemed so crushed over her failure.

"I'm sure he does. But he has a stubborn streak. Once he sets his mind to something—"

"That's not all bad," Pierce responded with a small laugh. "The old guy's got a lot of grit."

"Well, he didn't have. At least, he didn't for a long time." KC sighed. "This is getting us nowhere. Take me back, Pierce."

Pierce's pulse picked up. Maybe now they could get to why he'd waited for her. "Can we talk about something else first?"

"What else?"

"Us."

"Us!" KC attempted a small laugh. "There isn't any *us*, Pierce."

"There could be. Are you planning on seeing Rudman again?"

KC opened her mouth to speak, then closed it again. Why couldn't she just say no and be done with it?

The answer was simple. Even understanding Pierce's reluctance to "hurt" his friend, Dallas, KC resented the sheriff's interference. She also resented his assumption that last night had automatically made them a twosome. She would not get involved in a purely sexual relationship with a man she resented on other levels.

"I might be," she replied tonelessly, giving nothing of her thoughts away.

A pain darted through Pierce's system. He had the strangest conglomeration of feelings and thoughts to deal with where KC was concerned. It wasn't so much a matter of mistrusting her motives; it was that he couldn't quite get rid of the niggling doubts pestering him. And those same doubts carried over to her relationship with Rudman. She seemed so guarded whenever the banker's name came up. "I see," he said softly. "Let me ask you something. Do you feel anything for me?"

KC found the question ludicrous, given the short time they'd known each other. "Do *you* feel anything for me?"

"You know damned well I do, or I wouldn't have brought it up."

"What? What do you feel for me? What *could* you feel? We've known each other...how long? Two days? That's hardly enough time to develop real feelings for someone."

"Time has nothing to do with feelings. You either have them, or you don't. Obviously you don't." Pierce paused. "Or you want me to think you don't."

"Don't be silly," KC chided scornfully. "Why would I do that?"

"Good question, KC. Why would you do that?" Pierce moved close enough to KC's seat to drop his arms around her again.

"Please don't," she protested fretfully, and tried to pry his arms away. "Pierce . . ."

His face drew nearer hers, finally nesting in the hollow of her throat. "Feel my heartbeat," he whispered. "You excite me, KC."

Her eyes closed for a second, just until she realized she was succumbing to the mad beating of her own heart. Then she jerked her eyelids upward. "Stop it, Pierce," she demanded heatedly, again attempting to push him away. "What makes you think you can manhandle me whenever you feel like it?"

"I'm not manhandling you, honey," he growled softly. "You know what I'm doing, as well as I do." His breath was hot on her skin as his mouth moved down to her breasts. The dress was something slippery, lightweight. Through the fabric he could feel the rigidity of her nipples. "You're excited, too," he murmured.

Everything inside KC seemed to be losing form and slipping into a hot, molten mass. Mingled with all that heat were sharp, spiky thrills, piercing in their intensity, familiar only because she'd felt the same thing last night in this man's arms.

How easy it would be to just sigh and float into an affair with Pierce. That's what he wanted, and the only thing that constituted those "feelings" he'd talked about. There was no doubting he wanted to make love to her. The message came through in the tone of his voice.

What if he refused to stop? What if he went on and on, without her consent? He was big enough, and strong enough, to do anything he wanted to do. Should she be frightened in this dark van in this dark night, miles from anyone else?

Strangely, she wasn't. Any fear she felt was fear for what *she* was feeling, what Pierce made her feel with only sensual per-

suasion. He didn't have to use physical force, KC realized with
a throbbing weakness. He generated enough electricity to light
up the entire canyon highway.

A big hand rose on her back, seeking the nape of her neck.
KC turned her face, hoping to elude the kiss she sensed was
coming. "Please don't kiss me," she whispered hoarsely.

"You're not afraid of me, are you?"

"Should I be?"

"No. I'd never force a woman into anything she didn't want
as bad as me. But that's what I keep getting from you, KC.
There's all kinds of communication, and what you and I have
doesn't need to be said to be understood."

His mouth brushed a small kiss on one corner of her lips. KC
leaned back, as far as she could get. "I didn't come to Harmony for an affair," she groaned. "Don't push me into one."

"It's not me you're afraid of at all, is it? It's yourself."

"That's silly," she scoffed. But her voice was trembling as
much as her body, and Pierce heard and felt the tremors.

"You're shaking." They were in such an awkward position,
or he was. KC was still on the bucket seat, but he was perched
in the aisle. "Get in the back with me," he urged softly. "Let
me warm you up."

"I'm not cold," she denied quickly. "I'd like to go back to
the motel."

"Before or after I kiss you?"

"Pierce!"

His hands rose to her face, steadying it. He *was* going to kiss
her, no matter what objections she made. "I thought you didn't
force women," she whispered, just before his mouth reached
hers.

He tasted her lips briefly, then whispered back, "Maybe I'm
listening to that silent communication. It's saying, 'Kiss me,
Pierce. Make love to me.'"

"No..." The denial died in her throat as his mouth covered
hers again, this time completely, this time moving with firmness and purpose. He meant to inflame, she realized dizzily. He
meant to drive everything else from her mind but the two of
them, alone in the dark, a man and woman who really had to
answer to no one, and who each knew how strong and volatile
the chemistry was between them.

She could lose her way so easily, she knew, and desperately
tried to cling to a scrap of sanity. But being held and kissed,

caressed, teased into recognizing and admitting her own response, was weakening her grasp on reality.

KC moaned deep in her throat. She was on fire, with every cell in her body alive and needful because of this man's power. Pierce turned her on the seat, parted her knees to wedge his hips between them, drawing her closer. Her skirt slid up her thighs, and she felt his hands finding the tops of her hose, heating the bare skin between the sheer stockings and the legs of her panties. And all the while, kiss melted into kiss. Vaguely, as if from a great distance, she realized what was happening, that he intended taking her here, with him kneeling between her thighs, with her sprawled on the bucket seat.

Then, he seemed to change direction, to slow down. Breathing hard, his hands rose to her face again, and he broke the chain of passionate kisses to whisper raggedly. "It's still up to you. Are you saying the word?"

Was she? Could she? *Dare* she?

She wanted to. She'd never wanted anything more.

Oddly, she sought comfort from the very source of the turmoil in her soul. Her head dropped, and she pressed her forehead to Pierce's shoulder. His hands slid around behind her, weaving into her hair. He held her in that manner for some time, until KC's heartbeat slowed and her breathing was almost back to normal. Then she heard him say softly, "See what I mean. There's a wildness between us."

KC's reply was a muffled sigh. "Yes."

Pierce spoke more urgently. "Don't see Rudman again. He's not for you, KC."

She raised her head wearily. "And you are?"

"Can you doubt it? When a few kisses do this to the both of us? We've got something special going for us, KC. You must see it, too."

KC's mind seemed overloaded, bogged down with all that had happened since her arrival in Harmony. She'd made no headway with her grandfather, and she was wasting time with both Kyle Rudman and Pierce Wheeler. She should have had dinner and spent the evening with Dallas. Although if she examined her priorities closely, spending time with the man who understood her worries so well and wanted to buy the saloon and motel made better sense than what she was doing here with Pierce. Of course, she'd thought, she'd *hoped* to convince Pierce of the sensibility of her campaign here.

Instead, he'd done the convincing, and then tried to further their personal intimacy. And, Lord help her, she'd been putty in his big hands . . . again.

Drained, KC could hardly find the strength to rebut Pierce's summation of their relationship. "All you want is to make love to me," she whispered shakily, the strongest charge she could come up with.

Pierce's senses flamed. He hadn't expected such a straight-forward accusation, but could he deny it?

"Is that so terrible?" he asked low. "Isn't making love the obvious conclusion to desire? I do desire you, KC, and I won't apologize for it, either. How do you propose to handle *your* desire for me? And don't waste your breath denying you want me. It sparked between us the first time we set eyes on each other."

His arms were still around her, his hands on her back, his hips between her thighs. In the back of her mind she thought of how wrinkled her dress must be, and if it were light enough to really see, how debasing her position could appear. There was no one to see them, though, and even she could hardly see the man pressuring her every way possible. But she could feel him, and smell him, and hear him. And he was big and solid and persuasive, and he wasn't lying or imagining things, either. Of course she wanted him. And any attempt she might make to weaken his interpretation of the situation would be a lie.

But she didn't have to do what her body demanded. She was still in control of her baser urges, even if giving in to them would be far easier than denying them.

KC dampened her lips to speak. "You understand me only to a point," she said huskily. "The only common ground you and I have is this, Pierce, and I don't take sex lightly." KC reached behind herself, took his hands and brought them around her. "Will you take me back now?"

It took a few seconds for Pierce to answer, and then he gave it in two parts. First was a kiss, a tender meeting of their lips that rocked KC. Not only hadn't she expected another kiss at that moment, but she also wasn't prepared for one that contained only tenderness. Before she could recover, he whispered, "I want you tonight, but I can wait a little longer."

Then he moved back to his seat and started the van.

At first, KC sat with her mouth open. Pierce had surprised her. Within the tangle of her thoughts had been a doubt that he'd stop. Or had it been a crazy, foolish wish that he wouldn't? Whatever the case, while he turned the van around, she realized she hadn't expected him to give up so easily.

The dash lights softly illuminated the two of them, and Pierce gave her a warmly intimate smile. Realizing how disheveled she must look, KC quickly yanked her skirt down and turned in the seat to face the front.

Somehow, someway, she had to get this thing resolved with her grandfather and get out of Harmony. If she didn't leave soon, Pierce would win. He knew how strong the sensual bond between them was, and now, so did she. Last night hadn't been just a fluke; the man had much too much power over her senses.

On the way back to town, KC finally calmed down enough to speak her mind. She gave Pierce a sharp look. "I don't want to see you again."

"What?"

She'd stunned him, she saw. But she couldn't help that; he wanted too much. "I know we'll run into each other. As long as you're Granddad's friend, that can't be avoided. What I'm talking about is something like tonight. I'm not going to be in Harmony any longer than necessary, and I have no intention of using my time in a shoddy affair with you."

There was a harsh note in Pierce's reply. "Is that how you see this?"

"Yes, I do. I told you I don't take sex lightly, but it's obvious you do."

"What do you hold out for—a marriage proposal?"

KC sucked in a stunned breath. "I only think there should be something important between a man and woman before they fall into bed together. If that makes me a prude in your eyes, so be it."

"I told you I have feelings for you, didn't I?"

"Yes, but I know what those feelings are. You made them very clear."

"Dammit, KC, we've only known each other a few days. What do you want me to say?"

"My point exactly. We *have* only known each other a few days." KC saw the saloon and motel sign ahead. "I would appreciate it if you would stay away from me," she said evenly as the van pulled into the parking lot.

Pierce stopped the van beside her car. "Did you tell Rudman to stay away from you, too?"

KC's chin came up. "I would if he pressured me the way you do," she retorted. "Kyle's not a groper, for your information."

"Oh, I forgot," Pierce drawled sardonically. "*He's* a gentleman."

"You might not like it, but that's exactly what he is." KC reached for the door handle. "Good night."

Pierce waited until KC was inside the motel unit with the lights on, and then he drove away with a knot of perplexity in his gut.

At quarter after ten the next morning, a lull in business left KC and Dallas alone in the saloon. Dallas immediately got out the vacuum cleaner, but before he could plug it in, KC walked over to him. "Granddad, could you put that off for a few minutes? I'd like to talk to you."

"I suppose so. But I like to get the vacuuming done when the place is empty, honey."

"I know. But it's not empty often, and that's the only time we can talk during the day, too."

Dallas frowned, then nodded. "Well, all right. Wanna sit down?"

"Please." Going over to one of the tables, KC pulled out a chair. When they were both seated, she looked earnestly across the table at the elderly man. "Granddad, you know that I love you, don't you?"

Dallas's cheeks got pinker, but he nodded. "I love you, too, KC. I'm real proud of you, honey."

KC leaned forward, her eyes bright and hopeful. "May I speak frankly?"

Dallas sat back with a sigh. "You don't like this place, do you? I sure hoped you would."

"There's nothing wrong with the place, Granddad. What's wrong is you running it and living a thousand miles from home."

"Because I'm an old man?"

KC flushed, instantly chagrined. "I'm not trying to be cruel," she said softly. "But it's true that if you were twenty years younger, I wouldn't be concerned."

"I've been feeling real good, KC. Better than I've felt in years."

"I believe you. You're looking very fit. But right now the weather is perfect. What will happen this winter? It gets very cold here in the winter months."

Dallas studied his granddaughter. "What do you want me to do?"

KC hesitated a beat, then said quietly, "Come home with me. Sell the place to Kyle Rudman and come back to San Francisco. I can't stay much longer, and I'm terrified at the thought of leaving you here alone."

Dallas took off his glasses, wiped them with his handkerchief and settled them back on his face. "Well, now. It appears we have a problem. If I stay, you're unhappy; if I go, I'm unhappy."

Frowning, KC squirmed in her chair. "I'm only thinking of you, Granddad. Can't you be happy in San Francisco? That's your home. You've lived there your whole life."

"I've nothing against San Francisco, KC. But I'm happier here. I'm doing something, honey, something I really like. I've made some good friends, and you couldn't ask for a prettier little town, could you?"

"Harmony's pretty," KC agreed without enthusiasm. The beauty of the town and surrounding area wasn't the issue. "I know you've needed something to do. Anyone gets bored doing nothing. But there are probably dozens of things to keep you occupied at home. What about your old hobbies? You have a nice coin collection. Have you lost interest in that? And golf. You used to play golf years ago. I'll bet there are some senior citizens' golfing activities in San Francisco."

Dallas listened with a vacant expression. "I don't want to play golf, and I sold my coin collection."

"You did? When?"

"A few years back. Look, honey, I know you mean well. But I'm doing what I want to do right now. I don't like you worrying about me like this. If going back to California alone upsets you so much, why don't you quit your job and move here?"

KC's eyes widened. "And do what? How could I make a living here? Besides, I already quit my job. That's why I can't stay indefinitely. I've got to find another job."

"You already quit your job? Why? To come after me? Dammit, KC, that's a darned heavy burden to put on me. I thought you had a good job. And you left it just so you could make this trip!"

"No, no! It wasn't like that, Granddad. I'd been thinking of changing jobs for a long time."

Dallas looked doubtful. "Well, I sure don't remember you saying anything about it before."

"I did. Several times," KC insisted. She could see that Dallas didn't remember those incidents, which was troubling. She didn't want her grandfather shouldering the responsibility for something he hadn't caused. She'd been dissatisfied for at least a year, and quitting her position hadn't been an impulsive act at all. Of course, this trip had been a bit of a catalyst; it would have been a major undertaking to get the needed time off. But in any case she would have eventually turned in her resignation. "Believe me, Granddad, I didn't quit just to make this trip."

Dallas continued to look upset. "I'm disrupting your life," he said gruffly.

KC sighed poignantly. "You're not disrupting my life. But even if you were, I wouldn't care. You're worth it, Granddad. I'd do anything I could to keep you safe."

"Safe! KC, what do you think's gonna happen to me here?" Shaking his head, Dallas got up. "I've got to give all this some thought. How long can you stay in Montana?"

KC rose slowly. "Another few days, I suppose." She didn't like the forlorn expression in her grandfather's pale blue eyes. "I don't want you to be unhappy," she said soberly. "That's not my intent."

"I know it's not," Dallas sighed. "Give me a little time, KC. I need to think things through." And he picked up the vacuum cleaner's cord and plugged it into an outlet.

"Telephone," Dallas called out that afternoon, holding up the phone to KC.

"For me?" KC put down the damp cloth she'd been cleaning the bar with and hurried over to the wall phone. "Who is it?"

"Kyle Rudman."

Since their talk that morning, KC had sensed an odd petulance from her grandfather. He hadn't been treating her any differently on the surface, but underlying what appeared to be only normal behavior was something cool and distant. She was sure Dallas was thinking about their conversation, but she was worried that he was looking at it as interference on her part. Lord help her, she'd had enough of meddling herself the past few days—from Pierce Wheeler!

Now, after urging Dallas to sell the business to Kyle, KC felt guilty about receiving a telephone call from the banker, as though she were participating in a conspiracy against her own grandfather. She took the phone, smiling weakly at Dallas. "Hello, Kyle."

"I hope I'm not interrupting anything."

"You're not."

"Good. I have something to discuss with you. If I came by, could you take a little drive with me? It's about my offer, KC."

KC looked around for her grandfather and saw that he was busy with a customer. "I've been helping Granddad, but he wouldn't mind me leaving for a few minutes."

"That's very kind of you. Helping Dallas, I mean. I might have anticipated that, though, when I know how concerned you are about him. I'll be by in ten minutes, all right?"

"I'll be outside, Kyle."

It occurred to KC as she hung up the phone that Kyle might already be withdrawing his offer, and her spirit took a dive. Not that she had much hope left that Dallas was going to sell, but without a buyer there was no chance at all of getting him out of the saloon and motel business.

"I'm leaving for a little while, Granddad," she called.

Dallas gave her a brief glance, then turned back to his customer. Sighing, KC walked out of the saloon and headed for her room. Quickly she brushed her hair and refreshed her lipstick, and she was ready and waiting when the Mercedes pulled into the parking lot.

Kyle was resplendent in navy blue today, dressed in an excellently styled suit and vest, topped with a snowy white shirt and a navy-and-red striped tie. Spotting KC coming out of her room, he hopped out of the car to open the passenger door for her. "Thank you for coming on such short notice."

"Quite all right," she murmured as she settled onto the posh seat.

Kyle headed away from town, the same direction Pierce had taken the night before. The route looked very different in daylight, KC noted; it was scenically beautiful, although the sharp curves of the narrow road were actually breath-stealing in places.

"Something came up, KC," Kyle said somberly. "I can't go into detail, but it's imperative I either buy Dallas's property very soon or make up my mind to forget it. Have you made any headway with him today?"

KC released a dejected breath. "Very little, I'm sorry to say."

"That's too bad," Kyle sympathized. "He's going to kill himself in that place, KC."

All the worries that had stormed KC since Dallas's initial call to San Francisco battered her again in a shattering barrage. While Kyle's consolation was a harsh summation, it expressed KC's turmoil accurately. How could Kyle Rudman see the situation so clearly when Pierce Wheeler, and even Dallas himself saw nothing beyond the fun Dallas was having? Grit, indeed! What good was grit if an old man wore himself out adhering to a gutsy ambition?

"You're the only one who understands," KC whispered brokenly, forgetting that last night she had found this man dull. He might not set off flares in her libido, but Kyle Rudman's sensitivity knew no bounds. And yes, he was uncommonly handsome. A genteel man, with wonderful manners and tastes. A woman could certainly do worse than keep company with Kyle Rudman.

Kyle turned the Mercedes off the main road and followed a rutted, bumpy trail a very short distance to the river. Then he stopped, switched the motor off and turned in the seat. "You poor darling," he said softly, and slid over to draw KC into his arms.

She allowed the embrace and rested her head on Kyle's navy-blue shoulder. Sympathy and understanding were what she needed right now, not fireworks, so her completely bland reaction to Kyle's nearness was acceptable and even comforting. "I guess I might as well give up and go home," she sighed sadly.

"Please don't. Not yet. I was afraid of that happening, darling. That's why I had to talk to you. I'm upping my offer by another five thousand dollars."

KC lifted her head. "Another five thousand? Oh, Kyle, how generous!"

"Do you think it will help?"

"It might."

"And another thing, I'm also willing to reimburse Dallas for the sign and the parking-lot gravel. He'd get every penny of his investment back, plus a ten-thousand-dollar profit."

"That's *more* than generous," KC exclaimed, seeing a very substantial reason for broaching her grandfather one more time. "Why are you doing this?" she asked softly. "Why are you being so kind?"

Kyle smiled. "Two reasons: your grandfather and you. I'm as worried about him as you are. I can afford to be generous to help him make up his mind. And I've become very fond of you in a very short time." He reached for KC's hand and brought it to his lips, holding it there for a tender kiss to her palm. "I enjoyed last night very much, KC. Let's do it again tonight."

"Tonight?" Dismay struck KC. She didn't want a repeat of last night. "I better have dinner with Granddad," she hedged. "He's so busy during the day, I can hardly squeeze in a private moment."

Kyle nodded. "I understand. Yes, it would be best to talk to Dallas as quickly as possible."

"There's still a time limit on the offer, isn't there?"

"I'm afraid so, darling. I'm sorry about that, but it's really out of my hands."

He kept calling her darling, and the repeated endearment was beginning to bother KC. She also sensed Kyle wanted to kiss her, and the thought chilled her. It wasn't a bit fair that a nice man like Kyle repelled her physically while a bully like Pierce made her senses sing.

KC became very businesslike. "I should be getting back, Kyle. I told Granddad I'd only be gone a few minutes."

"Of course," he murmured, but he didn't move away. KC saw him gaze at her mouth, then at her breasts. Kyle's expression seemed suddenly sensuous, and she realized she'd been right; he did want to kiss her. His face came closer, and instinctively KC pulled back.

"You're very desirable," he whispered as his arm tightened around her shoulders. "I thought of you all night, darling."

KC stiffened, remembering, in the back of her mind, how she'd told Pierce that Kyle didn't grope. Well, it was apparent that Kyle Rudman had the same drives and passions as Pierce did. Only, Kyle was a bit more gentlemanly about the matter, and *she* felt nothing but a strong desire to get away unkissed.

"I really must get back," she said firmly.

His eyes were hooded with heavy lashes, something she hadn't really noticed before. KC suddenly felt a strange jab of wariness. Last night she'd sat in that van in a coal black night with Pierce. She'd felt how much he'd wanted her, and yet, she hadn't experienced any of the flutterings of uneasiness that gripped her now just because Kyle wanted to kiss her. And it was broad daylight, too.

There was tension in the Mercedes, but it wasn't the kind of tension she always felt around Pierce Wheeler. This was dark and disturbing, and KC had to deliberately force a smile. "Shall I call you after I speak to Granddad about the additional five thousand?"

Kyle sat without moving, just staring at her. Then, slowly, he nodded his head. "Please do that."

KC felt relief when he moved back behind the wheel and started the car.

Six

─────

Can we have dinner together tonight?'' KC asked as she and Dallas left the saloon together shortly after six.

Dallas shook his head. ''I have other plans, KC.''

''Other plans?'' KC echoed hollowly. Dallas wouldn't quite meet her eyes, and she was sure he was still upset over their talk that morning. ''Granddad, please don't be angry with me,'' she pleaded softly.

''I'm not angry,'' Dallas declared. ''I have someone I need to see tonight.''

Pierce? Of course. Dallas was going to tell the sheriff about the talk, probably ask for Pierce's advice. And Pierce would give it, gladly. The damned man gave advice without being asked; he certainly wouldn't be adverse to handing it out with an invitation.

Fuming again over the sheriff's involvement, but keeping her irritation to herself until Dallas had walked away, KC went on to her own room. Inside, she took off the jeans and T-shirt she'd worn all day and turned the shower on full blast.

Maybe it was time to admit failure and go home, she pondered morosely while she shampooed her hair. What was she accomplishing here? She was beating her head against a stone wall, and for what? Dallas didn't want her worrying about him; in fact, he seemed resentful about it.

If she only *could* stop worrying! She'd give a lot to be able to get in her car and drive away without worries.

Why did only Kyle understand how she felt? Dallas was almost childishly rebellious about her concern. As for Pierce, KC felt his bemused derision every time they talked about the problem. Pierce thought she was overanxious, worried about nothing, *foolish* even.

Was she?

While she bathed, KC attempted to see the situation unemotionally. Sighing, she quickly realized she couldn't separate her feelings that easily. She loved her grandfather too much to even think of him as someone with less influence on her emotions. All of her life, even before the accident that took her parents' lives, Dallas had been her hero. KC had deeply mourned her grandmother's death, but she had suffered more because of Dallas's loss than her own.

Since then she had tried to induce some spirit back into her grandfather. True, she hadn't pressed him into activities he hadn't shown enthusiasm for. The tour had been the first thing KC had suggested that Dallas had readily agreed to. And somewhere along that bus route, he'd regained some of his old spirit. For that KC was grateful. But the form it had taken— Dallas's strange burst of independence and his almost cavalier attitude toward living so far away from San Francisco and her—were very hard to accept.

Well, she had one more piece of ammunition, the additional five thousand dollars Kyle was offering. Perhaps Dallas wouldn't be gone long and she could talk to him again tonight. If that didn't do any good, she might as well make plans to leave Harmony.

After toweling off, KC dried and curled her hair, applied a few touches of makeup and dressed in a blue-and-green print skirt and a plain blue blouse with a scoop neckline. With a pair of low-heeled sandals on her feet and a white shoulder bag over her arm, she locked the motel room and went to her car. She would eat dinner in one of Harmony's cafés, then return to wait for her grandfather.

KC bought a copy of the local newspaper from a sidewalk stand, then went into Layton's Café. She found an empty booth, ordered dinner and picked up the newspaper, noting that it was a twice-weekly publication. Scanning the front page, she spotted an article on the new highway and read it with interest. Apparently the new road was finally a certainty, and she thought of how relieved Pierce must be.

Pierce. All day KC had managed to keep thoughts of him at bay. But now, sitting alone, bogged down with frustration over her grandfather, KC sighed, folded the newspaper and let Pierce Wheeler take over her thoughts.

The explosiveness between them wasn't normal. And it wasn't common, not for her. Maybe it was common for Pierce. Maybe he was so magnetic that women by the droves were willing bed partners. KC winced over that possibility, even while telling herself it didn't matter to her how many women Pierce took to bed. Why should it? In a few days, both he and Harmony would be nothing but a memory.

Still, there was no denying that the times in his arms were something special. If they had none of the present dissension between them, wouldn't she be in danger of falling for the handsome sheriff?

Honest enough to admit the truth of that conjecture, KC was no less disturbed to realize that no other man had ever reached her physical side so significantly. It was disturbing to realize that right now, just thinking about Pierce was increasing her pulse beat. She could sit here in full view of a dozen strangers and look perfectly serene, but with Pierce in her thoughts, she was a mass of inner turmoil. The man affected her, that was the bottom line, no matter how much she wished he didn't.

And speak of the devil!

KC stirred uncomfortably at the sight of Pierce coming through the door. And he was alone. Where was Dallas?

She grabbed the newspaper again and pretended a deep engrossment in the front page, hoping the sheriff would walk on by her booth without stopping. He didn't.

"Eating alone?"

KC looked up. "I thought Granddad was having dinner with you."

"Not with me," Pierce returned casually. "Mind if I join you?"

KC refolded the newspaper. Last night's request for Pierce to stay away from her lay on the air between them. But how could she enforce the demand in public? In the long run, did it really matter if they ate dinner together? She wasn't apt to be in Harmony much longer, no matter what transpired in this booth this evening.

"All right," she allowed tonelessly.

Pierce slid into the booth. "Catching up on the news?"

KC prepared herself to participate in a hopefully normal conversation with the sheriff. "Yes. I read that article about the new highway. You must be pleased."

"Very pleased."

The waitress came over, took Pierce's order and asked KC, "Shall I hold up your dinner until Pierce's is ready?"

Trapped into good manners, KC smiled thinly. "Thank you." She felt Pierce's dark gray eyes boring into her from across the table, and experienced a spurt of the resentment he seemed to cause so easily. Their "normal" conversation certainly hadn't lasted very long. "Stop staring at me," she whispered when the waitress had gone.

"I like staring at you. You're a fascinating woman, KC. In this light your hair looks like quicksilver. I was remembering how it feels." Pierce's hands were on the table, and he moved his fingers seductively, as if he were twining them through her hair right then. His graphic mime delivered a wave of heated memories, and KC blushed.

"You're impossible," she snapped.

"And you're beautiful, even when you're angry. Do you know how green your eyes are right now?"

KC glanced around. "Do you want the whole town to hear you?"

Pierce shrugged. "I don't care who hears me. I've got nothing to hide." The look in his smoky gray eyes became intense. "Do you?"

"I beg your pardon?" Dumbfounded at such a strange question, KC stared across the table. "Have I missed something along the way?"

"You don't have any idea what I'm talking about?"

Baffled, KC gave her head a shake. "What's this all about?"

Returning her puzzled stare for a stretch, Pierce finally broke eye contact. "Nothing important," he said. To throw her off the scent, he changed the subject. "How did you sleep last night?"

She looked him in the eye and lied. "Like a log."

Grinning, Pierce confessed, "Well, I didn't do that well. By this morning I'd just about decided to steer clear of—"

"Of me?" KC's cheeks were burning again. "As I recall, that's exactly what I asked you to do."

"I know. But it's impossible to avoid someone in this town, sweetheart. I walked in here with supper on my mind, and there you were. Looks like fate has something in store for you and me."

"Don't be ridiculous!"

"It doesn't look ridiculous to me."

"Well, it does to me."

Laughing softly, Pierce sat back. The waitress delivered their salads and left again. "Eat, KC. And let's talk about something else. Your constant references to sex are driving me loony."

She glared her indignation. "We weren't talking about sex, and you're not the least bit funny."

Pierce laughed again and picked up his fork. "How come you thought Dallas was having dinner with me?"

KC frowned. "Who *is* he having dinner with?"

"How would I know?"

"I suspect you *do* know."

Pierce grinned lazily. "I told you he has other friends. You just don't want to believe anything I say, KC. You've got a mental block where I'm concerned."

"With damned good reason," she retorted dryly. "From the minute I got to town, you've done your best to make me out a fool."

A shadow crossed Pierce's face, sobering his expression. "That's not true. I've got a few reservations about your wanting to haul Dallas back to San Francisco, but I've never thought of you as a fool."

KC concentrated on her salad, and when Pierce began talking about the new highway again, she was glad. Throughout dinner, they managed a reasonably sane conversation, but when Pierce reached for both checks, KC objected. "I can pay for my own dinner."

"But you're not going to. I'm paying."

"You're a terrible bully," she accused heatedly.

Pierce raised an eyebrow. "Because I insist on buying you dinner? Come on, KC, stop being so touchy. You're always looking for an excuse to be mad at me. Have you asked yourself why? From where I sit, it looks like you're afraid that if you let yourself be at all nice to me, you might be *too* nice. Is that what's bugging you? Are you afraid you might like me?"

While he was talking, Pierce was also getting out of the booth. *And* he walked off with both checks, leaving KC to stare after him, her heart thudding with all the tumultuousness he repeatedly aroused.

She was too emotional where Pierce was concerned, KC admitted, waiting outside the door while he took care of the bill. In fact, she'd been a bundle of nerves since she'd arrived in Harmony. Sooner or later something had to give. No one could function indefinitely with this kind of tension.

Pierce sauntered out with a smile. "Thank you for dinner," KC stated politely. "And goodbye." She turned and walked away, heading down the street to where she'd parked her car.

Chuckling to himself, Pierce followed three steps behind, taking the opportunity to admire KC's slightly swaying skirt and her pretty legs. Her hair was swinging, too, bright in the waning light, as alluring as Pierce had pronounced it earlier. A man could spend days lost in that silky hair...maybe a lifetime, he found himself thinking. The thought shook him a little, because he'd never placed a woman in that picture before. A lifetime? Hell, that sounded pretty permanent.

KC reached her car and turned to face the man behind her. "Are you following me?"

"No, ma'am. My car's a little farther down. However, I'd be happy to follow, if you'd be kind enough to invite me home with you."

KC wet her lips. Why was she hesitating for even one second? Just because Pierce was outrageously good-looking and appealing to everything female in her weren't reasons enough to compromise her standards. Yet she did hesitate, and she even heard herself asking inanely, "To my room?"

Pierce's eyes darkened. "Yes," he said softly. "To your room. Invite me, KC."

There was so much turbulence on their locked gazes, KC was almost swayed. What would it be like to forget everything else and do what Pierce wanted? Some women would. Some women would smile and flirt, or come up with a clever remark. Why couldn't she? She'd always known she had a rather serious personality, and certainly her past relationships had each taken a long time to develop. But this was different. Pierce was different. He was the kind of excitingly sexy man any woman would want to experience, given the opportunity.

Startled by the direction of her thoughts, KC shook her head. "I can't do that," she finally answered.

Pierce stared silently for a few moments. "You know something, KC? I have a feeling you don't think I'm quite real."

KC's gaze flickered. "What's that supposed to mean?"

"Aren't you a little curious about me? All you know is that I'm the local sheriff and that I rile the hell out of you because of my loyalty to your grandfather. Oh, yes, you know one more thing: you can have your way with me anytime you choose." Pierce ended with a smile, a broad, teasing smile that brought another flush to KC's face.

"You get a big kick out of teasing me, don't you?"

"Maybe I'd like to see you smile more."

KC looked away. "I haven't felt much like smiling lately."

"Maybe I can make you smile. Would you come with me for an hour or so? I'd like you to meet someone."

"Who?"

"A lady. Her name is Rose Dobrinsky."

Puzzled, KC frowned. "Why would I want to meet Rose Dobrinsky?"

"She'd like to meet you."

"I don't understand. Does she have something to do with Granddad?"

"No, KC. She has nothing to do with Dallas. She has to do with me. I'd like you to know that I'm as real as you are. Rose Dobrinsky is *my* family."

"Your family? But . . . the name . . ."

"Will you come? Do you have something better to do this evening?"

"I was going to wait for Granddad to get back. I need to tell him something."

"We won't be late. I'll have you back at the motel in an hour."

KC relented, although she wasn't sure why. In asking her to meet Rose Dobrinsky, Pierce had seemed sincere and not at all wolfish, or even teasing. Sincerity was usually influencing, and she couldn't deny some curiosity about Pierce's background. He was right; she knew very little about him.

KC drove her car back to the motel, noted that Dallas's white pickup was still absent and got into Pierce's van.

"Granddad is still out. I hope he didn't go far. I really do worry about his driving," KC said thoughtfully.

"I checked his driving, KC. He does just fine."

"You checked it?"

Pierce laughed. "He had a great time shopping for that pickup."

"It certainly surprised me," KC commented dryly.

"Well, stop worrying about it. He has to have something to get around town in."

"Not if he comes home with me, he doesn't. He used to be perfectly satisfied with a bus or a taxi."

Pierce shook his head. "You never give up, do you?"

KC looked away, not quite ready to admit she'd been thinking of doing exactly that.

They returned to town and took a side road that led away from the river. Pierce stopped the van in front of an attractive brick house. "Here we are." They got out and went through the gate and up the front walk. Pierce opened the front door and called, "Rose?"

A plump, smiling woman appeared. She had warm brown eyes and graying brown hair. A pink flowered apron covered the front of her blue-and-pink cotton dress. She—as well as what KC could see of the house from the foyer—was immaculate. "You've brought your friend," she beamed at Pierce.

"This is KC Logan, Rose. KC, meet the lady who straightened out a wayward sixteen-year-old boy and *kept* him straightened out."

"You?"

"Yes, me. It's a long story."

KC held her hand out to Rose Dobrinsky. "I'm very pleased to meet you, Rose."

Rose's two hands went around KC's. "You're as pretty as Pierce said you were."

"He did?" KC gave Pierce a curious look.

"Please come into the living room. Can I get either of you anything? Have you had dinner?"

"Just finished," Pierce answered. "We only stopped by for a few minutes. This is your bridge evening, isn't it?"

"Yes," Rose smiled. "But we have plenty of time. The group isn't due for another half hour." She turned to KC. "Do you play bridge, KC? Pierce is an excellent player."

KC nodded. "My grandparents belonged to a bridge club years ago. They taught me to play."

"Wonderful. Maybe we can get a foursome up some evening. How is your grandfather, by the way? Pierce hasn't brought him around for some time now."

"Oh, you know Granddad?"

Rose's laughter was contagiously bubbly, making KC smile. When she realized she was smiling, she glanced at Pierce and saw admiration in his eyes. "I get to meet a lot of Pierce's friends," Rose confided. "When he told me about you, I asked him to bring you by."

Pierce was sitting in a blue wing chair with his long legs stretched out in front of him. He looked happily content, KC noted, completely satisfied to be in Rose Dobrinsky's spotlessly clean and charmingly decorated living room. KC was busily formulating questions. If Rose Dobrinsky had raised Pierce since he was sixteen, were his real parents dead? And why had he told Rose about her?

"I don't quite understand the connection between the two of you," KC said frankly.

Pierce only smiled lazily, leaving the story to Rose. "My husband, Russ, was the sheriff of Levine County for years and years, KC. You do realize the sheriff's office is an elected position, don't you? Well, the people just kept voting Russ in, just like they're doing with Pierce. Russ would be very proud if he were still with us.

"Seventeen years ago we had a terribly cold fall. Blizzards every other day, it seemed. Just before Thanksgiving, Russ found Pierce wandering the streets. Well, he brought the boy home with him. Russ and I had four children of our own, but Pierce fit right into the family."

"They gave me a home," Pierce said softly. "Without the Dobrinskys, Lord only knows how I might have ended up."

"What happened to your own family?" KC asked the sheriff.

"I only had an abusive father, and I left him in Brooklyn when I ran away."

KC's eyes widened. "You're from Brooklyn?"

"I was born in Brooklyn, but my life began in Harmony," Pierce replied quietly. "Thanks to this lady and her husband."

"Pierce has been a joy," Rose put in with a fond glance at the tall, lanky sheriff. "Russ and I both came to love him just like he was another one of our sons."

KC gave Pierce a poignant look. "You were a very fortunate young man."

Rose asked KC about her family, and heard all about the boating accident that killed KC's parents and how Dallas and Harriet had raised her. "Well, your and Pierce's backgrounds aren't that far apart, are they?" Rose concluded brightly. At the sound of the front doorbell pealing, she got up. "My bridge group," she explained.

Pierce and KC stood, too. "We'll be running along," he said, bending over to kiss Rose's cheek.

It took several minutes to say goodbyes and get past the people on the front porch, but they were finally in the van on their way to the motel. "Well, what do you think of Rose?" Pierce inquired.

"She strikes me as a remarkable woman. Why did you tell her about me?"

"Does it bother you that I did?"

"No, but I'm curious why you did. Do you tell her about—"

"The other women in my life?" he finished softly.

"Well . . . yes."

Pierce took his eyes from the road and looked at KC. "And if I said no, what would you make of it?"

"I really don't know," KC mumbled, a little stunned by the implications of Pierce telling the only mother he'd ever had about her.

The van turned into the motel and saloon parking lot, and Pierce parked beside KC's car. Dallas's white pickup was still notably absent, and KC stared at the vacant parking space in front of unit two. "Who did he go to see tonight, Pierce?"

"You'll have to ask him."

KC's head jerked around. Pierce had turned the van's motor off, and the interior of the vehicle was quiet, with outside noises muffled and distant-sounding. "Does he have a lady friend?"

Pierce studied his companion. "How would you feel about that, if he did?"

"He mentioned meeting a woman, Mary." KC felt a strange, unsettled fluttering in her midsection. Her grandfather with a woman other than her grandmother? Oh, Lord, how *did* she feel about such a possibility?

KC's chin came up. Pierce knew. He knew exactly what was going on. "Mary who, Pierce?" she challenged.

He shook his head slowly. "I'm not discussing Dallas's personal life with you or anyone else, KC."

"Then he *has* a personal life?" KC was still trying to assimilate her feelings, but she realized her first reaction was negative. She was associating words like disloyalty and foolishness with her grandfather.

"He's entitled to a personal life," Pierce declared.

Again Pierce's defense of Dallas rankled KC. "Another of your unsolicited opinions, Sheriff?" she shot back. "How broad-minded you are with *my* grandfather. I wonder how generous you'd be if it were Rose who'd suddenly changed into a person you could hardly recognize."

"Is that the case with Dallas? Is he really a different man than the one he was in San Francisco? Or is it possible he was always the same underneath and maybe just a little bit smothered?"

"Smothered! By whom?" KC cried. "By me? Are you daring to infer I smothered my grandfather's natural tendencies? You've got a lot of gall!"

Pierce exploded. "Dammit! Are we going to end up in another argument? Talk about a mule-headed woman! KC, you've got a blind spot when it comes to Dallas. What makes you think you can live his life for him? As for my gall, little lady, if you treated your grandfather in San Francisco the way you're trying to do here, you bet you smothered him! No wonder he broke from the traces!"

KC narrowed her eyes at Pierce. How quickly their moods could change, she realized again. They sparked all kinds of emotions in each other, and right this minute she would love to slap him. Scathing words were the best she could do, though. "Last night I told you I never wanted to see you again. The next time you accost me in public, be prepared for a scene, because that's what you're going to get!"

Pushing the door open, KC jumped out and slammed it hard. She flounced angrily to her door and fumbled in her purse for the key. Sensing Pierce behind her, she spun around. "Just go away! I don't need or want anymore of your insulting observations."

It had grown dark. A small light beside the door of each motel unit and the brighter light on the tall sign Dallas had had installed illuminated the area quite well, though. KC dug through her purse again, and finally came up with the key.

"KC, I'm sorry," Pierce said low. "I know Dallas is a sore subject."

For some reason KC wilted. She was so weary of defending her position in this thing with her grandfather. In all honesty she wasn't the least bit sure she was right anymore. She'd come to Montana with such a distinct purpose, but it was no longer clear. Her mind was a muddle of new faces and unfamiliar attitudes. Dallas was as different as she'd proclaimed him, and she knew he resented her intrusion.

With the sudden loss of anger, KC felt drained, and she slumped against the door frame. "It's probably best if I just go home," she decided aloud, but with very little strength in the conclusion.

"Back to San Francisco?"

"Yes." Sighing cheerlessly, KC straightened up again and inserted the key in the lock. She felt Pierce's hand on her arm, and looked from it to his face. "I might be wrong about Granddad," she said dully. "But anything I've done was out of love."

A sense of shame hit Pierce. His damned suspicious nature had been working overtime with KC, and she didn't deserve such derogatory conjecture. "I know that," he said truthfully.

The new highway was in Pierce's mind again, along with the possibility of the state needing Dallas's property for the route and how that would affect the Logans. Millie, his secretary, was still checking on the ownership of the adjoining land parcel. She'd run into a strange turn. So far she'd discovered that every piece had changed hands in the last four months, but the new owner was a nebulous entity, a company with the name of Penn Holdings.

He could give KC hope, he realized. And he'd like to, especially now that he no longer doubted her sincerity. She'd been trying to force an issue that could very well be meaningless in a matter of weeks, maybe only days. But Pierce had such mixed feelings on the matter. While KC would be relieved if her grandfather was forced to sell to the state, Dallas wasn't apt to look at a forced sale so favorably. Pierce realized he couldn't reasonably be on both teams, on both Dallas's and KC's side, but that's what was happening. It wasn't that he agreed with KC, but she was reaching him in so many other ways he wanted to help her through this.

"KC, there's something you should know."

"About Granddad?"

"In a way. I think there's a chance that the new highway will come right through this place."

It took a few seconds for the full impact of Pierce's statement to sink in. KC had turned the key in the lock, and now she stood with her hand on the doorknob and stared blankly at the tall man beside her. "That would change everything, wouldn't it?"

"Yes."

"What makes you think ... I mean, do you have anything concrete?"

"No. But there aren't too many ways through this canyon. If the new road takes out the worst curves, which only makes sense, then it will have to come right through here."

"I see." KC said thoughtfully. "Do you have any idea how long it might be before we know for sure?"

"I'm only guessing, but it's my feeling that it won't be very long. From what I've been told, the surveyors are to start work in a few weeks, and I'm sure the route will be announced before the state sends surveyors in."

"A few weeks," KC repeated softly, understanding finally that if the state did buy Dallas's property, he would be free of responsibility again. Would he consent to going back to San Francisco then? Surely he would. What would he do in Harmony without his attachment to the saloon and motel?

A burst of loud laughter from the saloon startled both KC and Pierce. The night had grown a little chilly, which it always did in those mountains, no matter how warm the day had been.

Pierce saw KC shiver a little, but he was also watching the way her nipples had hardened from the chill and how they were pushing two arousing bumps into her blouse. She got to him, this half-pint of a woman. Every time they were together, no matter what else they talked about or even fought about, underneath it all KC kept proving how provocative she was. And she didn't even appear to be trying. Quite the opposite, really. Pierce knew she couldn't help being desirable to him. Something in KC and something in him just naturally created sexual friction.

He thought of her leaving, of one day vanishing from Harmony as abruptly as she'd appeared, and he knew he didn't want her to go. He hadn't been discontent before meeting KC. His job was satisfying and he knew almost everyone in the area on a first-name basis. Harmony was home, with all the complexities of feeling the word implied, and yet one woman's absence was going to create a void in his world.

Frowning, Pierce moved closer. His eyes were dark with the weight of his thoughts. His right hand rose to the back of KC's neck, and although she reacted with a small start, she didn't move away. "It just occurred to me that I don't want you to leave," he said in a low tone.

"I can't stay," she said huskily, immediately affected by this man's touch. They could argue until doom's day, and still they'd be physically attracted to each other, she thought with a strange sadness.

KC knew he was going to kiss her. What he'd done tonight, taking her to meet his "family," attempting to show her that there was more to him than the little she'd seen for herself, was influencing her thoughts.

The information he'd given her about the highway had also been an unexpected kindness.

So much had happened in the past few days and she was mired down with it all. Especially with the wild feelings Pierce created with a simple caress on the back of her neck.

She raised a hand to his chest, and felt the hard, steady beat of his heart through his shirt. If he wanted to kiss her, it was no more than she wanted, she finally let herself admit.

His mouth grazed hers, a too-brief excitement. But he did it again, and then caught her in a feverish embrace while his lips covered hers hungrily. His arms were hard around her, surrounding her with muscles and maleness, with scent and sensation. The kiss went on until she was dizzy and gasping for air. "Pierce," she whispered hoarsely, not even knowing why she'd had to say his name.

The door to the motel room was ajar, offering privacy from the passing cars and the people going in and out of the saloon. Pierce brought his hands down to her hips and pressed her closer. He could see in her eyes that she knew how aroused he was. "I want to come in," he whispered. "Invite me in, KC. We're not children."

Her nipples were hard against his chest, just as his most manly part was hard against her abdomen. She shivered, not from the night chill, but from the knowledge of what she was about to do. She wanted this beautiful big man, just as she knew he wanted her. And he'd been right: it didn't really matter that they'd known each other only a short time. Desire for each other had finally overpowered every other facet of their relationship.

She nodded her head slowly, then her senses leaped at the uninhibited excitement she saw on Pierce's face.

He pushed the door open with one hand, and with her cradled in his other arm, he led her into the room. It was dark except for outside lights filtering through the one window. She hadn't closed the drapes before she'd left for dinner, and the little room was soft with diffused lighting. With the door closed and locked, Pierce pulled her back into his arms.

Seven

Pierce kissed KC's lips again and again, nibbling their swollen softness, tasting her sweetness. She was like a small fragrant flower in his arms, petal soft, deliciously scented. He intended gentleness with her, but he wanted her with a desperation that was making his hands tremble and his body ache.

He scooped her up into his arms, kissing her while he crossed the dimly lit room to the bed. Laying her down, he stretched out beside her. "You're so sweet," he whispered against her lips before he kissed her again. She curled against him, and parted her lips for his tongue. His desire flamed as he probed the velvet heat of her mouth. "I want you so much," he whispered raggedly.

His hands began a greedy journey, traveling, touching, searching. He lingered at the soft, sensitive mounds of her breasts with their rigid little nipples, then traced the curves of her hips, her thighs.

"Pierce," she whispered, shaken by his urgency.

He heard, and understood, and forced his racing heart to slow down. Tenderly, he began to unbutton her blouse, and he was thrilled to feel her fingers at the buttons of his shirt. They both had too many clothes on. Pierce sat up and pulled first his shirt off, then his undershirt. He kicked his boots off, and returned to KC to peel her blouse away and unhook her bra.

Their ensuing embrace, with bare skin and soft breasts pressed into a furred chest, brought them both to complete abandonment. Their kisses became brief, gasping unions, until Pierce realized he was on the verge of losing all control. He didn't want to lose control with KC. He wanted to give her as much pleasure and satisfaction as he knew he would get out of their lovemaking.

He broke away from the excitement of her lips and raised his head. "Wait, sweetheart. We're moving too fast." Looking at her, adoring the passion on her beautiful face, he slowly caressed her breasts. "You're perfect. Beautiful and perfect." He lifted and shaped one breast, and lowered his mouth to it.

At that precise moment, the telephone rang.

Its shrill intrusion was like a splash of cold water. Pierce raised his head. KC stiffened. Neither spoke.

The phone jangled again.

"I better answer it," KC whispered ruefully, her mouth tingling from those passionate kisses. Pierce moved away, giving her room to reach out to the bedstand. She rolled over onto her stomach and stretched an arm out, then hesitated. She felt guilty, she realized, as if she were a kid caught with a hand in the cookie jar. She had to answer the phone, and it wasn't as though the caller could possibly know what state she was in. But Pierce's hand on her bare back was a hot reminder that this was an annoying and regrettable interruption, but still only an interruption.

"Answer it," he urged from behind her when the phone rang for a third time.

Reluctantly, KC picked it up. "Hello?"

"KC?"

It was Kyle Rudman. KC darted a nervous glance over her shoulder and saw Pierce's curious expression. It was such a strange situation to find herself in bed with one man and be connected by the telephone to another that KC was suddenly embarrassed. Her blouse was too far away to reach, but she snagged Pierce's shirt off the floor and held it to her breasts while she scooted up to a sitting position.

Her gaze met Pierce's fitfully while she said, "Yes, Kyle?"

She heard Pierce curse softly at the same time Kyle asked, "Have you talked to Dallas yet?"

Oh, yes, the five-thousand-dollar increase. She had promised to call Kyle with Dallas's response, hadn't she?

It came to KC in a flash of enlightenment that there were now *two* possible buyers for Dallas's business—Kyle and the state of Montana.

"No, Kyle, I'm sorry. Granddad went out this evening. I plan to speak to him during the first lull in business tomorrow."

"I see. Then you're all alone this evening."

KC froze. Something intimate had entered Kyle's voice, a prelude to a suggestion he come over and keep her company. Pierce was watching, almost glaring, vividly put out at Kyle being the caller. KC closed her eyes against the impressive picture of male sexuality Pierce made sitting beside her with his chest bare and a possessive scowl on his handsome face.

"I . . . I'm in bed," she stammered into the phone.

"Already?"

She lied. "Yes. I was . . . unusually tired tonight."

Kyle's voice became soothing. "Well, I'm very sorry if I awakened you. I'll be waiting for your call in the morning."

"Thank you. I'll call just as soon as I get a chance to speak to Granddad." KC was so embarrassed and sorry for lying that she added, "I really am going to try hard with Granddad, Kyle. I hope you know that."

KC put the phone down and looked at Pierce. "What was all that about?" he asked sharply.

KC slumped against the headboard with her head back. "That was terribly uncomfortable," she groaned.

"What did Rudman want?"

Just like that KC realized how damaging the call had been. Pierce wasn't radiating desire now; he was deeply, genuinely upset. Hugging the shirt to herself, KC shrank into a small ball. "He wanted to know if Granddad had reconsidered his offer," she said cautiously, wondering how honest she dare be. It was so obvious that Pierce didn't like Kyle, and if it was because of her, then that dislike was based on petty jealousy and was ridiculous.

"Why is he asking you about it? Why not Dallas?"

Why, he sounded like an interrogator! KC's eyes flashed. "I don't have to explain every move I make to you."

Pierce's voice dropped. "And what move are you and our illustrious banker planning, KC?"

"Just what are you getting at?" she flung back. "For your information, Kyle's as concerned about Granddad working too hard in this place as I am."

"Bull!" Pierce snorted derisively. "I can't believe that you'd go for that line of hooey. Whatever Rudman's up to, it's to benefit himself."

KC's eyes blazed with indignation. "Why don't you like Kyle?"

"Because he's a damned phony! I can't believe you're naive enough to be taken in by fancy clothes and a sickening smile."

KC felt like a fool, sitting on the bed half-clothed and arguing. The cloud of passion that had destroyed her defenses such a short time ago had evolved into a murky regret. This man had much too much influence on her. And she wasn't doing a very good job of dealing with it.

She swung her feet around to the floor and stood up. "Where you going?" Pierce called out just before she disappeared into the bathroom. The door closed without an answer, and Pierce flung himself off the bed, cursing under his breath. KC had the disconcerting habit of stalking off without any warning.

He switched on a lamp and closed the window drapes. Then he prowled around, waiting for KC to come back. The thought of her with Kyle Rudman kept gnawing a hole in his gut. He had very unusual feelings for this particular woman, he realized dourly. He could accept an interrupting phone call right in the middle of very meaningful lovemaking, but he couldn't deal with the caller being Kyle Rudman. Or the possibility of KC and Kyle putting their heads together to separate Dallas from Harmony.

With a dozen aggravating thoughts nagging at him, Pierce picked up his undershirt and yanked it on. He would have put his shirt on, too, if KC hadn't hauled it into the bathroom with her. Anymore lovemaking was out for tonight. He'd lost the mood, anyway.

Maybe it was for the best. KC was becoming too important. She'd been on his mind ever since their first meeting, and telling Rose about her proved she wasn't just a passing fancy.

And this thing with Rudman. What was that jerk up to? He sure wanted Dallas's property. And whatever was going on, KC was all for it.

While Pierce was wrangling with everything going on, so was KC. Looking in the mirror at her tangled hair and kiss-swollen lips, she had to wonder why she had rushed to Kyle Rudman's defense when she wasn't even sure how she felt about him anymore. Today, out by the river, hadn't she been uneasy with him?

That wasn't his fault, though. Just because some irritating character flaw in herself seemed to prefer an opinionated know-it-all like Pierce over a genteel, sensitive man like Kyle Rudman, it certainly wasn't Kyle's fault. Pierce's accusing attitude with the banker was pretty hard to take.

No, she hadn't been wrong in defending Kyle. Pierce was just jealous, unbelievably possessive, given the short span of their relationship.

"Oh, damn," KC whispered, placing her hands on the sink and letting her head fall forward dejectedly. Why was she getting so involved with Pierce? Without Kyle's phone call . . .

KC studied her reflection again. She must feel something important for Pierce to have gone so far with him, she realized. What was going on with her and the sheriff? Was it something real, something lasting?

Was she forgetting how angry he repeatedly made her feel over Dallas? And yes, even over Kyle?

Good Lord, how complex and convoluted her life had become!

The bathroom door finally opened. Lost in Pierce's large shirt, KC stepped out. "Sorry," she murmured, walking over to the chair for her blouse. "I should have taken this with me," she added, turning back to the bathroom.

"Just a minute." Two long strides brought Pierce close enough to take her arm. "Don't turn away from me, KC," he said quietly.

She saw the white undershirt he was wearing with relief; he wasn't talking about picking up where they'd left off. She looked into his eyes. "We don't agree on even one small thing, Pierce. I think it's time we faced that, don't you?"

"You don't care for Rudman; you care for me."

"Do I? There are times when you get to me. But that—" she nodded at the bed "—seems to be our only common ground. It's not enough."

"*That's* important. Without *that*, a relationship is pretty damned empty," Pierce drawled sardonically.

KC shook off his hand and continued on to the bathroom. "We'll talk later," she said as she closed the door behind her.

She was out again in minutes, wearing her blouse. She held the shirt out to Pierce, and he took it and put it on. "Pierce, this kind of thing seems to keep happening with us. I think we should be adult enough to prevent it in the future, don't you?"

"Or maybe we should be adult enough to ask ourselves *why* it keeps happening." Pierce tucked the tails of his shirt into his jeans. "If the phone hadn't rang—"

"But it did ring," KC interjected sharply. "And I'm glad it did!"

He'd been thinking it was best, too, but hearing KC say it didn't set right. He knew damned well that he'd pressured her into inviting him in, and that she'd been sincere in that statement about not taking sex lightly. He always had, until now. Sex had simply been another bodily urge to satisfy, like hunger and thirst and the need for a good night's sleep. He was positive his past partners felt as he did, or if they hadn't, he hadn't gotten the message. With KC, the message couldn't be ignored. Not any longer.

He felt tender toward this woman, he realized suddenly. Tender and protective. Her pride in her own high standards was becoming his pride. He wanted her desperately, but desire was becoming tempered with caring. A warmth for her felt special, different than anything he'd ever experienced. Even with that nebulous area of doubt between them, that portion of her life inhabited by Kyle Rudman and her determination to get Dallas away from the saloon and motel, Pierce knew that what he and KC had was special.

A step toward her caused a wary look in KC's eyes. Pierce stopped, and the look in his eyes appealed to her. "If we're going to be completely adult here, let's shoot for honesty. I feel something for you that I'm not sure I've ever felt before. What about you?"

KC took a startled step backward. "What are you saying?"

Pierce rubbed the back of his neck for a troubled moment. "I wish to hell I knew. All I do know is that I don't want you going out with other men."

KC hit Pierce with a head-on look. "And then what?"

He frowned. "What do you mean, and then what?"

"Didn't you just suggest honesty? All right, let's be honest. What do you want from me, Pierce? Do you want me to be your girl? Your woman? What?"

He colored slightly. "Do we have to label it?"

Yes, become a Silhouette subscriber and the celebration goes on forever.

To begin with we'll send you:

4 new Silhouette Desire® novels — FREE

a lovely 20k gold electroplated chain—FREE

an exciting mystery bonus—FREE

And that's not all! Special extras— Three more reasons to celebrate.

4. **FREE Home Delivery!** That's right! We'll send you **4 FREE** books, and you'll be under no obligation to purchase any in the future. You may keep the books and return the accompanying statement marked cancel.

If we don't hear from you, about a month later we'll send you six additional novels to read and enjoy. If you decide to keep them, you'll pay the low members only discount price of just **$2.24*** each — that's 26 cents less than the cover price — AND there's no extra charge for delivery! There are **no** hidden extras! **You may cancel at any time!** But as long as you wish to continue, every month we'll send you six more books, which you can purchase or return at our cost, cancelling your subscription.

5. **Free Monthly Newsletter!** It's the indispensable insiders' look at our most popular writers and their upcoming novels. Now you can have a behind-the-scenes look at the fascinating world of Silhouette! It's an added bonus you'll look forward to every month!

6. **More Surprise Gifts!** Because our home subscribers are our most valued readers, we'll be sending you additional free gifts from time to time — as a token of our appreciation.

FREE! 20k GOLD ELECTROPLATED CHAIN!

You'll love this 20k gold electroplated chain! The necklace is finely crafted with 160 double-soldered links, and is electroplate finished in genuine 20k gold. It's nearly 1/8" wide, fully 20" long — and has the look and feel of the real thing. "Glamorous" is the perfect word for it, and it can be yours FREE in this amazing Silhouette celebration!

SILHOUETTE DESIRE®

FREE OFFER CARD

4 FREE BOOKS

20k GOLD ELECTROPLATED CHAIN—FREE

FREE MYSTERY BONUS

PLACE YOUR BALLOON STICKER HERE!

FREE HOME DELIVERY

FREE FACT-FILLED NEWSLETTER

MORE SURPRISE GIFTS THROUGHOUT THE YEAR—FREE

YES! Please send me my four Silhouette Desire® novels FREE, along with my 20k Electroplated Gold Chain and my free mystery gift, as explained on the opposite page. I understand that accepting these books and gifts places me under no obligation ever to buy any books. I may cancel at any time for any reason, and the free books and gifts will be mine to keep!

225 CIS JAY9 (U-S-D-02/90)

NAME
_____
(PLEASE PRINT)

ADDRESS _____ APT _____

CITY _____ STATE _____

ZIP _____

SILHOUETTE "NO RISK GUARANTEE"
- There's no obligation to buy — the free books and gifts remain yours to keep.
- You receive books before they're available in stores.
- You may end your subscription anytime — just by letting us know.

PRINTED IN U.S.A.

FILL OUT THIS POSTPAID CARD AND MAIL TODAY!

Postage will be paid by addressee

BUSINESS REPLY CARD

FIRST CLASS   PERMIT NO. 717   BUFFALO, N.Y.

SILHOUETTE BOOKS®

901 Fuhrmann Blvd.,
P.O. Box 1867
Buffalo, N.Y. 14240-9952

NO POSTAGE
NECESSARY
IF MAILED
IN THE
UNITED STATES

KC sighed and turned away. "It doesn't matter. I can't stay here much longer, anyway."

"Why not?" Pierce came up behind her. "KC, instead of trying to get Dallas back to San Francisco, why don't you stay here?"

"Stay here! I've got to earn a living, and I don't think there's much call for an advertising executive's assistant in Harmony."

"That's what you do in San Francisco?"

KC went over to the window and moved the drape aside enough to see out. "That's what I did. I'm presently among the unemployed."

Pierce stared as that piece of KC's personal history registered, unhappily recognizing it as a reason why she might need money. "You weren't unemployed when you arrived, were you?"

"I resigned my position two weeks before I left San Francisco." Dropping the drape, KC faced Pierce with a weary sigh. "Let's call it a night, okay?"

"Okay." Pierce moved to the door, then turned and took the few steps back to her. "We're going to see each other again. When?"

"Oh, Pierce," she sighed dispiritedly. "What's the point?"

"There's no point if you don't care," he said softly.

She let him search her eyes, and she battled with a deluge of uncertainties, knowing he was watching the emotional war. They were vastly different people, worlds apart on matters as basic as her feelings for Dallas.

"You're thinking awfully hard," Pierce remarked lightly.

He was astoundingly handsome with his unruly hair flying every which way from their short stint on the bed. And did any man have more expressive, influencing eyes?

Suspecting that he could probably talk her into anything, if he really tried, didn't alleviate the persuasive pull KC felt. Maybe it was what she wanted anyway, she admitted weakly. She could tell herself a thousand times that continuing a relationship with a man she would only be leaving behind very soon was pointless, but how could she fight that intoxicating pull she constantly felt from him?

"All right," she finally agreed. "But I'm not sure it's all that wise."

His fingers kneaded her shoulders, conveying approval and relief. "I'll pick you up around noon on Saturday. I'd like you to see my place. We'll have lunch there."

KC nodded with thoughtful resignation, felt his hands slip from her shoulders, and watched him walk to the door.

"Good night," he said before opening the door and leaving.

The tiny, little room suddenly seemed big and empty without him in it. She cared, KC realized suddenly. She cared too much for her own good.

KC awoke in the night, damp with perspiration from a disturbing dream. She forced the frightening remnants of the nightmare from her mind by thinking of the present, and when she was well saturated with Harmony and its complexities, she concentrated on Dallas and the business he'd purchased.

She'd seen the white pickup return shortly after ten, but had decided to save her final plea for morning. If Dallas should suddenly see reason and accept Kyle's offer, her worries would be over. If he remained stubborn, she could leave or wait for the state's decision on the new highway route. Those were her options, like them or not.

Of course, beneath those seemingly simple choices lay a few posers. For one, Pierce's opinion that the new road would take out the saloon and motel. Would it be terribly underhanded to accept Kyle's offer without telling him of Pierce's conjecture? After all, if Kyle thought he was buying a business to improve and operate indefinitely, its demise could be quite a blow. She would have to tell him about Pierce's theory, KC decided; it was only fair.

Sighing, KC let Pierce take over her thoughts. She had asked him what he wanted from her, but wasn't it time she asked herself what she wanted from him? Or if she wanted anything at all?

What was wrong with enjoying a man's company without an emotional involvement? She had certainly done that before. A single woman stayed home alone a lot if she didn't date just for the fun of an evening out. No, there was nothing wrong with casual dating.

Only, with Pierce, their relationship had never been casual. Not even for a day. He'd ignited fiery emotions in her right from the first. Ordinarily she wasn't a volatile, impulsive person, but she looked at how often she'd lost her temper with Pierce. When had she ever called a man disparaging names in anger? With Pierce, she was a different woman.

It was with Kyle that she was more her usual self. It was very easy to maintain an unemotional level with Kyle Rudman as she had no racing pulse to deal with, nor flashes of temper.

With Kyle, she was no more emotionally stimulated than she was with female friends, KC admitted with a touch of sadness. The sadness was for Kyle, because she knew he felt quite differently toward her. She had sensed several times his hope of a more personal bond between them. And that was something she couldn't give him. As nice as he was, the thought of kissing him or of any other intimacy repelled her.

How complex human emotions are, KC pondered with another sigh. A man she preferred liking did absolutely nothing for her, while a man who could and did drive her up the wall on a relatively consistent basis brought her to life with a look, a touch, a word.

She was playing with fire with Pierce, wasn't she? Did she want to get burned? Was *that* what she wanted from him?

KC finally dropped off to sleep again, but she returned to dreams that were no less disturbing than the one that had awakened her.

Dallas was quiet and introspective the next morning, going about his duties with little of the glee KC had been noticing. His change in spirit was so apparent, KC became worried that he might not be feeling well and bustled around the saloon in an effort to alleviate some of the elderly man's work load.

KC had spent enough time in the saloon to recognize some of the regular customers now. They greeted her as warmly as they greeted Dallas, and she was discovering, for the most part, that the people around Harmony were exceptionally friendly. She was also realizing that the saloon was not just another tavern. While beer was a good seller, so were ice cream and soft drinks. People even brought their children in for cones and hot dogs. KC hadn't yet spent an evening in the saloon, but the daytime business was very family oriented.

KC waited all day for an opportunity to initiate a private conversation with her grandfather, but as luck would have it, the place was constantly busy from morning until Mrs. Seberg arrived at six. Thus, when she and Dallas walked out together, KC still hadn't had a chance to mention Kyle's increased offer.

Topping her desire to pass on that information, though, was concern for her grandfather's health. "Haven't you been feeling well today, Granddad?" she asked the moment they had cleared the doors of the saloon.

"I feel fine," Dallas returned crustily.

KC frowned. "Well, you haven't been acting like it."

Both of them saw the silver Mercedes with Kyle Rudman sitting in it. "Looks like you've got company," Dallas remarked dryly.

KC felt guilty of gross negligence. She had promised to call Kyle and hadn't done so; she'd kept delaying the call because she'd had nothing to relay. Kyle was getting out of the car, and KC turned to Dallas. "Do you have plans for tonight?" she asked quickly.

Dallas looked her right in the eye. "Just a talk with you, KC."

Something in Dallas's manner alerted KC. He'd been strangely withdrawn all day, and she had interpreted it wrong. He hadn't been ill at all; he'd had something on his mind. Something quite serious, by the look of it.

"I'll speak to Kyle and be right back," KC said soberly.

"I'll be in my room," Dallas announced, and struck off toward room two.

KC turned to see Kyle Rudman approaching. He wasn't smiling, nor did he look very calm.

"I thought you were going to call. What did Dallas say when you told him about the extra five thousand?"

Not even a hello? Why, he looked haggard, didn't he? There was tension at the corners of his eyes and around his mouth.

"Kyle, I'm truly sorry. But the place was busy all day. I'm on my way to Granddad's room right now to talk. I'm certain that I'll have an answer yet tonight."

"Damn!!" The word was a small explosion, and KC saw aggravation in every line of Kyle Rudman's expensively clad body. "KC, time's running out."

"You said a week. Has that changed?"

"I need an answer right away. This whole thing is getting just a bit annoying."

For her, too, KC realized. Why the big rush? She couldn't *make* things happen with her grandfather. At least, lately she hadn't been able to. "I said I was sorry," she said coolly, and saw a change come over Kyle. Right before her eyes, he became the man she'd thought he was—controlled, calm and collected.

"Of course you did," he said smoothly. "I'm the one who should be apologizing. Forgive my impatience, KC, but I'm getting pressure from . . . well, let's just say that banking is not always an easy business."

"Is the bank making the offer, Kyle? I've never been clear on that point, whether it was the bank or you personally."

He stumbled over his reply. "No, no, you mustn't misunderstand. The bank has nothing to do with this. I'm not at liberty to explain, but . . ."

KC waited, but the sentence was left dangling. "Would you like me to call you at home later?" she finally asked.

"Yes, please do." Kyle took out a card and scribbled something on the back of it. "This is my home number." When he pressed the card into KC's hand, he maintained a much longer contact than was necessary and smiled down at her. "Actually, I'd like it very much if you came by the house instead of calling," he said warmly.

KC withdrew her hand. "I'll probably call. I have no idea how long I'll be with Granddad. He mentioned wanting to talk to me about something, and we'll probably have dinner together. It could be a long evening."

"Yes, well, if it isn't, feel free to just drop in."

"Thank you. I'll keep that in mind." KC started away, then stopped abruptly. "Oh, I almost forgot. Kyle, do you know anything about the new highway coming through Harmony?"

"What?"

Startled, KC watched the man blanch. Frowning, she proceeded a little more cautiously. "It was in the newspaper. Surely you read about it."

Kyle cleared his throat. "Well, yes, of course I read about it. Heard about it, too. People are talking about it. Why?"

"I wanted to pass something someone said about it on to you is all. He thinks there's a possibility of the new road taking out Granddad's business. It wouldn't be fair to accept your offer without . . ."

"Who said that? Who thinks that, KC?"

There was a frantic edge to the banker's questions, and KC realized how right she'd been to tell him about this. He might very well withdraw his offer right now, but as much as she hoped he wouldn't, she was glad she hadn't concealed the information. "The sheriff, Kyle. Pierce Wheeler told me that."

Kyle grabbed KC by the arm. "*The sheriff!* My God! Does he have official information? What did he say?"

"Kyle! It's only conjecture. He only told me about it because..." KC stopped talking because Kyle was no longer listening.

Drawing a deep breath, he relinquished his hold on her arm. "I'm sorry. You just took me by surprise."

"I'll understand if it makes a difference in your offer," KC said uneasily, fearing that that's exactly what was going to happen.

But Kyle shook his head adamantly. "No, no. My offer's still open. I don't believe the sheriff's theory for a minute." He smiled, quite himself again. "Rumors are vicious things sometimes, aren't they? By the way, how is Dallas doing? I would imagine you're becoming quite anxious to get him away from ten, twelve hours of work everyday."

KC sighed. "Yes, I am. But to be perfectly frank, and you should be completely aware of this, I don't have a lot of faith that I'll succeed." She watched the man's mouth waver between grimness and a weak smile.

"But you still plan to try."

"One last time. I'm going to talk to Granddad tonight and tell him about the additional five thousand. If that fails..." KC shrugged, conveying a sense of finality.

"You'll do your best, I'm sure," Kyle mumbled vaguely, and began moving toward his car. "Call me...or come by... whichever you prefer."

"You'll hear from me for sure," KC called, then headed for Dallas's motel unit.

Dallas had showered and put on clean clothes. He was brushing his hair in front of the mirror over the dresser when KC rapped once and opened the door. "Come on in," he said. "Did Kyle leave?"

"Yes. Granddad, should I get ready for dinner, too? It would only take me about ten minutes to shower and change."

"Let's talk first." Dallas put down the hairbrush. "Sit down, KC."

"All right." There was something in the air, something about Dallas that alerted KC again. He looked determined, even a little stubborn, and those qualities, so often apparent these days, warned her that the "talk" might not go the way she wanted.

KC settled into a chair and Dallas took the other one. "First off, let me say that I appreciate your concern, KC. I know you came here only because you thought you were doing the right thing. I've been thinking about everything you said, and I've decided to lay my cards on the table."

"Please do."

"I plan to. But don't rush me. I've got quite a few things to say, and I want to say them in my own way."

KC swallowed a nervous smile. "I won't rush you, Granddad."

"Good. Now, you know that your grandmother and me had a good life together."

KC nodded somberly. "Yes, I know that."

"And you know how hard it was for me to accept her passing."

KC nodded again. "It was terribly hard."

Dallas pinned her with a penetrating look. "There are a few things you don't know, young lady. Your grandmother and me had a long-standing agreement. I don't know if other couples do this, but they should if they don't. We agreed that whichever one of us went first . . . well, the other one wasn't to spend the rest of their life alone. Now, you didn't know that, did you?"

"No," KC whispered.

"I have a lady friend, KC. You didn't know that, either, did you?"

KC sank farther into the chair. "I suspected it."

"Well, you're a bright girl. That doesn't surprise me at all. Anyway, that's where I was last night—talking to Mary."

"I see," KC said weakly.

"No, you don't. I can see on your face that you don't like me having a lady friend. You think it's disloyal to your grandmother."

There was a lump the size of an egg in KC's throat. "Please go on, Granddad," she barely managed to get out.

Dallas got up and went over to the window. His back was to KC, and she looked at his slender frame sadly. "Her name is

Mary Collier. She's the lady I met while I was sight-seeing. I'd like you to meet her."

Could she? KC felt only like crying.

"Anyway, she has nothing to do with this business," Dallas said, turning around and walking back to the chair. "I bought this place completely on my own. I wanted something to do, *needed* something to do. Now I'm beginning to wonder if I want to keep it when it has caused you so much unhappiness."

KC sat up straighter.

"Yes, I'm thinking of doing what you want, KC. But whether I sell the business or not, I've made a final decision on one thing. I'm not going back to San Francisco. I like it here and I like Mary. We're going to be married."

"Granddad," KC whimpered softly.

Dallas looked unrelenting. "You're a young woman, KC, with your whole life ahead of you. You'll be getting married yourself one of these days. Nothing would please me more than if you should decide to stay in Harmony. You've got two young men interested in you right now—Kyle Rudman and Pierce Wheeler. For my part, I favor Pierce, but I wouldn't presume to tell you who you should marry. I expect the same courtesy from you."

KC realized the sly old fox had her on that point.

But he was also angling to best her on the business, too, wasn't he? Laying responsibility for selling the place on her unhappiness? It was *his* health KC was worried about, not *her* happiness. Her unhappiness only resulted from worrying about him!

KC was recovering a little from the shocks Dallas had handed her. It was time to get a word in. "Kyle upped his offer," she stated quietly.

"Upped it? And he came to you with it? Why not me? Who owns this danged place, you or me?"

"Granddad, don't get upset!"

"I'll get upset, I'll get plenty upset! What kind of sneaky game is Rudman playing? What does he think I am, senile or something?"

"My Lord, no! Granddad, he's been very nice."

Dallas snorted. "Well, I'm not so sure I want to sell to a man who would go behind my back like that."

"Granddad!"

"Don't you 'Granddad' me, young lady. Where I come from, a man looks you in the eye when he talks business, and doesn't go behind your back to your granddaughter!"

Oh, hell, she'd botched the whole thing. Pierce was sure right about one thing: there was nothing wrong with Dallas Logan's mind!

KC stood up. "He's offering you every penny of your money back, *plus* the five thousand he initially promised, *plus* another five thousand," she recited.

"What for? Why does a banker want an old saloon and motel so much he keeps upping his offer? Use your head, KC. Doesn't it look a little odd to you?"

"Oh, Granddad," she sighed hopelessly. "What do you care why he wants it? He wants it and he's willing to give you a ten-thousand-dollar profit."

"Well, I don't like it," Dallas exclaimed pugnaciously. Then he grinned. "Let's go have dinner. I'm as hungry as a bear."

Eight

Pierce had business around the county that day and got back to town around seven. He drove directly to his office to check his messages before going home. Thumbing through the stack of notes on his desk, he saw one from Millie, his secretary.

Pierce, call me. I'd like to bring you up to date on Penn Holdings. Millie.

Perching on the corner of his desk, Pierce dialed Millie's home number. "I just got back, Millie. Did you find out who's behind Penn Holdings?"

"Everything I've run across points to Kyle Rudman, Pierce."

"Are you sure?"

"Well, how sure do you want me to be? I talked to Louise Nash in the assessor's office, and they've been instructed to mail the property-tax billings on that property I've been researching to Kyle's home address."

"I see." Pierce suddenly saw the whole picture clearly. No wonder Rudman wanted Dallas's property so badly; it was the only parcel on that end of town he didn't already own.

Millie went on. "I wormed a little information out of Sherry Ridgley over at the title company, Pierce. On every one of those purchase transactions, Kyle brought in cash."

"Cash? Not a check?"

"Cash. Greenbacks."

"Interesting. Anything else?"

"That's about it. Because of your weekend off coming up, I thought you should get the information tonight."

"Thanks, Millie. I appreciate it."

Pierce put the phone down thoughtfully. There was nothing illegal in Kyle Rudman buying property, but why had he hidden his activities behind Penn Holdings?

Sliding off the desk, Pierce walked over to the detailed wall map of Harmony and frowned. On impulse, he went back to the phone and called Millie again. "Is there a list around here of those parcels of land you checked?"

"In the locked file cabinet behind my desk, Pierce. The folder is labeled For the Boss."

Pierce laughed. "You're kidding."

"I had to call it something," Millie laughed. "Anyway, it should be right in front in the third drawer down."

"Thanks."

Locating the file folder, Pierce returned to his office and the wall map. With thumbtacks, he designated each piece of property from Millie's neatly compiled list. Then he stood back at the visual evidence of what he'd already figured out. There were eight thumbtacks, and they were completely surrounding Dallas Logan's property. Dallas was sitting right in the middle of a good-sized chunk of land owned by Kyle Rudman, via Penn Holdings.

Now why would the banker suddenly buy up that much land?

Pierce smiled grimly over the answer. Because Rudman *knew* that the new highway was going right through that land! Somehow, Kyle had learned of the state's decision before anyone else in the area. Then he'd figured out the most sensible route, just as Pierce had. Kyle had gotten very busy after that.

Pierce sat behind his desk to digest the matter. There was nothing criminal in anyone buying property. But there was something damned unethical about a banker using privileged information to feather his own nest! How would Rudman have learned of the state's decision before anyone else in Harmony, other than through banking connections? Someone in Helena had talked out of turn, obviously, and big-ears Rudman had pounced on the slip.

And now, to be securely in the catbird's seat for negotiating an outrageous sale price with the state, all Kyle needed was Dallas's property.

Pierce stirred uneasily. KC wasn't in on this, was she? What was it she'd said on the phone to Kyle last night? Oh, yes. *"I'm going to try real hard with Granddad, Kyle. I hope you know that."* Pierce's stomach churned as he waged an inner battle about KC's possible involvement. She and the banker had hit it off right from the start. Had Kyle seen an immediate ally in Dallas's granddaughter. The lure of money was a powerful incentive, and making a little profit while accomplishing her own goal, that of getting Dallas away from the business, might not even seem nefarious to someone without a job.

Pierce was deeply shaken by the whole mess and wondered what he should do about it. One thing he didn't want to do was cause another delay in the road construction. That new highway was badly needed, even if Rudman—and maybe KC—were unscrupulous enough to make money on it.

Maybe there was nothing he could do, anyway, except warn Dallas to hold on to his property until he heard from the state.

On the way back from having dinner, KC noticed Pierce's van in the rearview mirror. She hadn't expected to see him until the next day, and her heart speeded up alarmingly simply because he was close by and apparently planning to see her tonight. She had no more than pulled into the saloon's parking lot, however, when Katie Seberg came rushing out. "Thank goodness you're back. I've got to leave, Dallas. An emergency. My husband took a fall, and I've got to drive him to Missoula."

Pierce walked up. "Anything I can do, Katie?"

Katie had fiery red hair and worried blue eyes. "I sure would appreciate a driver, Pierce. My hands are shaking. Tom's been painting the living room at home and he fell off the ladder. My neighbor, Cathy Miller, just called me."

"Maybe we need an ambulance."

"I don't think so. It's his arm. Cathy said it looks like a broken wrist to her."

"I'll be glad to drive you and Tom to Missoula." Pierce turned to Dallas. "I need to talk to you about something, so if I get back early enough I'll stop by."

"Sorry to leave you in the lurch, Dallas," Katie called over her shoulder, already on her way to Pierce's van. She stopped suddenly. "Dallas, I called Jeff to see if he could work my shift, and his wife said he was working tonight at The Blue Mountain Lodge."

"Don't worry about it, Katie," Dallas called back, then said to KC, "Well, looks like I better get back to work. Jeff's the only relief bartender I know."

KC had been staring after Pierce. He'd hardly even looked at her, and after last night, she couldn't figure out his abnormal reserve. "Nothing doing," she said absently, then brought her complete attention back to Dallas. "You've already put in a long day. I'll take care of the place tonight."

"Are you sure?"

"Positive. You go and get a good night's rest. I insist, Granddad."

"Well, the place is a little different at night, KC," Dallas cautioned.

KC scanned the half dozen or so vehicles in the lot. "I can handle this many customers. Please. You look tired."

Dallas finally gave in with a very readable expression: he *was* tired, and business was light tonight. KC could probably handle everything just fine.

At Dallas's okay, KC hurried into the saloon and went behind the bar. One table was occupied by two men and three women, and six people sat at the bar. "Hi," she said with an all-encompassing smile.

"Did Katie leave?" she heard.

Explaining as she went, KC emptied ashtrays, filled beer orders and kept the bar wiped clean. The group was congenial, enjoying music from the jukebox, laughing and teasing each other. Every so often someone would leave and someone else would wander in, but the number of customers remained right around a dozen.

The saloon didn't serve hard liquor and everyone who came in knew it. They were content with a few glasses of beer, canned music and visiting with friends. KC sold potato chips, pretzels and hot dogs, besides beer, soft drinks and coffee. Popcorn was free, sitting in bowls up and down the bar and on any occupied table.

By midnight she had taken in a nice sum of money, and no one had gotten rowdy or intoxicated. No matter how well the evening had gone, though, KC's inner conflict had kept her on edge. Throughout the hours, she'd watched for Pierce rather anxiously.

Dallas's stand about getting married and not going back to San Francisco, whether he kept the saloon or not, had affected KC diversely. At first, she'd been only stunned. But then, as they'd eaten dinner together, and Dallas had gone on and on about Mary and how contented he was in Harmony, KC had begun to recognize an emptiness in herself as big as the Grand Canyon. She'd been able to give the painful feeling a name by the end of the meal, and if it wasn't "desertion," in its most literal sense, it was very close.

Deserted. KC didn't like the word, nor the feeling, yet she hadn't been able to shake the sensation of being truly alone for the first time in her life. The long trip back to San Francisco without Dallas loomed as a frightening undertaking, and the vision of taking up her life, looking for a new job and developing a new routine day by day *without* Dallas was close to unthinkable.

Oddly, Pierce Wheeler seemed like some sort of lifeline within the maze of such unanchored thoughts. KC realized she was anxious to talk to Pierce, although what he could do or say to make her feel better wasn't clear. Especially when she knew very well that anything Dallas Logan did was A-OK with Pierce Wheeler.

At twelve-thirty, the only people still present were a man and a woman, who were rather romantically inclined at one end of the bar. They ordered coffee and laughingly promised to leave as soon as they drank it. KC assured them that there was no hurry, and busied herself wiping down the beer and soft-drink spigots behind the bar.

The front door opened and KC looked up. Pierce was walking in, big, handsome, self-assured, and KC felt the knot in her stomach that she'd endured all evening relenting somewhat.

Pierce said hello to the couple at the bar, then walked to the opposite end of it. "Where's Dallas?" he asked quietly.

With the damp cloth she was still carrying, KC wiped at the already clean bar top. "I worked for Granddad tonight. He was exhausted. Can I get you anything? The coffee's still fresh."

"Thanks."

"How's Mrs. Seberg's husband?" she asked as she went to the pot and filled a cup, noticing in the process that her hands weren't quite steady.

"His wrist is broken in two places."

"Did he have to stay in the hospital?"

"Just for tonight. Katie stayed in Missoula, too. She said to tell Dallas that she'd be back to work tomorrow. So, you ran the place tonight. How did it go?"

"No problems, really."

"Well, this never has been a rowdy place." Pierce splashed some cream into his coffee and stirred the mixture while he watched KC. There was something different about her, something keyed up. Her eyes were a little too bright, her voice a little too breathy. He thought of why he needed to see Dallas, and wondered if the situation was becoming a little too much for KC to handle.

"Anything wrong?" he asked.

Was anything right? KC darted a glance at the remaining couple, then turned bewildered eyes on Pierce and whispered huskily, "I need to talk to you . . . or to someone."

Pierce drew a sharp breath, positive now that KC was into something way over her head and regretting it. "You can talk to me. I'll hang around."

"Thank you." With nervous energy, KC busied herself with the final cleaning behind the bar, waiting for the couple to finish their coffee and leave. Every so often her eyes sought Pierce's and their exchanged glances seemed heavy with emotion.

KC tried to analyze Pierce's hold on her, and why she was turning to him now. For the first time she realized that he seemed to see her more clearly—or more nakedly—than anyone else. And there was speculation in his every gaze, and desire, and something alive and hot that touched her soul. He was a fascinating man, but he was also solid, strong and down-to-earth. And that's what she needed: contact with something or someone firmly planted.

The couple at the end of the bar finally got up and called out, "Good night." KC walked past Pierce and crossed the room to the door. After securing the lock and turning off the outside lights, she came back to the bar.

"Tired?" Pierce asked softly.

"A little." KC refilled his cup and poured one for herself. Then she came around the bar and sat on the next stool. She took a sip of coffee, then set the cup down.

"Did you tell Dallas what I said about the new highway possibly taking this place out?" Pierce asked.

"Yes." KC's mind wasn't on that particular moment of the evening. Nor had Dallas's been when she'd mentioned Pierce's speculation. "It didn't seem to affect him all that much," she said low. "Pierce, Granddad's getting married."

Pierce blinked, then broke out into a grin. "You're kidding!"

"Did you know?"

"No, I didn't know. Did he tell you about it tonight?"

"Just before we went to dinner." A drop of coffee on the bar drew KC's attention, and she wiped it off with her forefinger. "I feel..."

At her hesitation, Pierce urged, "How, KC? How do you feel?"

Tears suddenly blurred KC's vision. "Lost," she whispered.

Pierce hadn't been planning any fast moves. Last night he'd made a decision to go slower with KC. In between stops around the county today, he'd commended himself for the wisdom of that decision. He had no doubt that this was a different kind of relationship than he'd ever been a part of, and his feelings were fast advancing beyond the sexually unrestrained philosophy he knew very well he'd been guilty of in the past.

Not that he wanted KC any less. Just looking at her, simply by being in the same room with her, his body was shrieking demands. But he knew he was beginning to think about loving and permanence, sometimes with dismay, sometimes with an unfamiliar euphoria. In either case, he was sailing in unknown waters, and a little caution seemed advisable.

Still, with her close enough to touch and fighting tears, he didn't have the strength of will to stop himself from touching her. His hand rose and his fingertips brushed her cheek. She was wearing a dark color, navy-blue or black, indistinct in the dim saloon lighting, a blouse and slacks, and her face was a pale oval about the garments.

KC hadn't meant to invite a caress. But when Pierce touched her, she wondered if that wasn't what she needed from him tonight.

For a few moments they sat that way, the merest tips of his fingers on her cheek, neither speaking, eyes glued to one another. Then Pierce growled, "Aw, hell," and gathered her up. Her arms went around his waist while his wound completely around her, and they were suddenly tightly, passionately locked together.

She put her head back, her face up. "I . . . think I want you to kiss me," she whispered.

Pierce hesitated, torn between KC's unexpected mood and the decision he'd made earlier. "You know I want to. But you also know where a kiss leads for us, KC."

He'd spoken almost solemnly, verbalizing what they both knew only too well. Tension prickled her scalp, and an image of driving away, of packing the car and heading back to San Francisco flashed through her mind. There was every chance she would never see Pierce again after she left Harmony. Hot tears were stinging her eyes and draining down her throat. Too much had happened. She felt at loose ends, discouraged, disheartened. "Just hold me for a minute," she whispered in a gravelly, teary voice.

He was glad to hold her, startled by the show of tears, but getting too lost in the warmth of her nearness to keep questioning her mood. His hands moved on her back, and the scent of her hair was saturating his senses. His body was responding naturally to a beautiful woman in his arms, but with the added excitement this special woman created.

KC's mind was working, but in a strange way. In Pierce's arms, the evening's unnerving events were losing their sharp edges. There was warmth and security and a spine-tingling comfort in being held by this particular man. There was also the very real and solid sensation of maleness, of a hard chest and strong, muscular arms, offering whatever kind of comfort she should seek.

Her thoughts were indistinct, her nerves on edge, her emotions raw. She needed something he'd planted and kept alive within her throughout her troubled days and nights in Harmony.

She snuggled closer, a deliberate invitation. She heard Pierce's swift intake of air, felt his surprise. During every other encounter, he'd been the pursuer. A responsive tensing of his body conveyed his cooperation; he would follow wherever she led.

Her face lifted again, her lips parted and a groan of acquiescence rumbled in his chest as his mouth came down on hers. His lips were warm and firm and exciting, and KC's molded with the ardor of a demanding male mouth. Pierce moved them both from their stools to the floor, and with her heart pounding wildly in her breast, she pressed against him, taking his tongue, sliding her hands up his chest to clasp together behind his head.

The kiss was intensely arousing, requiring another, and neither of them said no. Again and again their lips met, sometimes briefly, sometimes clinging until they needed air, but always with increasing hunger.

Pierce was the first to finally speak. His voice was gruff, hoarse. "Do you know what you're doing to me?"

Her answer was a breathless, "Do you know what *you're* doing to *me*?"

"I know what I want to do."

It was what she wanted, too, wasn't it? Why was she in his arms at all? A crazy recklessness was making her dare fate, throw caution to the winds. "Then do it," she whispered in a husky challenge.

He thought of asking, "Why tonight?" Why, after the roller coaster of advances and retreats they'd been on since they'd met, was she so bold tonight? Surely Dallas's marital intentions hadn't put KC in this strangely abandoned mood.

But he asked nothing, losing both thought and reason when she whispered again, "Do it, Pierce. I want you."

Never had those words affected him like they did now. His blood seemed to explode in his veins, rushing to his head in a dizzying roar. "Where?" he growled thickly.

She didn't care where. She didn't even want to think about where. Somehow the step she'd been afraid to take before had disappeared. Her fingers wound into the thick hair at the back of his collar. "Kiss me again," she pleaded huskily, rising on tiptoe to reach his mouth.

His compliance was a passionate explosion. And while their mouths clung and moved and tantalized, he yanked the hem of her blouse from the waistband of her slacks and groped beneath it. Her skin was hot and silky, igniting his thoughts.

Where? On a chair? A table? The floor was too used, with a million footprints in the not very clean carpeting.

He could make do, he could make love to her anywhere. Standing, sitting, in any position. But that wasn't what he wanted. He wanted her on a bed, as they were last night. Only tonight, nothing would stop them. Nothing.

He tore them apart and grabbed her hand. "Let's get out of here," he commanded urgently.

Dazed, KC let him take control. They left through the backdoor, and it was Pierce who remembered to lock it. The distance to her motel room was covered in seconds, and it was Pierce who found the door key in her purse.

"Don't turn on the lights," she whispered, and walked back into his arms to taste his mouth again. With the saloon's outside lights off, the room was dark, and she didn't stop to wonder why she wanted it that way. She only knew how consumed she was, how hot and vibrant her need was.

Her blouse came off, then his shirt. They both knew where the bed was without light, and they gravitated toward it, even while seeking kisses and bare skin. He unbuttoned her slacks, and she felt them slide to her ankles. She kicked them away and reached for the buckle on his belt, then his zipper.

His body was hot and throbbing, and her hands closed around him.

Growling with intense pleasure, he let her explore. But they were still standing . . . and he urged her to the bed.

She'd never felt so wanton, KC acknowledged somewhere within the steamy regions of her mind. Pierce's hands were liquid heat, altering her flesh to the same hot liquidity wherever they roamed. And they roamed everywhere . . . possessing her breasts, her hips, her thighs . . . making every part, every inch, of her his.

Yes, his. Whatever came after this, for this incredible moment in time, she belonged to Pierce. And she felt possessive toward him, too, staking claim to his furred chest, to his long, sinewy thighs, to that breathtaking, impressive maleness at the base of his tight belly.

It seemed an eternity from their initial meeting to this moment, and yet she knew it had been just under a week. From the first, though, this had been inevitable. If time had allowed she could have delayed this intimacy for months, and it still would have happened. Eventually.

She felt alive, more alive than she could ever remember feeling. She held his face and kissed his lips again and again while he caressed her breasts. She knew she wasn't thinking, and she didn't care. His mouth traveling down to her nipples was all she cared about. She would deal with tomorrow, tomorrow. For now, she only wanted to *feel*.

And listen to the pulsing rhythm of her own heart keeping time with Pierce's hoarse whispers. "You're beautiful. Tell me what you like. I want to please you."

She moaned softly as his hand urged her thighs apart. "You're pleasing me," she gasped.

"This?" His fingers moved with a delicious, knowing stroke.

She brought his head down, conveying her pleasure and desire through a mind-dazing kiss. He spoke against her lips. "We need protection. Give me a minute."

Her mind numbed while he left her. She heard what he was doing and was grateful he'd thought of protection, but she was cold and alone without him, and afraid of changing her mind. The return of his heat and bulk was welcome, and she clung to him with a new desperation.

His voice soothed. "I'm back. Don't be alarmed."

"Pierce. Oh, Pierce," she whispered brokenly. "I'm afraid."

"Of me?"

"No...I don't know. Hold me tight."

"Anytime, sweetheart, anytime."

She was held and comforted, and his kisses rained on her face, then on her lips. "I adore you," he whispered. "I've never felt this way before. I've never wanted a woman more." His hands began a feverish journey, his mouth right behind them. The brief foray into his wallet was soon forgotten as thrill upon thrill compounded in the wake of his lips and tongue.

He was an able, generous lover, wanting to give as much pleasure as he was receiving. But it wasn't always this way for Pierce, and he recognized again how differently he felt about KC. Her pleasure was his pleasure; her excitement his. He reveled in the desirous, gasping little breaths she was taking, in the way she kept moving under his caresses, meeting them, telling him in heated body language just how he affected her. It was heady to arouse an especially desirable woman to writhing, moaning need, but it was also arousing him unmercifully.

His voice cracked. "I need you now."

"Yes," she gasped huskily, and opened her thighs to him.

He moved between them, lifted her hips and slid his aching shaft into her velvety heat. Her body squeezed around him, pulsated around him and a growl of passion built in his chest. He no longer felt gentle; the time had passed for gentleness. He felt powerful, masterful, indomitable, and he began the ride to rapture with a gruff cry of conquest.

There was no mistaking who was in command: Pierce was. He stopped the tempo long enough to demand, "I want to see you." And he reached for the lamp switch, startling KC with the sudden infusion of lamplight. She blinked up at the man above her, and watched as he lowered his upper body again until his face was only an inch away.

Her heart was beating erratically. His eyes were dark, drugging pools, boring into her. "You're beautiful," he whispered, and moved within her. She couldn't escape his eyes, and she stared into them, mesmerized by their passion and sensuality.

This was a mistake, she suddenly and painfully realized. How could anyone make love like this and then forget it? Frightened by the future she was burdening herself with, KC closed her eyes tightly.

But Pierce growled, "Open your eyes," and her eyelids jerked up in surprise. "Don't shut me out," he commanded, sensing the subtle change in the woman beneath him.

"You . . . you shouldn't have turned on the lamp," she whispered, trying to elude the hot light in his eyes by looking elsewhere.

"We're doing the same thing, whether it's dark or light. Look at me. I'm not letting you turn away from me, KC." His movements became provocative, seductive, and he rested on his forearms, placed on each side of her head, and watched her reactions. "Nothing that feels like this could be wrong, sweetheart," he whispered. "Tell me you like it."

She swallowed. "Pierce . . ."

"Tell me!"

She should have known he would want so much. For certain she'd known that making love with Pierce would be wild and hot. And it was. Every cell in her body was on fire. Her stomach ached with a tension that coiled tighter with his every slow and deliberate thrust. What she hadn't known was how emotionally involved she would be. This far surpassed the physicality she'd anticipated and needed. And she feared that no matter how physically sated she might be afterward, she wasn't going to get out of this bed emotionally unbruised.

His lips grazed hers. "Tell me, sweetheart," he said softly, and punctuated the gentler plea with a blood-heating slide deep into her body.

Her truth arose. "You make me feel...things I've never felt before."

Elation fired Pierce's passion, emotions that built to a hot throb in his system. But a streak of gentleness had also returned to his desire, as though he'd conquered and could afford the less macho attitude. His eyes held hers. "This has been coming from our first meeting."

Her head bobbed once, and her tongue dampened her lips in a slow circle. She thought it strange that he wanted to talk through this, but had to admit eye contact and soft, husky words were erotically stimulating. It struck her that he was an expert lover, unhurried despite an undoubtable ardor. She didn't want to compare her other few sexual encounters with this one, but she couldn't direct her thoughts very well within the searing blast of their sexuality. And everything else she'd ever experienced came off second best, less than second best.

Her breaths were small pants, her expression a drift of emotions, her eyes a smoky green. Pierce brought his mouth down to hers, and teased the soft fullness of her lips with the tip of his tongue. Her fingernails dug into his back, and he thrust deeper into her heat and whispered, "Give me some scars, sweetheart. Let yourself go."

He was demanding everything she was. No part of her was to remain private and unscathed. She was approaching total and complete vulnerability, on the verge of tears and words she was afraid of saying. Internally she was dissolving, losing bone and muscle and form and identity. No longer were they a separate man and woman; she was an extension of his maleness, a quivering mass of concupiscence that molded and moved at his direction.

He was hypnotizing, intoxicating, with his tireless, tormenting plunges. She was reaching a height of sexual attainment she'd never even come close to before, she feverishly recognized just before the drab little room exploded into a million starlit pieces.

Her nails dug—just as he'd asked—and a low moaning began in her throat. His kiss took the moans, but his faster, harder thrusts only created more of the whimpering sounds. She scratched, she bit, she writhed and then she collapsed into tears, barely aware of his passionate shout of fulfillment.

They were sweaty, both of them, breathing hard, united in weakness as they'd been in strength. Pierce's head rested on the pillow beside hers, his lips against her ear. "KC... sweetheart... you're fantastic," he whispered raggedly.

Her? No, not her. Him. He was the fantastic one. A demanding lover, yes, but one as concerned with her pleasure as his. He was that rarity among men, an unselfish lover. It took ages for her breathing to quieten and her pulse rate to return to normal, and she knew she'd been as thoroughly made love to as any woman could ever dream of.

Her body felt at peace, every cell replete and satisfied. She should be only content.

And she would be, she realized, if all she wanted from Pierce was sex. But, Lord help her, she wanted more, didn't she?

She was at the brink of an emotional precipice, she thought unhappily, falling in love! And she'd been doing that from the moment they'd met. Tonight had merely iced the cake of her secret and sadly one-sided feelings.

Nine

While strength flowed back to his body, Pierce's thoughts would have lifted KC to a dizzying plateau. But she had no way of knowing that "I love you" was on the tip of his tongue. The closest thing to that kind of emotional confession had been his I adore you, but it had been said in the deepest throes of passion; it was lovely to remember, but hardly something to rely on once passion had faded.

He was heavy, but such a welcome weight. She wanted to hold him to herself, to prolong this moment of shared warmth as long as possible. But she relaxed her arms when he raised his head, kissed her tenderly and moved away. With a strange ache in her heart, she watched his naked retreat to the bathroom, admiring the wonderful symmetry of his powerful body and long legs. Then, sighing, she scooted beneath the bed's top sheet and stared at the ceiling.

She was falling in love, she admitted unhappily. If she hadn't been so involved in other problems, she might have figured that out before she'd gone this far. *That's* why she'd turned to Pierce tonight. It was only natural to seek solace from a man as important to her as Pierce was becoming.

Pierce reappeared and approached the bed. KC's eyes flicked over him in rapt absorption of his masculine beauty. His body was strong and beautiful. The black hair on his chest was thick, narrowing in its downward plunge, denser again at the juncture of his thighs. His muscles were evident but supple-looking, his skin smooth where it wasn't bristled with hair. She dared to stare and was rewarded with a blatant conclusion: Sheriff Pierce Wheeler was all man, with or without his badge.

KC's gaze lifted to the gray eyes watching her. "Are you all right?" Pierce asked quietly.

She nodded slowly. He bent over, picked up his briefs and pulled them on. Then he sat on the edge of the bed and looked at her. KC sat up, too, stacking the pillows against the bed's headboard for support. She tucked the sheet across her breasts and under each arm.

"You're a very special woman," Pierce said in a low voice.

They studied each other, each searching for something. KC wet her lips, wondering what he'd say if she blurted out her true feelings. No, she felt things she couldn't possibly say. Pierce had touched her deeply. He'd possessed her heart and soul along with her body. He'd known her as intimately as one person could know another. He was an artful and caring lover. But, she suspected sadly, she was special to him only because she'd been a passionate and responsive partner.

He placed one hand on the bed on her opposite side and leaned over her, while, with the other hand, he brushed wisps of golden-taffy hair back from her forehead. It was a tender gesture and denoted, to KC, how physically pleased and satisfied he was.

"Shall I go... or stay?" he asked softly.

She hesitated over the sudden quick beat of her heart. Having Pierce in her bed the rest of the night was a provocative thought.

But it was an impossible dream. "Your van can't be parked outside my door in the morning."

He probed the sea-green depths of her eyes for a moment, then sighed. "No, I suppose not. We're still on for tomorrow, aren't we?"

"If you wish."

His mouth came down on hers in a provokingly sweet kiss. "I wish," he confirmed. "I'll pick you up as planned, around noon."

KC watched as he stood up, collected his jeans and pulled them on. "Are you in any mood to hear why I came back here tonight?" he asked.

"There's nothing wrong with my mood, Pierce." Her tone was slightly argumentative, a little resentful. Which she had no right to be, she knew. Tonight had been her doing, not Pierce's. And she shouldn't blame him if her feelings were getting out of hand.

"You just look very relaxed, sweetheart. I don't want to ruin that."

KC stirred, recalling how Pierce had ignored her while Katie Seberg had explained the emergency with her husband. "You came by earlier to see Granddad about something, didn't you?"

Pierce pulled his shirt on, his expression sobering. "Yes. About Rudman and what he's up to."

"Kyle?" If Pierce hadn't wanted to ruin her mood, he'd picked the wrong topic. She was suddenly tense again, and just a bit disgusted. "I don't want to hear anything negative about Kyle," she announced rather sharply. "And there's no reason for you to be stirring up trouble for him with Granddad, either."

Pierce froze in place, his fingers on the buttons of his shirt, his face darkening. "Well, I think you'd better hear this," he drawled sarcastically, shaken again by KC's consistent defense of the banker.

Pierce quickly finished buttoning his shirt and tucked it into his jeans. Then he sat down to pull on his socks and boots, deliberately choosing the bed over the chair, deliberately nudging his seat against KC's sheet-covered thigh. His mouth was a grim line, a far cry from its previous array of ardent expressions. "I can't believe how you leap at the chance to defend that creep."

"And I can't believe how you take every opportunity to insult him!"

"Maybe I wouldn't insult him if you weren't so damned defensive."

"And maybe I wouldn't be so defensive if you tried a little human kindness for a change!"

Pierce faced her. "You're going to hear this, whether you want to or not. Our wonderful neighborhood banker bought every piece of property within the corridor for the new highway that he could lay his hands on. The reason he wants Dallas's land is because it's a missing piece of the puzzle. Without it, his chance of holding the state up for an exorbitant price on the whole package is a helluva lot weaker." Pierce's eyes narrowed. "Or maybe you already knew all that. Did you?"

KC's eyes were snapping. "That's absurd," she flung, missing Pierce's accusing question in her reaction to his ridiculous story. "Kyle wouldn't do something like that."

"How do you know what he'd do?" Pierce's eyes narrowed to two accusing slits. "How close are you two?"

"We're not close at all," she gasped. "How dare you imply...?"

Pierce took her shoulders and brought her up from the pillow. His face was dark with emotion and only inches from hers. "I want you to think about what I just told you. It's not a figment of my imagination. A company by the name of Penn Holdings has bought every inch of ground on this side of town except Dallas's. Rudman's the only local link to the company. If he's not the only person behind Penn Holdings, he's a very important part of it."

KC glared. "You're saying Kyle used me to influence Granddad into selling."

"If you didn't know about it in advance, then he used you, yes."

She stared into hot gray eyes, then looked away. "I don't believe it. He's been genuinely concerned about Granddad working too hard."

"How naive are you?"

She'd had too many shocks tonight, and even the physical calm she'd just attained hadn't eradicated their effects. Pierce had played a mighty big role in Dallas's eccentric behavior, and KC suddenly remembered that. Anger curled in her eyes. "Naive enough to have invited *you* into my bed," she hurled, hoping to inflict just a little dent in Pierce Wheeler's armor of irritating confidence.

It worked. His jaw clenched. "Are you sorry you did?"

She wasn't going to answer that, KC decided. In fact, any answer, either negative or positive, would be merely words. She didn't know how she felt about it yet.

And then, for some unknown reason, she remembered the several innuendos Pierce had just made about whether or not she'd known what Kyle had been up to. "Why, you bastard," she whispered.

"What?"

"You think that I've been conspiring with Kyle to get Granddad to sell for some selfish reason of my own! *That's* what's been eating at you all this time, isn't it?"

Pierce started as though slapped. Coming out of KC's mouth, his own damned suspicions sounded bad, very bad. He wanted to explain, but only got out, "KC—"

"Do you want a good laugh? I actually believed your dislike of Kyle was because you were jealous. Funny, huh?" Squirming, KC tried to shake his hands off her arms. The sheet slipped, and she grabbed at it and held it in place over her angrily heaving breasts. "Your opinion of me is really uplifting, you snake in the grass."

"KC, please..." There was a frantic note in Pierce's voice. If she were truly innocent, then he deserved every ounce of disdain she was heaping on him.

"Please, what? Why don't you just get out of here!"

"Not like this. Not with you spitting bullets and madder than hell at me."

"I suppose I shouldn't be mad?" KC held her glare for another moment, then slumped wearily. "What's the use? It doesn't matter, anyway. I'm going home, and..."

Pierce felt as if he'd just been kicked. "You're really leaving?"

"Yes," she cried, perversely glad that her impending departure had caused the pain she could see in his eyes.

"KC..." Pierce swallowed and slowly lowered her back to the pillow. She made a pretty picture with her hair spread out and mussed around her face. Her shoulders and arms were bare, and the full, female roundness of her breasts was clearly delineated through the white sheet. "Why are you in such a hurry to leave?"

"I explained that before. Granddad made it very clear tonight that he's going to do exactly as he pleases. I have you to thank for a very large part of that stubbornness."

"Me! Why in hell me?"

"Oh, good Lord! Don't pull that innocent act at this late date! We've gone round and round on that subject before. And don't worry about Kyle getting this place," she added with sarcasm. "I have a very strong hunch that Granddad will even balk at the state's offer, if and when it comes through."

At least that was good news. "Then he's definitely not selling to Kyle?"

"I'm sure he's not. I plan to tell Kyle.... Oh, no, I forgot I promised I'd call after I talked to Granddad! I'll have to contact him first thing in the morning."

Pierce got to his feet. "I'm sure he'll be thrilled to hear your voice," he drawled. "But I'll bet you ten bucks he goes into shock when you tell him Dallas isn't selling."

KC was hit with a burst of uneasiness. She'd wondered why Kyle wanted the business and why he'd seemed increasingly pressured. She didn't want to believe Pierce, and yet there were now seeds of doubt planted in her soul. Maybe she just didn't want to face disappointment with one more person. She liked Kyle. She had been amazed and gratified with his wonderful understanding, and to hear now that it had all been a sham, a facade, was like a stab in the back. On top of that, Pierce had been thinking she'd plotted right along with Kyle, if that's really what the banker had been doing.

Actually, everything that had gone wrong seemed more like Pierce's fault than anyone else's. Like an omen of things to come, he'd been the first person she'd met in Harmony. And from that moment on, he'd influenced every single phase of her time here.

It suddenly appeared important to prove him only meanminded and spiteful about Kyle. Yes, she was sorry she'd given in to her baser urges and invited intimacy with Pierce. And it was only ridiculous to have imagined herself falling in love with him. Without him slapping Dallas on the back and praising his achievements, the elderly man might already be back in San Francisco with her. And suspecting her of double-dealing her beloved grandfather was too damned much.

KC's gaze was coolly resentful. "I think it best if we call tomorrow off." Her heart did a fearful flip over the dark glower she saw appear on Pierce's face. And his advance looked entirely too purposeful! "Stay away from me," she cried.

"Stay away, hell!" Pierce reached the bed, grabbed her upper arms and hauled her upright. The sheet slid down and his eyes seared her naked body. Her nipples hardened under his relentless gaze and her every nerve leaped to alertness. His fingers dug into her arms while he took his time looking, and when his interest lingered on the patch of golden hair between her legs, KC exploded.

"Take your hands off me!"

"No way, sweetheart," he growled. And he yanked her closer and brought his mouth down on hers, hard. It was a bruising kiss, one that contained dark emotions, and KC knew that something had frustrated Pierce to near violence. Was it Kyle and her defense of him? Or breaking tomorrow's date? What?

Her mouth was stinging when he broke away. His eyes were stormy and hard. "I'll be by at noon tomorrow to pick you up. Take care of your business with Rudman before that."

Her voice was weak. "You can't order me around like that. Just who do you think you are?"

His reply lashed the air. "I'm the man who—" He stopped just short of confessing his real feelings. I'm the man who loves you, who wants to love you! But let her find out about Rudman first, he decided. Tomorrow, when she told Rudman that Dallas wasn't selling to him under any circumstances, KC was bound to see a different person than the fawning, sickeningly sugary man she seemed to find so appealing.

KC was waiting with a discordant throb in her body. Pierce had started to say something, and she wanted to hear the rest of it. It had sounded like the start of something important, something she would want to hear. "You're the man who— what, Pierce? What were you going to say?"

"Nothing. We'll talk tomorrow." His gaze roamed her face while he let her slide back to the bed. "I'd better be going. It would be damned easy to crawl back into this bed with you." Leaning over without touching her, he kissed her lips. KC closed her eyes and did everything she could to fight the delicious sensation threatening to sweep her away again. But it didn't last long, and she raised her lashes to see Pierce looking down at her.

"I'll see you tomorrow," he said confidently.

She didn't argue, but in the back of her mind was denunciation. She was going to see Kyle tomorrow and get this thing straightened out once and for all, before she did anything else.

KC awoke the next morning with a throbbing headache and a horrible case of the blues. Pierce and Kyle and Dallas had all haunted her dreams, leering and laughing at her from a hodgepodge of senseless scenarios. The first thing KC did when she painfully opened her eyes was crawl out of bed and find some aspirin tablets. The second was burst into tears.

Her thoughts exploded. She was weak where Pierce was concerned, and that made her sob. It was possible that Kyle had used her, and that made her sob, too. Then, when she thought of how completely she'd failed with Dallas, she fell back on the bed and cried until she was weak.

Finally, the utter absurdity of lying in a heap and crying her headache into monstrous proportions sank in, and she pulled herself off the bed and went and stood under the shower. Ten minutes of alternating hot and cold spray helped clear her head, and when she got out and dried off, she was able to function almost normally.

At nine KC dialed the number Kyle had written on the back of his business card. Mrs. McCollum answered the telephone. "Rudman residence."

"Mrs. McCollum, this is KC Logan. Is Kyle there?"

"No, he isn't. But he left a message for you, Miss Logan. He had to go to Helena on business, and he wondered if you would have dinner here at the house with him tonight."

"Dinner?"

"He should be back in town around seven. If you could be here then?"

KC wanted to slam down the phone, but didn't like to take her anger out on Mrs. McCollum. She'd wanted this thing with Kyle behind her as quickly as possible, certainly before Pierce appeared at noon. She had visualized telling him that he was completely off-base where Kyle Rudman was concerned, and she wasn't only disappointed that she wouldn't be able to, she was *furious*!

She had to forcibly calm herself down, recognizing another phase of the jagged emotional state she'd awakened with. Still, her voice contained very little warmth. "I'll be there at seven."

Dallas was in high spirits when KC walked into the saloon. She'd delayed going over until she felt more controlled, and it was close to eleven before the need for a cup of coffee got the better of her good intentions.

"Hi, honey," Dallas called, sounding so much like his old self KC found herself responding with a smile, if one without much heart in it. "You look chipper this morning," she commented.

"Honey, I *feel* chipper. How did it go last night?"

Last night? Oh, the saloon. For a moment there KC had thought only of Pierce, and she didn't want to think of Pierce. Thinking of Pierce only made her want to cry again, and she'd already done enough crying that morning. "Everything went fine," she replied tonelessly. "Pierce came by and said that Mrs. Seberg will be back to work tonight."

"That's good." Dallas patted her hand. "Are we friends again?"

KC's lower lip trembled, and she turned away from Dallas's keen blue eyes. "Granddad, we've never been anything but friends."

"You've been crying."

"Over nothing. Please, I really don't want to talk about it."

Dallas looked confused for a moment, then wandered off to wait on a customer. KC poured herself a cup of coffee, then walked through the storage room and back to her room. She was in no condition to deal with the public today.

And as far as getting into another discussion with her grandfather, there was nothing she could do but accept his transgressions. She loved him too much to get truly angry with him, and she certainly wouldn't leave Harmony with any bad feelings between them.

But today she didn't feel up to coping with much of anything.

It never occurred to Pierce that KC wouldn't be ready and waiting for him at noon, and he was determined to have an enjoyable day with her. But more than that, he was hoping for some serious conversation. They had a lot to iron out, and he was prepared to make a few heartfelt apologies for thinking she'd been in on Rudman's scheme. Then, too, the thought of her leaving Harmony tore Pierce up, and he kept trying to figure out an enticement to make her stay.

Would a marriage proposal do it?

The very thought curled his hair. Was he ready for marriage? Was what he felt for KC the real thing? How in hell did a man know?

Sure, he wanted her physically. More than ever after last night. He'd awakened in the night wanting her, and some vivid imagery had caused him discomfort this morning. If she'd been in his bed, he could have taken care of that discomfort very nicely. But did an almost permanent erection mean he was really in love?

They hadn't known each other long enough for a serious commitment. If he didn't come up with something, KC was going to leave. And he had a very strong feeling that if he let her go, he'd be sorry for the rest of his life.

Pierce parked the van and strolled into the saloon. Dallas was behind the bar and smiled rather cheerlessly, Pierce thought. "Good to see you, Pierce."

Pierce's grin was masculinely companionable. "I hear congratulations are in order." He shoved his hand across the bar, which Dallas shook firmly. "When's the big event?"

"Don't know. I'm leaving that up to Mary. We're in no hurry. In fact..." Looking around to make sure no one could overhear, Dallas leaned forward. "This is between me and you, right?"

"Whatever you say, Dallas."

"Well, it's like this. If we get married, Mary's gonna lose some of her social-security benefits. And she really don't like that idea. We've been considering just moving in together and pretending we're married. We don't want anyone to know, especially KC."

"I understand," Pierce said solemnly. "Don't worry, my friend. Whatever you do, you've got my blessing."

Dallas picked up a bar rag and wiped the place in front of Pierce. "Can I get you anything?"

"Is KC around?"

Dallas's face fell. "I'm real worried about her, Pierce. I don't think she can take everything that's been going on. She came in and got a cup of coffee about an hour ago, and I could tell she'd been crying."

Pierce frowned. "Is she at the motel?"

"I hope she is. How come you're looking for her?"

"I thought we had a date," Pierce said quietly, rethinking last night with a few misgivings.

Dallas grinned then. "Well, great. That's just great. She's probably in her room waiting for you." His eyes suddenly shone with impish cunning. "Sure would be great if she married some nice fella from around here and stayed in Harmony, wouldn't it?''

Hesitating a moment, Pierce finally laughed and nodded. ''It sure would be, Dallas.'' He slid off the stool and leaned across the bar. ''But if she did, how would you pull off a fake wedding ceremony?''

Startled, Dallas stood back. ''Why, I didn't think of that.''

''See you later, old friend.'' Touching his forehead in a casual salute, Pierce laughed and left the saloon. Dallas was a great old guy, always full of surprises. But he'd boxed himself in playing matchmaker today.

Pierce stopped short when he saw that the parking space in front of room five was empty. He hadn't noticed that on his way in, but then he hadn't questioned that KC would be here, had he? Choked with emotions he couldn't quite identify, Pierce returned to his van and got in. This was something he hadn't expected. Why had KC been crying this morning? Had he hurt her last night with his blatant innuendos more than he'd realized?

She'd told him last night that the date was off. Hadn't he believed her, or was it that he just hadn't listened?

She wasn't a windup toy, dammit. What had made him think she would act like one?

He really was in love with her, wasn't he? To hell with time and what was normal or considered proper in a courtship. When had he ever worried about what was proper, anyway? Hadn't he said essentially the same thing to her that night? Either you had feelings or you didn't. Well, he had them, right along with a gutful of apologies. If those things weren't enough to keep her in Harmony, would anything else he could say be?

Reaching for the ignition key, Pierce started the motor. He'd find her, he thought grimly. And when he did, they were going to do some serious talking.

The riverbed was lined and layered with rocks of all sizes, from tiny, smooth ''skipping'' stones, to massive, craggy boulders. The river water was likewise a diverse mixture, calm and moving lazily in places of green, murky depths, then rushing and tumbling in shallow areas. Sunlight danced across the river's surface, a golden glow here, a splashing, diamondlike brilliance there.

It was mesmerizing to watch the river's movement. Seated on a large flat rock, her back to the spot she'd left her car, KC stared at the water through a blur of tears. This was the same spot Kyle had brought her to only a few days before, and she'd returned only because it was a quiet place to try to collect herself.

It was also a place Pierce might not think to look when he realized that she'd slipped away. She didn't want to see Pierce right now. In fact, there was a good possibility that she wouldn't want to see him again at all before she left Harmony. That was one of the things KC needed to think over.

She felt weighted down with all she had to think about. It was time to make some decisions and she didn't feel capable of doing so. It was perhaps the oddest sensation she could ever remember having: she felt terribly adrift from the rest of the world.

It was because of Dallas, she knew, but Pierce had a lot to do with it, too. And she didn't even have a job. That was her own doing, to be sure. But it added to the oddly rootless sensation tormenting her. What *did* she have besides a lonely apartment in San Francisco and a thousand-mile drive ahead of her?

KC closed her eyes. Damn, she hated people who wallowed in self-pity, and that's exactly what she was doing. Even worse she knew what she was doing and still couldn't rise above the despondency in her soul. Nor could she control her tears.

KC sat there for about an hour, just watching the water and brushing away tears, despising her mood, but finding nothing either in her own thoughts or the beautiful, sunny day to lift her spirits. Perhaps she could have handled every other shock but the one Pierce had given her last night. Now she remembered all of the other hints he'd made that something wasn't quite on the up and up with Kyle. And she'd thought his reservations had only been based on jealousy!

What a fool she'd been. What a stupid, moronic fool.

KC sighed when she heard a vehicle traversing the rutted, bumpy road from the highway and realized that her solitude was about to be invaded. Wiping her eyes she stood and dusted off the seat of her blue shorts. A desultory glance toward the motor noise made her flinch. Pierce had found her, after all.

She walked to her car, then stood quite still until the van stopped. Pierce got out and called to her.

KC steeled herself for a derogatory remark about her absence.

"What are you doing way out here?" Pierce came up, leaned against her car and hooked his thumbs in his jeans pockets. He saw immediately that KC had been crying again. Her eyes also contained that little-girl vulnerability that never failed to wring him out.

"How did you know where I was?"

He spoke gently. "I didn't. I've been driving around looking for you."

KC looked away. "Aren't you going to say something about me not waiting for you?"

Pierce studied her. "You're a big girl. If you didn't want to wait, you didn't have to."

Her head snapped around. "How very understanding!"

"Do you want to fight?"

"I want to be left alone! I would think that uncommon understanding you've just developed might have told you that."

"We need to talk."

"Do we? About what, Pierce? Have you come up with a few more insulting accusations to toss my way?"

Pushing away from KC's red sedan, Pierce paced a few steps. "You've got a right to be mad. I'm sorry. That's all I can say, KC. I'm sorry as hell."

Tears burned a path to her eyes again, and KC blinked hard. Dammit, why did one kind word make her feel like completely letting go and bawling like a baby again? What was wrong with her today?

To gain a moment to get rid of that choked feeling, KC turned and walked back to the riverbank. She knew Pierce was following, but thank God, he stayed a few steps behind.

Shoving her hands into the side pockets of her shorts, KC gave her attention to the river, aware that Pierce had picked up a handful of pebbles and was tossing them in the water, one at a time. Even with the river's natural rushing sound the *kerplunk* of the stones was audible, and absently KC counted six splashes.

"Feeling better?" she heard, and darted a glare in Pierce's direction.

"I feel just fine."

Slate-gray eyes were squinting at her. "You don't look fine. You look tense enough to bite my head off. Is that what you want to do? If screaming at me for a while would help, go ahead.''

"Oh, stop it," KC heatedly demanded. "Since when did you get so noble and understanding?"

Pierce gave her a long, penetrating look. "Since I realized I might lose you," he said softly.

KC's eyes widened. She turned and started running back to her car. Halfway, Pierce caught her from behind and wrapped his arms around her struggling body. She tried to tell him to let go of her, but only a series of garbled sobs came out of her throat.

"Easy," Pierce said huskily, and held her until she was no longer fighting to escape. Her tears fell on his arms across her breasts, and she stood with her head down and wept. He pressed his lips to the back of her hair. "Tell me what's so bad, honey. Talk to me."

KC sniffled. "I need a tissue. There are some in my car."

"Right. I'll get them." Releasing her, Pierce moved to the red sedan, crawled in and found the box of tissues. KC had come up, and he held the box out to her. Grabbing a handful, KC walked away and blew her nose. She ended up at the edge of the river again, and sensed Pierce standing a discreet few feet beyond her.

"You can't lose someone...I mean, I never belonged to you," she finally said tensely.

"I know. I think I'm talking more about what could be, KC. There's a lot more between us than sex."

She was feeling so low, she couldn't even visualize Pierce having any real feelings for her. "What?" KC faced him. "Tell me what else there is."

They stared at each other. "It hurts me to see you cry," Pierce said softly. "I like your smile and that independence you show the world. It's not very deep, though, is it, honey? You put on a tough exterior, but underneath you're not tough at all."

KC stiffened. "I don't even know what you're talking about."

Rubbing the back of his neck, Pierce walked a small circle, and when he stopped again he was close enough to touch KC. "What's the real reason you came after Dallas?"

"Are we going to play twenty questions now? Why I came after Granddad has nothing to do with you and me," KC hurled angrily.

"Indirectly it does. Hasn't that been the cause of most of our arguments?"

"Don't forget Kyle Rudman," she said coldly.

Pierce grimaced. "I'd like to forget Rudman, believe me. I'm not through with that guy yet, and I'm damned sorry I ever thought you might have thrown in with him. But the obsession you had about getting Dallas out of here was pretty tough to swallow, KC."

"Obsession! I resent that. Loving and caring about my grandfather doesn't make me crazy."

Shaking his head, Pierce put a hand on her shoulder. "You're not easy to talk to, KC."

"I'm sorry. I . . . I'm so mixed up."

"I can see that," Pierce said thoughtfully, and after a moment added, "Would you come to my place so we can really talk?"

Did she want to discuss feelings she couldn't even understand? How could she explain anything to anyone when her mind was only a muddle? She'd sat out here for at least an hour, trying to make heads or tails of everything that had recently happened, and she'd gained nothing except maybe a very small peace from the pretty spot. The thought of prying into her emotions, of tearing herself apart, was only disheartening.

"Not today," she whispered, evading Pierce's eyes.

"Tomorrow, then?"

KC took a breath. "I promised Granddad I would meet Mary Collier tomorrow."

"You're upset about meeting Mary, aren't you? Honey, you'll like her."

KC gave a shaky laugh. "I don't think it matters much to Granddad whether I like her or not."

Pierce had never seen anyone so completely unhappy before. "Come home with me, just for a few hours. Don't shut me out, please."

Ten

When KC didn't answer, Pierce began looking for a reason for her low spirits in earnest. He knew this was more than a bad mood and immediately thought of Kyle Rudman and that KC had planned to talk to the banker that morning. "I think I finally understand what's going on. Rudman gave you a bad time, didn't he? KC, if he said so much as one word out of line to you, I swear I'll—"

"I haven't seen or talked to Kyle today. I tried, but his housekeeper said he'd gone to Helena on business," KC rebutted wearily.

Scowling, Pierce looked away long enough to collect his thoughts. If Rudman wasn't the cause of KC's blues, what was? Did it have something to do with last night? They'd attained such togetherness in each other's arms, but then he'd ruined it with his blasted accusations. Yes, that no doubt was part of the cause of KC's melancholy. But there was more, too, something that went deeper and was obviously very painful for her.

Certainly she wouldn't be this upset over Dallas getting married, would she?

Narrowing his eyes on KC, Pierce's thoughts went in a whole new direction. KC had lost her parents as a child, then her grandmother not too long ago. Last night, in the saloon, hadn't she admitted feeling lost? Was it possible she was just bone-deep scared of losing Dallas, too? Was it also possible that she didn't understand why she was so scared, and was battling the lonely sensation with tears and anger simply because those were her only available weapons?

It was one explanation for that vulnerability he'd spotted before and was so recognizable today, and it also could be why KC was having such a hard time over the meeting with Mary Collier. Yes, she'd like Mary, if she let herself. But in her present frame of mind, could she like anyone?

That applied to Pierce Wheeler, too, he realized. This wasn't the best time to start talking about love, was it?

This was a touchy situation. Now Pierce understood last night and why KC had turned to him. She'd needed comfort badly.

She wouldn't have turned to just any man. There was something strong, real and vital between them, no matter how fervently she'd questioned it.

Pierce suddenly felt like a fool for not understanding KC better before this. He was usually a little more perceptive, but then his judgment had never before been clouded by falling in love.

In the next breath he wondered if she was through with Kyle or still planning to contact him. Pierce stirred uneasily, not very thrilled with the idea. "KC, don't see Rudman again. You don't have to prove anything where he's concerned. I can't even believe that I could have connected you to his rotten little game."

KC's reply was quick and sharp. "I have to see him. I don't happen to believe your story."

"And you think you're going to prove me wrong."

"Yes!"

"You can't, and it could be dangerous."

KC bristled. "I suppose you're going to accuse him of being a threat now, too? I'll have you know that Kyle has been nothing but a gentleman around me."

"KC, he needed you. He was getting nowhere with Dallas on his own. And once you destroy the reason he needed you, I have a feeling you're going to find out his true nature. Please stay away from him. Talk to him on the phone, if you feel you must, but don't go around him. Will you at least do that much?"

"No. I'm having dinner at his house tonight."

Anger swirled in Pierce's brain. "Have you heard anything I've said?"

A flush stained KC's cheeks. "Of course I have. But you're not the final authority on everything that goes on in Harmony just because you're the law! Now, if you'll excuse me, I'm going back to town."

KC walked back to the car with Pierce right on her heels. As she reached for the door handle, he reached for her hand and held it. "Do you know what this comes down to? You'd rather believe Rudman than me."

"No." Confused, KC stammered over a denial. "That's not true."

Pierce's stormy gaze held hers. Kyle Rudman was no longer worth arguing about, and Pierce felt he better understood KC's feelings about Dallas. But he was still only human and couldn't stop himself from bringing up what was bothering *him* the most. "What about last night? I know damned well you don't bed-hop, and it was me you wanted. What about that?"

She hesitated, but only to gather enough strength to say aloud what had been nearly destroying her. "*That* was a mistake," she choked out, and jerking free of his hand, she climbed behind the steering wheel of her car.

Pierce stayed at the river after KC had driven off. Things had gotten tense around Harmony since KC Logan's appearance. He restlessly raked his hair into snarls as he paced the riverbank.

This was a serious situation to her. But it was crucial that someone should convince her she wasn't losing Dallas just because he was supposedly getting married and staying in Harmony.

Even more upsetting to Pierce, though, was how KC was rejecting him. He should have told her about his feelings last night, before they'd ever started discussing Kyle and that can of worms. Now KC's emotions were so raw and shattered, she probably wouldn't let herself believe he was in love with her, no matter how he presented it.

Maybe he needed a little help with this, Pierce mused. Maybe he should talk to Dallas. But even Dallas didn't really understand KC's true state of mind. Still, if they put their heads together, surely the two of them could come up with something to alleviate KC's emotional state. She'd looked and acted

as if her heart had been broken, a condition one simply didn'
argue away. She was going to have to be shown.

There had to be a way.

Pierce left a little later with a prayer in his heart. He had a
plan, which he felt positive Dallas would go along with. And i
would also protect KC from any problem with Kyle when he
found out he wasn't going to get his greedy paws on Dallas'
property.

With very little enthusiasm, KC dressed for her dinner date
She chose the black dress this time. She moved listlessly, giv
ing only a few minutes to her makeup and hair. She simply did
not care if she looked her best, not for a dinner engagemen
that she would rather do almost anything else than attend.

KC eyed the telephone and speculated on making a call to
Kyle rather than going to his house. Not because Pierce had
asked her to, either. But during the hours between leaving
Pierce and getting ready for the evening, she'd lost every dram
of desire to prove that the sheriff was an imaginative trouble
maker. It didn't matter anymore. If Kyle was a petty crook be
neath all of that expensive clothing, so be it. By the same token,
if he wasn't, Pierce would find out that he'd jumped to con
clusions.

KC at least knew that her lassitude had nothing to do with
Kyle Rudman. Her despondency had to do with Dallas and
Pierce. She had all kinds of indistinct feelings about Dallas and
Pierce, but one thing was becoming painfully clear: she loved
them both, yes, *loved* them, and neither one of them really gave
a damn, did they?

Oh, Dallas loved her very much. She knew that, just as she'd
always known it. But their lives were splitting, taking differen
directions. It was something she would eventually get used to
even if today she could hardly keep from crying every time she
thought about it.

As for Pierce, well, Pierce's feelings were concentrated be
low his belt. They had to be. It hurt so much to think that he'd
actually believed she could have conspired against Dallas, with
or without Kyle, that KC knew she could never forgive him
Especially when he'd done everything possible to get her to bed
while harboring such despicable suspicions about her.

Deeply involved in her own unhappy thoughts, KC jumped when someone knocked on the door. She'd worked in the saloon a few hours that afternoon at Dallas's request, the first time he'd actually asked her to do anything around the place. "I've got an errand I can't put off, honey. Would you mind?" As lousy as KC had felt, she hadn't had the heart to refuse, and had even hoped the forced activity would help her mood.

Then Katie Seberg had arrived to take over before Dallas had gotten back, so KC was surprised to see her grandfather at the door. "Oh, it's you, Granddad," she said dully. The few hours waiting on customers hadn't worked any kind of magic, and KC still felt as low as she had all day.

"Yep, sure is. Can I come in for a minute?"

"Of course." KC stepped back and held the door.

"You sure do look pretty."

"Thank you."

"About to leave?"

"Yes, but I've been considering just calling Kyle rather than going to his house."

"Well, that's what I'm here to talk about. I've been doing some thinking about his offer, and I'd like you to give him a message."

"Wouldn't you rather just call and talk to him yourself?"

"Nope. The man seems to prefer going through you." Dallas grinned slyly. "Let's let him have his fun, all right?"

KC sighed. "What's the message?"

"That I'm ready to discuss his offer."

If Dallas had suddenly kicked her in a shin, KC couldn't have been more startled. "I don't understand. I thought you were dead set against selling to him."

"Maybe I am and maybe I ain't."

KC shook her head, amazed. "What's going on now, Granddad? You've got something cooking in that head of yours, I can see it in your eyes."

"I want to talk to the man," Dallas said innocently. "And since he's been going behind my back with you, you're the one who should deliver my message. Will you do it?"

After scrutinizing the elderly man for a moment, KC sighed again. "What exactly do you want me to tell him?"

"That I'll meet him in the saloon at eight sharp tonight."

"How will you talk business with a dozen people around?"

"I'm closing up early. I've already told Katie."

Recalling that the evening with Kyle was to include dinner, KC frowned. "What if he doesn't want to meet you at eight?"

Dallas chuckled. "Oh, I'm sure he'll come." He peered closely at KC. "Does that ruin your evening?"

"Lord, no. I told you I was thinking about just calling. All right, I'll go and deliver your message."

"And come right back here?"

"Where else would I go?"

Shortly after, KC drove to Kyle's house. And for the first time that day she felt something other than depression: avid curiosity. She knew that Dallas was up to something, in spite of his show of innocence, but she also knew that she'd lost any ability she might have once had to second-guess her grandfather.

One of the garage doors was open and Kyle's Mercedes was parked within, so KC parked on the opposite side of the driveway. Kyle opened the front door before she could ring the bell. "KC, you look absolutely ravishing. Come in, my pet."

My pet? KC found herself inwardly groaning at the drippy endearment. Kyle really was a bore, wasn't he? And not just because she was in a lousy mood, either. He'd *always* been a bore.

Smiling weakly, KC allowed herself to be steered into Kyle's sumptuous living room. Within seconds a crystal glass of iced white wine was pressed into her hand. "Thank you," she murmured and sank onto the posh couch.

"I can feel it in my bones," Kyle gushed with a toothy grin, seating himself on the next cushion of the long sofa.

"Feel what?" KC asked, startled.

"That you have good news for me. You do, don't you?"

He was going right for the gusto, wasn't he? No preliminary conversation, no "How are you?" or "Great weather we're having, hmm?"

KC felt rather lifeless again as she was suddenly stricken with an enervating conviction. Pierce was right, wasn't he? Dammit! Kyle *had* been using her. That smile was as phony as a three-dollar bill. Why hadn't she seen through this jerk before?

Dismayed and uncomfortable with herself, KC took a slow sip of her wine. She didn't like being used, especially when she'd trusted and believed and stood up for Kyle so ardently. She'd made mistakes in Harmony and it wasn't very clear why she had. But her eyes were open now, at least to this man, and

he honestly wished that she didn't have a message to deliver
and could tell him that he was never going to own Dallas's
property.

Well, she didn't have to rush into her "good" news, did she?
And she was in the proper frame of mind to pay Kyle back, just
a little.

She rolled another sip of wine around in her mouth. "What
delicious wine. I'm sure it must have been very expensive."

"Quite," Kyle concurred tersely.

Deliberately sweeping the room with her eyes, KC drawled,
"But then, everything you own is expensive, isn't it?" Tonight, Kyle was dressed in California casual, cream-colored silk
pants, a matching silk shirt that was open almost to his belt,
gold chains around his neck and a stunning bright green blazer.
The man might be a jerk, but he had a flair for dressing dramatically.

"I like nice things," Kyle returned, and KC caught the im-
patient gleam in his hazel eyes. "Let's get to the point, KC. Did
you tell Dallas about the additional five thousand?"

"I most certainly did."

"And?"

She dared one more delay. "I've been wondering all day what
Mrs. McCollum would prepare for dinner. She really is a wonderful cook."

"KC!"

"Yes, Kyle?" Such theatrical innocence proved beyond a
shadow of a doubt that she was Dallas Logan's granddaughter, and KC almost giggled over the thought.

"What did Dallas say?"

The man was practically bursting at the seams, KC noted.
She dropped her eyes to the wine in her glass, then raised them
slowly. "I told Granddad you wouldn't want to do it on such
short notice, not with our dinner plans, but he felt sure that you
would." Kyle was close to gritting his teeth, KC saw.

"Do what, KC?" he asked, enunciating each syllable distinctly.

"Meet him at the saloon at eight tonight. He's ready to discuss your offer."

In another age, Kyle might have jumped up and shouted
"Eureka," KC realized. Actually, she thought he exhibited remarkable restraint when it was so apparent he was overjoyed.

"Eight?" Kyle pulled the sleeve of his green blazer back and studied the thin gold watch on his wrist. "Eight," he repeated, then gave KC a rather sheepish grin. "I'm afraid I'll have to cancel dinner tonight, my pet. You do understand, don't you?"

She'd had enough. "Implicitly," she returned icily. "By the way, I'm not your pet, nor your darling." Rising, KC looked for a place to set her glass down, then, deliberately avoiding the coaster, she placed it on the coffee table. As she stalked from the room, her last glimpse of Kyle was of him rushing to save his tabletop from a damp ring.

"Jerk," KC muttered, her temperature running several degrees higher than normal. Oddly, though, once she was in her car, her anger vanished and she felt only drained again.

Pierce had been right and she'd been dead wrong. Kyle was elated at Dallas's request to meet tonight, but what if her message had been negative? What would Kyle's reaction have been if she'd have told him that Dallas had definitely and finally refused his offer, which was the way KC had seen it until Dallas knocked on her door tonight.

My Lord, was that the reason for that damned message? Merely a means to shield her from a possibly bad scene with Kyle?

If so, then Pierce was behind it. It was Pierce who'd been worried about Kyle's reaction, not Dallas. What were those two cooking up for Kyle? Ten to one, Pierce would be at that meeting tonight.

Well, so would she! Dallas wouldn't care if she sat in.

Or would he? He certainly hadn't let her in on the reason for that message, had he?

With her heart pounding nervously, KC drove back to the motel. Sure enough, Pierce's van was there, but it was parked *behind* the saloon. She could see it from the motel, but there was a very good chance that Kyle would pull in and park in front of the saloon and miss the van entirely.

KC hurried into her room, kicked off her high heels and tore off her dress and hose. She was running on nervous energy and adrenaline, she knew, keyed up from the long, upsetting day, unnerved from the meeting with Kyle.

After dressing in jeans, a navy-blue, long-sleeved T-shirt and sneakers, KC opened the window drapes just a fraction, only enough to peek out. Once Kyle got there and was inside the saloon with Dallas and Pierce, she was going to sneak in the backdoor and listen to their meeting. Only one thing would stop her—if Dallas had locked that backdoor.

If he had she'd take it as an omen, KC decided anxiously. If the door was unlocked, then that would mean she wasn't doing anything underhanded. If the door *was* locked . . . well, she'd just have to come back to her room and stew until Kyle left. Although in that case, she'd probably never know what really went on.

KC didn't have to wait long. At precisely eight, Kyle's silver Mercedes pulled into the empty parking lot and stopped as close to the saloon's front door as Kyle could get it. "Bingo," KC whispered, knowing that the banker had no idea that Pierce was inside with Dallas.

The minute Kyle went into the saloon, KC slipped out of her room and ran across the parking lot. Holding her breath, she very quietly tried the knob on the backdoor, and breathed again only when it turned. Telling herself that she'd been involved in this mess from the beginning and had every right to hear what Pierce and Dallas had in store for Kyle, she cautiously and silently stepped into the storage room and closed the door.

Voices from the saloon carried quite well, and she moved to the wall beside the open doorway to listen.

"Well, I still don't see why you want him here, Dallas. He doesn't have a damned thing to do with our deal."

"He's my best friend, Rudman. Take it or leave it."

They were arguing over Pierce's presence, KC realized, and wished she could have been there soon enough to hear Kyle's initial reaction to the sheriff being a participant in the meeting.

"I'm not here in an official capacity," Pierce drawled.

"Oh, really?" Kyle said snidely. "Now, why do I have a little trouble believing that?"

"Beats me." Pierce laughed.

Dallas took the floor. "Do you want to just forget this, Kyle? If you do, just come right out with it."

Kyle sounded sullen. "No, I don't want to forget it. This is important to me."

"A little too important, I'm guessing," Pierce put in.

KC heard Dallas clearing his throat. "The first thing I want to get out in the open is the way you've been going behind my back with KC, Kyle. That little gal means the world to me, and I think you've been using her."

"No, Dallas, that's not true. KC is a lovely woman. I have only the highest regard for her."

"You'd better have," Pierce snarled. "I plan to marry her, and by all that's holy, if I ever find out you've done one thing to hurt her, I'll . . ."

"Now, Pierce, let's not get carried away here. I'm sure Kyle never made any undue personal advances to KC. His interest in her was only because of this property. Am I right, Kyle?"

KC missed Kyle's reply entirely. She was still back at Pierce's statement: *I plan to marry her.* Her heart had been pounding before that, but after those words, it was like a jackhammer in her chest. Why would he say that to Kyle and Dallas when he'd never so much as even hinted at a future together to her?

Eavesdroppers usually got what they deserved, KC admitted.

"That's all beside the point, Dallas," Kyle was saying. "Let's get to the bottom line. Are you interested in selling or not?"

"Nope."

"Then why in hell did you ask for this meeting?"

"So I could tell you myself. KC was going to, you know, and frankly, Rudman, I wasn't sure what a man who'd go behind a fella's back might do to a woman who gave him that kind of news."

"Why, you old son-of-a . . ."

"Watch your mouth, Rudman," Pierce growled. KC nearly stumbled over her own feet to look through the doorway when she heard a scuffling noise and realized something physical was happening.

Then she couldn't believe her own eyes. Kyle took a swing at Pierce, and Pierce popped him on the jaw so neatly and quickly, KC barely saw the blow. The next instant, Pierce caught the reeling banker and plopped him down on a chair. "Sit there until you cool off," Pierce ordered.

KC jumped back out of sight, her pulse beating a mile a minute. Dallas and Pierce had planned this whole thing, just to keep her from any possible wrath Kyle might have. And he was madder than a hive of hornets. She had misjudged Kyle on every count.

Shivering, she wished she could leave, but she was shaking so badly she wasn't sure she could get out silently. Her face was burning from Kyle's litany of curses, and then Pierce was speaking again.

"We know exactly what you've been up to, Rudman, but I do have one question. How come you paid for all that property you bought with cash?"

"There's no law against buying something with cash," Kyle said with a sneer.

"Not if it's your cash, there isn't. Was it?"

"That's for me to know and you to lose sleep over, Wheeler."

"Maybe a visit from the bank examiners would change that tune, Rudman."

"Do anything you want. You're not scaring me."

"No? You think you're pretty damned smart, don't you?"

"Smarter than a hick sheriff any day of any week, Wheeler."

KC covered her ears with her hands. This was far worse than she'd imagined.

Chair legs scraped against the floor. "I'm leaving," Kyle announced harshly. "Dallas, if you change your mind..."

"Don't look for that, Kyle. I won't be changing my mind."

"You'd make more money on my offer than the state will pay you."

"Maybe, maybe not. Besides, there are times in a man's life when profit isn't as important as principles, although I kind of doubt if you'd understand that."

"You're right," Kyle scoffed. "I've never found principles a particularly tasty dish at the dinner table, and I like to eat well."

After a moment KC heard the front door open and close, and she put her head back and released a long, troubled breath. The silence from the saloon was broken then. "How about a cup of coffee, Pierce?"

"Thanks. Dallas, I'd like to talk to you about KC."

"What about her?"

"Several things. I meant what I said about wanting to marry her, but before I get into that, I need to know how you feel about her coming here and trying so hard to get you away from this place?"

KC's mouth dropped open.

"Listen, Pierce. There's not another person in this whole danged world who means as much to me as KC does. That little gal can do no wrong, as far as I'm concerned."

"Even after she sided with Rudman?"

"She did that with the best of intentions. Whatever KC did was because she loves me."

"And what about Mary?'

"KC and Mary will get along. I'm a little worried about pulling off that phony wedding, but if you're planning to keep KC here, then Mary and me will figure something out. If it wasn't for Mary losing so much of her social-security check, we wouldn't even consider such a thing. I just can't tell KC about it, Pierce. I wouldn't want her living with a man without marriage, so how could I expect her to condone me doing it?''

Tears were dripping down KC's face. She knew she should get out of there, but her feet wouldn't move. She strained to catch the next exchange between Pierce and her grandfather.

"I'm in love with her, Dallas. I haven't told her yet, but I'm going to. Do you think she's back at the motel now?''

"Probably. Finish your coffee, Pierce. I've got one more thing to say. KC's lost a lot of people in her life. She was only a little kid when her folks were killed. That was a bad time for all of us. Losing our son and his wife was real bad. Harriet nearly died from grief, and me, well, it was a long time before I could laugh again. KC's the only reason Harriet and me made it, to be real honest about the matter. She was a joy, Pierce, a ray of sunshine in a mighty bleak old world.

"Then she lost her grandmother. That was a bad blow for both KC and me. You know what I think? I think KC's scared of losing me, too.''

"It's possible, Dallas. But you're entitled to a life of your own. KC's got me, if she wants me. And I want kids. Do you think she does? Has she ever said?''

"Heck, yes, she loves kids. Holy smoke, I just realized something. When KC has babies, I'll be a great-grandfather. Ain't that something, Pierce?''

KC couldn't take anymore. And how she made it out of that storage room without alerting Pierce and Dallas, she would never know. Blinded by tears, she stumbled across the parking lot and flung herself through the door of her room. Then she threw herself across the bed and cried so hard, the mattress bounced.

She'd heard much too much. That part about Dallas and Mary only pretending to get married, for one thing. And Pierce's admission of love, and his desire to marry her. And Dallas saying that she could do no wrong.

She was wrong to even be in Harmony. She'd been wrong to come here, wrong to expect Dallas to drop everything and go back to San Francisco, wrong, wrong, wrong.

Was her real reason for making the trip as simple as Dallas had theorized? That she was afraid of losing him, too?

Shuddering, KC sat up. She had a lot of soul-searching to do, didn't she? And what about Pierce? What was she going to say when he told her he was in love with her? She loved him, too, didn't she?

Oh, Lord, could she even trust her own feelings now? She'd made so many mistakes in Harmony, with Dallas, with Kyle, and yes, probably with Pierce. And he was talking about love and marriage and *kids*!

He could be on his way over right now! Sniffling and wiping her eyes, KC hurried to the bathroom to wash her face. Whatever happened, he must never know that she'd been in the storage room tonight and had overheard so much. *He must never know!*

Eleven

Pierce and Dallas shook hands and exchanged a solemn "good job done" look. They had agreed that very few people would be able to resist the lure of the storage room during that meeting, and their prediction had been right on the money. KC had heard everything they'd wanted her to hear.

The two men parted, with Dallas heading for his motel unit and Pierce heading for KC's. Pierce walked slowly, taking time to compose himself. He wanted the right expression on his face when KC opened the door, one that told her he knew nothing about her little adventure this evening. He also wanted her to think that their episode at the river was forgotten and behind them, nothing of any import.

Light seeped through a narrow separation of the window drapes, and Pierce saw KC's shadow as she came to the door at his knock. They both had a monumental acting job coming up, but Pierce felt that now they were both ready for the next step in his plan.

"Oh, Pierce," KC said, displaying surprise.

"Hi. The meeting's over, and I thought I'd stop by and tell you about it before I left."

KC closed the door after Pierce came in. "I was surprised to see your van out there. Apparently Granddad wanted you at the meeting."

"Yes, he did." Pierce tried hard not to stare at her puffy eyes, but finally decided that ignoring them would be out of character. He moved closer and raised her chin. "You've been crying again."

KC blinked several times, a flutter of long lashes that she hoped would dispel the urge to bawl again. What she'd overheard was beating like a drum in her brain, but she managed to force a little laugh. "I've just had a bad day, Pierce. Actually, I feel much better tonight. The world always looks a little brighter after one's windows are washed, don't you agree?"

A joke? Pierce's heart melted at the brave attempt. His voice got deeper, gentler. "Much brighter, honey." His gaze moved over her features, one by one. "You're the prettiest thing," he said softly. "The first time I saw you, I couldn't look at you hard enough."

That encounter hadn't been that long ago, and KC remembered his detailed scrutiny very well. She also remembered her own response at that initial meeting, and flushed as she realized where this conversation could be heading. She wanted to hear of Pierce's love, but her own uncertainties made rushing headlong into the moment impossible.

Brightly, she spun away. "Tell me what happened at the meeting with Kyle."

Pierce put on a grin. "Dallas and I kind of ganged up on him. We had it all planned."

"Then Granddad refused Kyle's offer, after all?"

"In spades, honey. I wish you could have been there."

"But why did Granddad want the meeting then?" KC pushed back a wisp of hair from her forehead, aware that her hands weren't quite steady. "From what he said earlier, I halfway expected him to accept Kyle's offer."

"He wanted to tell him no face to face, man to man. Dallas has been really put out over Kyle pressuring you."

KC frowned thoughtfully. "Yes, I know that now."

"You do?"

"I mean that I figured it out," KC quickly amended. Flustered over her slip, she indicated a chair. "Would you like to sit down?"

"I really should be going."

"Going?"

"Well, you're probably tired. Aren't you?"

Tired? What about what he'd told Dallas? Nervous suddenly, KC smoothed her hair down with both hands. "I'm . . . really not . . . very tired," she stammered.

Pierce's eyes lit up. "Maybe you'd like to go out for a few hours then. I thought I might stop at the Buckhorn for a beer on the way home."

"A beer? Well, no, I really don't feel up to that kind of atmosphere. Thanks, anyway," she said wistfully.

"A ride, then? Maybe you'd like to take a ride somewhere? It's a great night for a drive."

KC looked away, totally confused. She knew what she'd heard, and this didn't sound like "I love you and want to marry you" to her.

"Or," Pierce said softly, "we could go to my place."

"Your place?"

"My place. I've wanted you to see it, anyway."

Along with the pounding of her heart, KC's thoughts ran wild. Going to Pierce's house would be inviting intimacy and also provide an opportunity for him to speak frankly about his feelings. Was she ready for that? What was her response going to be when he did?

She simply did not know, did she? Her own feelings were locked so deeply inside of herself and then layered with all kinds of resentments and doubts, she really didn't know if she would ever be able to turn them loose. Especially when she no longer trusted them.

Nevertheless, and perverse as it seemed, she couldn't face leaving Harmony without giving Pierce the chance to express himself.

KC slowly nodded. "All right. We'll go to your place. I'd like to see it."

"Good," she heard Pierce murmur behind her as she went for her purse and the motel key.

They were all the way through town before KC caught on. "You don't live right in Harmony?"

"No. I have five acres and a cabin on the top of a mountain. It's only eight miles out of town, a beautiful spot. You'll like it."

KC smiled doubtfully. "Will I be able to see it in the dark?"

"It's beautiful at night, too. You can almost touch the stars from my back deck."

Unable to keep what she'd overheard at bay, KC brought it up again. "So Kyle took Granddad's refusal pretty hard?"

Pierce chuckled. "He took a swing at me."

She'd seen that burst of violence for herself, but it still made her stomach turn over. Some kind of comment was called for, though. "Did you swing back?"

"Just a little tap on the jaw to cool him off."

"I see." KC's thoughts advanced to what had happened after Kyle had gone, and she knew she was skating on thin ice, but she couldn't stop herself from pushing just a little. "You and Granddad stayed quite a while after Kyle left, didn't you?"

"Just talkin'," Pierce said offhandedly.

"About the business?"

"Mostly about you."

"Me? Why were you discussing me?"

Pierce glanced at her. "Well, Dallas is worried about you, for one thing."

"He shouldn't be."

"He loves you, KC."

She swallowed the lump rising in her throat. Did she believe Dallas's theory about her being afraid to lose him, too? All she could honestly admit was that she felt like crying every time she thought of it. When had she gotten so darned emotional that anything the least bit poignant touched her to tears?

"He'd sure like you to stay in Harmony."

"I . . . don't want to interfere in his life anymore."

"He doesn't look on your concern as interference."

KC's voice was thin. "That's what it's been, all the same."

Pierce signaled and made a left turn. They were immediately surrounded by dark, dense forest and traveling on a paved but much narrower road. It was a safe, impersonal topic. "Don't you have trouble getting out of here in the wintertime?"

"This is a county road. They keep it plowed."

"Winters are quite harsh around here, I would expect."

"They're wild. But I love the snow, and there's nothing more satisfying than sitting in front of a roaring fireplace and listening to a blizzard howling outside. Ever had that experience?"

"We don't have blizzards in San Francisco. Lots of rain and some wind, of course, but no blizzards." KC heaved a long, soulful sigh. She simply could not stay disassociated from the present.

"What was that for?"

"Granddad's arthritis. Cold weather is tough on him."

"Mary will take care of him."

"Yes, I suppose she will. I...really do want to like her," she added, her voice muted with circumspection, then feeling relief that it was true and that she'd reached that point.

Pierce smiled in the dark. "If I tell you a secret, will you promise to keep it to yourself?"

"A secret? About what?"

"You have to promise first."

KC already knew what the "secret" was, that phony marriage Dallas and Mary were planning. It was easy to promise not to mention it because she knew she would never have the courage to even hint that she knew about it. Nevertheless, she had to respond as she would have normally. "Well, secrets are sometimes hard to keep. Maybe you shouldn't tell me, especially if you can't let me know in advance what it's about."

"All right, I can tell you that much, I guess. It's about Dallas."

"Granddad?" KC threw her head to the back of the seat with a dramatic groan. "Oh, Lord, what's he up to now? Nothing would surprise me."

"This will," Pierce chuckled. "Do you promise?"

"I won't breathe a word."

"Well, he and Mary are only going to pretend to get married so she won't lose any of her social-security benefits."

"You're kidding!"

Pierce almost exploded with suppressed laughter. KC was one fine little actress. Someday, a long time into the future, he'd tell her what really happened tonight, but for now he'd play the game. This whole night was going to be mighty interesting.

The "secret" had been deliberately divulged during his and Dallas's conversation in the saloon, a ploy to solidly convince KC that no one knew she was in the storage room. Besides, after discussing it that afternoon, Dallas had really preferred that KC knew the truth, and tonight had been a good way to let her in on it without a heart-to-heart on the subject.

"I think it's great, don't you?"

"Great? Well, I don't know if I'd go that far, but it does make a certain amount of economic sense," KC returned dryly.

The van's headlights revealed the road's sudden sharp incline. They'd been climbing gradually since the left turn off the highway, but this upward slant was much more pronounced.

"I moved out here a little over five years ago," Pierce said. "The place was pretty run-down, so I made a good buy. It's home now, and I wouldn't trade it for town living for anything."

"You've never lived in a city, have you?"

"I'd call New York a city, wouldn't you?"

"Oh, yes, I forgot. But you were just a kid when you left Brooklyn."

"Sixteen, KC, but, yes, just a kid. A dumb kid, too. Oh, I knew how to survive on the streets, I did that quite well. But the rest of the world was a complete mystery. I hitchhiked west, which proved how dumb I was," Pierce laughed. "At that time of year, I should have headed south."

"You were really alone, weren't you?"

At the wistful note in her voice, Pierce darted a glance at her. "All alone, honey."

"You must have been terrified."

"Actually, I was so damned glad to get away from my alcoholic father, I didn't even think about anything else. When I left Brooklyn I had twenty-six dollars in my jeans, and I had stolen that from another kid. Over the years I've often wished I knew where that guy was so I could send his money back with interest. The best I can do in reparation, though, is to help other kids in the same fix I was in. I work with kids' groups all over the state."

"Very commendable," KC commented quietly.

"Well, here we are." The van nosed around a curve, its headlights flashing across the front of a brightly varnished, peeled-log house. Pierce pulled to a stop in a driveway that stopped at the doors of a log garage.

After cutting the engine and switching off the headlights, Pierce murmured softly, "Just listen to that quiet. That's what's so great about this place, KC. A person can breathe and think up here. Come on, let's go in. Get out on my side. It's dark out, and I don't want you tripping over something you can't see."

KC stepped out of the van right into Pierce's arms. She didn't know if she'd expected this so soon, but oh, Lord, it felt good. He was big and warm, and his arms felt like a security blanket around her. She sighed into him, molding into the dips and curves of his body. His hands moved down her back, then splayed around her waist, and she felt the brush of his lips on her right temple and heard, "Let's go inside."

Slightly surprised that he was satisfied with such a brief and passionless embrace, KC only nodded wordlessly and allowed Pierce to lead her into the house.

The interior of the log house was cozy and comfortable. As Pierce walked around and switched on lights, KC took in the nicely sized rooms, the modern kitchen, the color scheme combining polished wood and several shades of blue. "I'm impressed, Pierce."

"Glad you like it. What should we have to drink? Coffee? Tea? Or maybe you'd like something a little more stimulating. Brandy, maybe?"

KC was standing at the fireplace, looking at the several framed photographs on the mantel. She recognized Rose Dobrinsky in one of them. "Coffee will be fine, thank you. Is that Russell with Rose in this picture?"

"Yes. Those other photos are of friends. Make yourself comfortable while I put on a pot of coffee."

"Thanks, I will." There was a bookcase with a variety of books, and KC spent a few moments reading titles. Sports and news magazines all but covered the top of the coffee table, and a tray holding record albums sat beside a stereo system. A television set was situated on a small cart with wheels, and KC decided that the blue tweed recliner chair placed at a good viewing angle must be Pierce's favorite.

The aroma of perking coffee drifted from the kitchen. KC went to the doorway. "Smells good."

Pierce looked up. "How about a sandwich? Did you have dinner?"

"No, did you?"

"I had a late lunch is all." With KC safely tending the saloon that afternoon, he and Dallas had met at Layton's Café to discuss Pierce's plan, and they'd both eaten a hamburger.

KC helped, and with a plate of ham sandwiches and their coffee, they went back to the living room to eat. Pierce stacked the magazines and they both sat on the couch, with the food on the coffee table in front of them.

Halfway through a sandwich, Pierce asked, "Well, what now, KC?"

"I beg your pardon?"

"What are your plans?"

She blinked disbelievingly. What about *his* plans, the ones he'd told Dallas about? She could hardly ask him about them, not when he didn't have the slightest idea she'd been listening.

"Are you still planning on leaving Harmony?" Pierce casually inquired.

KC frowned at her sandwich. "I...need to find another job," she said numbly, wondering what was going on. She'd heard him correctly from the storage room, hadn't she?

Pierce chewed and swallowed, then remarked, "Anyone around here who really wants a job has one, you know."

KC lowered her cup. "Meaning that I could find a job in Harmony if I tried? Doing what, Pierce? Other than a part-time receptionist job during my college years, I've worked in advertising. I don't believe there's an advertising firm in Harmony, is there?"

"Do you type?"

"Of course I type. But..."

"Then you could find a job."

A bit of anger began festering, but KC didn't want to get mad. She'd had enough of anger and arguing in Harmony to last her a good long time. Before she could say a word in defense of her position, however, Pierce shot her an amiable smile. "A job shouldn't be the deciding factor in whether you leave or stay, KC. That's the only point I'm trying to make."

"Oh?" she remarked warily, her pulse beat picking up speed, positive that he was now heading into more personal territory. "What should?"

Popping the last bite of his sandwich into his mouth, Pierce picked up his coffee cup. "What you *want* to do, of course. It seems pretty simple to me. If you really want to go back to San Francisco, then that's what you should do. But if you'd rather stay here, close to Dallas, then you should stay."

KC sank back against the sofa. The guilelessness in Pierce's gray eyes was confusing her. Why had he talked that way to Dallas, confessing love and very serious intentions, and now acted as though his interest in her went no further than her own plans?

"I'll get the coffeepot." Rising, Pierce disappeared into the kitchen and returned with the pot. He topped off her cup, refilled his, then took the pot back to the kitchen. KC watched his long-legged stride carry him through the house, and when he was back on the couch and oh-so-nonchalantly drinking coffee again, she began to smell a rat.

She hadn't heard wrong earlier tonight, and there was nothing faulty with her memory. There was something a little out of kilter going on here. Narrowing her eyes speculatively on her companion, KC's mind whirled. Just what was this all about?

Pierce was laughing softly. "Is something funny?" KC asked, sitting up straighter again and reaching for her cup.

"Just the look on Rudman's face when Dallas told him he wasn't going to sell."

So, you're not quite through with Kyle yet, are you? KC thought with a sudden devilish impulse. Whatever sport Pierce was amusing himself with, why couldn't two play?

"Poor Kyle," she sighed tragically.

"What?" Pierce's smile disappeared into thin air. "Why, poor Kyle?"

"Don't you feel just a little sorry for him? I mean, he's such a nice man, and—"

"Nice! Don't tell me you still think of him as quality, for God's sake! He's a con artist, KC, and maybe worse. I'm planning to notify the proper authorities on Monday that the bank examiners should make an immediate and thorough check of the bank's records. Rudman paid for an awful lot of property with cash, and I'm betting..." Pierce broke off abruptly, suddenly remembering that KC had heard all about that only a short time ago. She knew damned well that he suspected Kyle of embezzlement, so what was she pulling?

This double-agent stuff is getting complicated, he thought.

Pierce almost gave in to an overwhelming urge to roar with laughter when he thought of the maze of who knew what and how they were each guarding their recent activities, and barely squeaked out of it by swallowing a mouthful of scalding hot coffee. Coughing and sputtering, he put the cup down and fell back against the sofa.

"I know you like Kyle," he said with exaggerated sadness. "But I truly believe he's a thief, KC."

"A thief? Oh, how terrible. Are you sure?'

Such shock, such pathos. She should be on the stage, shouldn't she? Pierce continued to look unhappy. "All I have are suspicions, KC, just suspicions."

Bristling, KC reverted to her real self. "Well, I have first-hand experience with your suspicions, and—''

Pierce reached for the small hand in her lap and stroked it while he spoke forlornly. "Will you ever be able to forgive me for that? What can I do to prove how sorry I am? I'll do anything. I want us to be friends."

Friends? Startled again, KC stared down at their clasped hands. His was so big and solid, hers was practically lost in it. Maybe it was time to drop a small bomb herself. Whatever game Pierce was playing was wearing thin.

"We can be friends," she said quietly. "As good of friends as people can be a thousand miles apart. I'm leaving on Monday, Pierce."

He'd anticipated that and had a doleful sigh all ready for it. "I guess you have to do what you think best."

KC stared. Why, he hadn't even flinched! Wasn't he even going to try to talk her out of it?

Too agitated to sit still any longer, KC jumped up. Crossing her arms over her breasts, she walked around the room.

"What's wrong, honey?

"Nothing!" Pacing nervously, KC stopped at the mantel for a second, then went to the sliding-glass door and peered out into the black night. She could see nothing but her own reflection in the glass, and she looked pretty bleak, she realized. The only way she could ask Pierce about that conversation with Dallas would be to admit she'd been hiding in the storage room.

"How about taking a look at the stars? I promised a great view, remember?''

The reflection in the glass allowed KC to see that Pierce had stood and was coming up behind her. He reached around her, prickling her spine with the brush of his body against hers, and slid the door back. His breath was warm on her scalp. "This leads to the deck," he said softly.

For one delirious moment KC considered just leaning back and closing her eyes. He wouldn't reject a personal advance, would he? If he did, it would be the first time in their short-lived relationship. What had happened to all those steamy looks and outright declarations of wanting her? Even at the river today she'd felt his desire. What had altered that between then and now? And why, in heaven's name, had he talked so bluntly to Dallas and now seemed almost cool? Which was the act, those few minutes in the saloon or this?

Stifling the impulse, KC stepped outside. The night air was cool. She shivered, then wondered if it was from the fresh air or from Pierce's baffling behavior. The lights in the living room went off and KC whirled.

"I turned them off," Pierce explained as he came through the door. "You can see the stars better without lights on."

"Yes, of course," KC murmured, and turned again and stepped over to the deck railing. She truly felt on top of a mountain, she realized when she examined the skyline. As her eyesight adjusted and the heavens became brighter, the irregular demarcation of coal-black forested peaks against a velvety starlit background was awe-inspiring. "It's utterly beautiful," she said with genuine sincerity.

Two strong arms closed around her, and KC's pulse made a wild leap. She felt Pierce's chin come to rest on the top of her head, and she leaned back against him, exactly as she'd wanted to do a moment ago.

"Makes you feel small and insignificant, doesn't it?" Pierce said, his voice low and intimate.

"Very."

"Gives a person perspective, too."

"In what way?"

"When you really take note of God's creations, man's are pretty puny. Problems don't seem quite so unmanageable up here, either. I sit out here a lot during the summer."

"And during the winter?"

"During the winter I sit by the fireplace," Pierce drawled dryly.

KC laughed softly, then brought her hands up to curl around Pierce's arms across her breasts. His wrists and forearms were hair-roughened and solid, warm and comforting. At her back his body heated hers from the top of her head to just below her hips.

Why was he holding her now? And was this only an embrace of friendship? Was that truly all he wanted from her now?

Sighing over the void within her that just seemed to be getting bigger and bigger, KC absently toyed with the watch on his left wrist.

"What are you thinking?" she heard, hearing, too, the way his voice rumbled deep in his chest. She could stand this way forever, couldn't she? Locked in this man's arms, encircled by his strength? But that wasn't something she could confess. Not with him acting as if there'd never been anything the least bit personal between them.

"Nothing very profound," she said softly. Why had he so openly talked about love and marriage to Dallas and was now saying nothing about his feelings to her? Experiencing a gripping sadness, KC stared at the night sky and tried hard to ignore the ache in her heart.

"Cold?"

"No. You're generating enough heat for the both of us."

A lazy laugh preceded his reply. "A man holding a beautiful woman just naturally generates heat, honey."

He was getting aroused. KC could feel the masculine strength developing in his jeans, and her own senses began heating up. Little fingers of responsive desire had begun licking at her insides, fueled by the memory of how exciting and satisfying making love with Pierce was.

He still desired her. For a while she'd thought that was gone, but apparently it had only been held in check. How odd that he would change tactics so dramatically, KC thought, trying again to make heads or tails out of this strange evening. There was something uncharacteristically subdued about Pierce tonight, something almost . . . suspenseful.

KC frowned at the stars. Was Pierce waiting for an indication from her that she would be receptive to the frankness he'd given Dallas?

How would she be behaving now if she hadn't been in the storage room during that discussion?

She would still be angry and distant with him, just like she'd been at the river today. Why wasn't he questioning her all too obvious about-face? What was going on?

Before KC could get her thoughts reorganized, she felt Pierce shift his weight and unclasp his arms in front of her. His hands moved to her waist and drew her back into a tighter fit against him. The tenor of the embrace changed instantly, especially when his mouth moved against her ear. "You smell better than any woman I've ever known."

"And you've known a few," she whispered.

"A few," he admitted. "None like you, though."

His voice had become husky, reaching deep inside KC and garnering a trembling response. A hundred small flutterings of bittersweet excitement darted here and there in her body, over-riding her thoughts and uneasy questions.

His right hand slowly moved upward and then opened around a breast. KC's breath caught at the instantaneous flame in the pit of her stomach. He nuzzled her ear and the side of her throat while he caressed first one breast and then the other, stimulating both nipples to tormenting rigidity.

KC dampened her lips, not sure she should be letting him touch her like that, then admitting that he couldn't touch her enough to satisfy that terrible yearning he created so easily. Why didn't he say, "I love you, KC," and make this wild desire all right?

His hands dropped, both of them, and stopped on her hips. With just a little pressure, he urged her behind back and curved his lap around it. "I want you," he whispered hoarsely, which was completely unnecessary when it was so obvious from the hard mass pressing against her buttocks.

If she hadn't heard him declaring his love for her to Dallas, what would her response be? KC wondered dizzily. There was something crazy about tonight, something that not only didn't add up, she was almost afraid to try to add it up. They were both different, and she knew why she was, but she couldn't figure out why Pierce was. And why he wasn't resolutely curious about *her* inconsistencies.

"Pierce," she whispered, confused. "We should talk. I don't quite grasp..."

"Later, honey. We'll talk later. Right now..." The thought was completed by the rasping sound of the front zipper in her jeans being opened. KC sucked in a sharp breath, but she didn't lunge away from the big hand that slid into the opening. Nor did she elude the fingers that eased beneath the lacy band of her bikini panties.

And then she could think of nothing but the burning, consuming need to just let go, to stop worrying about every damned moment of every damned day and just do what she herself felt like doing.

The thought was so brand-new and stunning, KC stiffened briefly, so briefly that Pierce never even caught the momentary emotional withdrawal. Besides, he was so involved with hot, wet, female flesh and the ache in his own body, he might not have noticed a sudden downpour.

"Let's go inside," he whispered thickly, hungrily.

Her voice was gravelly and breathy. "To talk?" she dared to tease, already recognizing a bolder, more reckless quality in herself.

"To make love. I'm on fire, sweetheart, and so are you."

"Yes," she agreed breathlessly, memories of a deep voice flitting through her mind. *"You either have feelings or you don't, KC."*

"I intend marrying her."

"I love her. I'll tell her tonight."

If this was part of the game Pierce was playing, it was the most intensely honest part. It wasn't in her power to deny what they both wanted so desperately right now.

"Kissing you is like catching the tail of a comet, KC."

Turning in his arms, KC stood on tiptoes and slid her hands up his chest to the back of his neck. "Yes, let's go inside," she whispered. "I want you, too."

Twelve

What had started as a twinge of uneasiness out on the deck rapidly developed into a full-fledged guilt attack by the time Pierce had KC at his bedroom door. He certainly wasn't a man without faults, but deceit wasn't a congenital or an ingrained part of his personality. While the plan to show KC that she was far from being alone or deserted was working beautifully, its success was due to deception.

KC stopped at the strange expression on Pierce's face. He answered her unspoken question. "You were right. We should talk before..." Pierce wasn't so high-minded that he intended confessing the setup at the saloon tonight. KC would be furious if she knew she'd been manipulated. But he could talk around it and still make headway with her fears and frustrations, which had been the whole point to the charade after Kyle had stormed out.

He could see the confusion in her eyes—and the questions. The normally concealed little-girl part of her, that unprotected, sensitive side of her that had wrung him out on the first day they'd met, accounted for the almost dazed bafflement deep within that lambent green. She'd heard him tell Dallas that he loved her, and certainly must have expected to hear it again, here, at his house, and she didn't understand why she hadn't.

He had a lot to clear up before he rushed her to the bedroom, he knew, although he'd forgotten everything else out on the deck but how she felt in his arms. "Let's go back to the living room," he said gently.

A soft, stolen breath through parted, pink lips nearly made Pierce change his mind, but then she said in shaky tones, "All right."

While KC perched on the edge of the couch, not knowing what to expect next, Pierce dumped the cold coffee from their cups and refilled them with fresh, hot coffee. Then he joined her on the couch.

"We haven't known each other very long," he said quietly.

KC studied him for a long moment before agreeing. "No, not long at all." She was undergoing the strangest sensations, a chill of foreboding, a fever of desire. Pierce wanted to talk, and KC knew that now she was going to hear—for the second time tonight—that he loved her. She felt so . . . so *false*, sitting here as though she hadn't the slightest idea of what was coming. Why hadn't she dashed into the saloon after Kyle had left and announced, "I'm here. I've been here!"

"But something rather earthshaking happened when we met."

She nodded slowly, weakly. "Something unusual. For me, at least."

"For me, too." Pierce picked up his cup and watched her over the rim while he took a swallow of coffee. "I don't want you to leave on Monday."

KC looked down. "You've known all along that I had to leave eventually. We've both known it."

"What about Dallas?"

Yes, what about Dallas? She didn't want to leave him; she still had the same worries and concerns for him that had brought her to Harmony. Despite his theorizing about her being overly afraid to lose another loved one, which, no doubt, had some merit, he was elderly and dear to her. Admittedly, she hadn't had enough time yet to accept or denounce the theory. But it was also one of those cases where, it really didn't matter. Something had driven her, and that same something would hound her the rest of Dallas's life. Figuring out whether her fears were selfish or unselfish wouldn't make any difference.

"Granddad will have Mary," she said quietly.

"Then you've come to grips with their relationship?"

"I can't run his life."

"True, but have you really accepted that?"

Sighing, KC slumped back against the sofa. "I think you should know a few facts about the past. The man you met, the Dallas Logan who came to Harmony, is not the man who got on a tour bus last June and left San Francisco. That man was old and sad and not very well. *That's* the man I came to Harmony to take back home with me, just so I could care for him as I'd been doing since my grandmother's death.

"I have an apartment, Pierce, but in the past two years I haven't spent a combined total of one month in it. I stayed with Granddad, seeing to it that he got a hot meal in the evening, making sure his house was clean and his laundry done—most of all, just being there so he wouldn't be alone."

Pierce's frown contained a bit of self-castigation. He'd fully accepted KC's concern for Dallas, but he'd still believed it to be somewhat exaggerated. "Why didn't you tell me those things before?"

"Would you have believed me? The man you defended so stoically is a totally different person. I saw the changes in Granddad right away—the independence, the pride, the renewed spirit. Perhaps the hardest thing to accept is what caused those changes."

"Mary."

"Yes." KC rose and walked about the room. "A new love," she said softly. "I guess love transcends age." She sighed again. "At any rate, it made a new man out of Granddad. Anyway, don't ask me if I've accepted not running his life anymore. I never wanted to run his life, but when a person you love is just fading away before your very eyes, you don't sit back and do nothing. At least, I don't."

"So when he called you and said he'd bought a business in Harmony..."

"I was astounded, to say the least. I was positive someone had taken advantage of him."

Thinking of his theory about KC simply being afraid to lose one more loved one, which he'd passed on to Dallas so the elderly man could mention it and KC could overhear it, Pierce felt like a fool. He also realized that he didn't understand KC as clearly as he'd thought.

"We haven't talked like this enough," he said gruffly.

KC raised an eyebrow. "No, we haven't. But then, you were such a staunch ally, and positive I was in cahoots with Kyle...."

A deep flush colored Pierce's face. "You have a right to rub it in."

"I'm not rubbing it in, Pierce." She smiled suddenly, a poignant smile. "Granddad's such an old rogue, you know. I wouldn't doubt that he's enjoyed me chasing after him and you fighting his battles."

"You're kidding."

"No, I'm not kidding. That twinkle you can see in his eyes had been absent for quite a while, but he used to love being the center of attention."

"He's a great old guy, KC."

"Yes, and he was a great young guy, too. He just lost his way for a few years." KC blinked back a few tears. "Well, he's made a new life for himself, and I *have* to face it. That's really the bottom line, Pierce, not if I've willingly accepted it or not. He and I have always had a special relationship, and I hope we always will."

"You can't miss," Pierce said softly.

"Let's discuss Kyle Rudman now," KC said determinedly, after clearing her throat.

Pierce's face fell. "Why?"

"Because I need to." KC's chin was up, her eyes bright. She was so pretty Pierce kept staring at her. He'd orchestrated the evening before they'd reached the bedroom door, but since they'd returned to the living room, KC had gradually been taking control.

Well, that's what he'd wanted, wasn't it? And the reason for that bit of drama in the saloon tonight? She'd desperately needed a catalyst to force her to sort things out, and now that she'd gotten started, it looked as if she was going to delve into every aspect of her time in Harmony.

Pierce settled back, suddenly interested in how she viewed Kyle now. Besides, he had a feeling that in her present mood, sooner or later she would get to them, to Pierce Wheeler and KC Logan. And that was the ultimate target for him, the real reason for his plotting and planning tonight.

There was an odd strength flowing through KC's body. She was on an emotional roll, gradually propelled by the events of the past few days to a point of having to get her feelings out in the open. Those feelings were oddly gaining distinction now, and broiling with honesty. If she could only express herself accurately by admitting she'd been in the storage room tonight, then she wouldn't hesitate to do so.

Across the room, KC met Pierce's gray eyes squarely. "I liked Kyle," she said distinctly. "I *wanted* to like Kyle."

Pierce cleared his throat, doing his best to keep a small burst of uneasiness at bay. "You had a reason, I expect?"

"I believe so. Kyle projects a lot of appeal. You can make fun of him all you want to—and you did—but most women appreciate good manners. His style of dressing isn't for everyone, but he carries it off well."

Pierce glanced down at his own snug-fitting jeans, black T-shirt and cowboy boots, and grinned wryly. The fact that KC was wearing jeans, too, was immaterial; jeans were only a part of her wardrobe. For him, they were practically a uniform.

"You're a jeans and boots man, Pierce," she said calmly, without censure or disapproval. "Clothing preference is a personal choice, and the only reason I even mentioned it is that you denigrated Kyle's clothes on several occasions."

"And you were impressed by them."

"Impressed? Not singularly. But whether you can admit it or not, Kyle knows how to lay on the charm."

"When he wants something," Pierce growled.

"Oh, definitely. I'd be the last person to debate that point. But then, we're all a little guilty of that, don't you think? Aren't we all a little more charming, a little nicer, when we want something from someone?"

"He's a smooth operator, KC," Pierce insisted.

"Very smooth, Pierce. Like I said, I wanted to like Kyle. He's an attractive, appealing man—on the surface. Which is all one sees at first." To collect her thoughts, KC took a few silent steps. "I was thrilled with his offer to buy the business," she then said earnestly. "Yes, I wondered why he wanted it, but for my intents and purposes, his reasons weren't that important. All I wanted to do was separate Granddad from something that I felt was too much for him."

KC turned to face the man on the couch. "I despised your interference."

"I know. And you wanted to despise me, too, but you couldn't do it, could you?"

The air was suddenly heavier, and before KC could come up with any kind of reply, Pierce had bounded off the couch and reached her. He put his left hand on her shoulder and, with his right, raised her chin. "You couldn't despise me, could you?" he pressed.

Their gazes locked, KC's clouded with uncertainty again, Pierce's dark with masculine tension. "You . . . you're the man who impressed me," she finally whispered. "Not Kyle, you."

"Even though you wanted to like Kyle, it was me you were drawn to."

"Yes."

Pierce pulled her close, one big hand cradling the back of her head. "I love you, you know," he said softly.

KC closed her eyes at the joyous flip of her heart.

"I think I fell hard the first time I set eyes on you," Pierce added. "I know I wanted you on sight." He held her tenderly until he realized she hadn't said anything, then he tilted his head back to look at her. "No comment?"

Extricating herself, KC moved away, putting space between them. Pierce watched with a puzzled expression, and she felt his perplexity and apprehension clear across the room. "I love you, too," she finally announced, and held up a hand against Pierce's movement to close the gap between them. "This isn't a novel or a movie, Pierce. This is real life, and contrary to what the poets say, love does not conquer all."

"What are you getting at?"

"I'm getting at the problems between us," she said, rather sharply. "And if you don't think there are any, then we have one more that I never even thought of."

Rubbing the back of his neck, Pierce prowled the room, giving her small space a wide berth. "I don't see anything that can't be worked out," he finally declared.

"With time," KC amended. "How do we get the time?"

"You're not still thinking about leaving! Dammit, KC, even if you couldn't find a job right away, what the hell do you think loving you means to me? Anything I've got is at your disposal. I'm talking about marriage." As if she didn't know! Those damned secrets, about who was supposed to know what, were beginning to grate on Pierce's nerves.

"Oh, you are? Well, I'm not a mind reader, am I?"

At the look of exasperated frustration on Pierce's face, KC made a wild leap for the sofa, plopped down on her stomach and buried her face in the upholstery. Her shoulders were shaking, and funny little noises were coming from her and Pierce felt a slamming wave of remorse. He sure hadn't intended to make her cry again, he thought, hurrying over to the couch and kneeling beside it. "Honey, I'm sorry. Please don't cry. I know you're not a mind reader. And that was a helluva stupid marriage proposal."

And then he realized she wasn't crying; she was laughing!

He sat back on his heels, frowning at first, finally grinning in response to KC's uncontrollable laughter.

But what was so funny?

Gasping and wiping her eyes, KC finally turned over. "I'm sorry. My system is really screwed up, Pierce. All day I've been either crying or on the verge, and just now, you had such a frustrated look on your face."

"My frustration is funny?" he asked dryly.

"Only because—well, I've got to tell you something. I thought I could keep it to myself, but I just can't."

She was going to confess the storage-room incident. Well, there was one very effective way to stop that. Honesty had a strange way of breeding more honesty, and if she confessed, so might he. And he was afraid of how she might react to hearing she'd been engineered tonight.

She was on her back stretched out full length, an inviting position, in any case. Moving quickly, Pierce leaned over her, bringing his lips down to within a fraction of hers. "I'm tired of talking," he whispered, ignoring the surprise in her eyes and firmly mating their mouths.

KC's mind reeled for a moment, but tucking away her "confession" wasn't at all difficult to do with Pierce's lips on hers. A delicious deluge of desire accompanied the kiss, and she raised her hands to his hair and curled her fingers into it. His tongue was pure velvet, slipping into her mouth, uniting with hers, retreating, advancing, an intoxicating eroticism.

"I love you," he whispered.

"I know. That's what I have to tell..." Another kiss, and another, and then KC made no further attempt to tell him anything, except, "I love you."

His hands went under her shirt and found her breasts. "You're not going anywhere," he growled. "You're staying right here, with me."

"My apartment... and furniture," she whispered.

"We'll get your furniture, if that's what you want." He took her lips again in a long, drugging kiss, then broke away and got to his feet. "Come on, this couch wasn't designed for making love, sweetheart."

KC lifted a hand to the one he held out and allowed herself to be pulled up. She expected to get to his bedroom on her own two feet, but Pierce swooped her up into his arms. She laughed huskily and wrapped her arms around his neck. "You're an impetuous lover, darling."

At the endearment, Pierce's eyes lit up, although his voice and expression remained serious. "I'm an anxious lover, KC. I want you naked, I want your body around mine, I want to bury myself in you."

She plumbed the depths of his beautiful gray eyes. "You're also slightly naughty," she whispered.

"Have I offended you?"

"No, never. You're a passionate man. I knew that right from the first."

Pierce began striding down the hall to the bedroom. "I'm a man in love, and you're the woman I love. Nothing will ever change that, KC, nothing."

A small frown tautened the skin between her eyebrows. Would he be saying that if he knew what she'd done tonight? Pierce's honesty was unquestionable; hers wasn't anything to be particularly proud of, not after sneaking around the way she had.

Her feet slid to the floor beside the bed. Pierce was saying sweet, wonderful things between lingering, warm kisses. "You're so beautiful, I ache when I look at you. You're intelligent, bright—so special, honey, so very special."

Without passion melting her insides, KC knew she would blurt out everything. Even turning into warm jelly, the need to confess her transgression remained in the back of her mind. But it was impossible to speak with his mouth and hands moving over her.

Her T-shirt was lifted over her head and tossed, and she pulled the hem of his from the waist of his jeans. Pierce got rid of it quickly, then unsnapped the back of her lacy bra. The straps slipped down her arms, and the garment fell to the floor, unnoticed. He kissed her bare breasts, his head bent forward, and KC closed her eyes while she explored the muscles of his shoulders and back.

He was so solid, such hard, warm flesh, so much man. Her head swam dizzily as desire built. Her hands moved over him, her fingernails etching trails from his back to the whorls of dark hair on his chest. His tongue teased a nipple, then his mouth opened around it and a staggering jolt of pleasure liquefied KC's knees.

She reeled, and Pierce caught her by the waist and brought them both down to the bed. He gathered her up into an embrace that welded them from breasts to thighs, and their kisses were no longer even slightly playful. Boots and sneakers were kicked off. Her jeans were unzipped and pushed down; his went next. Underwear was a trivial matter, discarded without even a pause in the passionate, needful kisses they were exchanging.

They were lying on top of the spread, legs intertwined, arms around each other, moving, writhing, gasping with an urgency neither could nor wanted to control. Burned by his heat, seared by her own, KC undulated against the hard shaft of manhood between them. It was she who initiated the final act, she who reached down and took him and directed him to the intolerable ache in her body.

"Now?" he whispered, surprised that she was ready so fast.

"Now," she rasped hoarsely, needing him so badly she couldn't see straight.

Gladly, eagerly, Pierce slid into her feverish body. And then, locked together, united as nothing else could unite a man and woman, he held her and watched the emotion on her face. Her eyes closed, opened, closed. "Make love to me," she whispered. "Now, Pierce."

His hips moved automatically, creating a long stroke out, then back into her heat, and she took a deep, shaky breath. He was completely absorbed with her reactions, understanding that they were sharing the purest form of communication. "I love you" was in her eyes, but also "I love this." Never, he vowed, never would he ever do anything to mar or alter the perfection of their physical relationship. What kind of problems couldn't be overcome if a man and woman had such perfection in intimacy?

He didn't hurry her, he pleasured her. And he could see that pleasure on her face and feel it in the hands that stroked his back, his shoulders, his arms. Her eyes turned dreamy for a while, and a small smile played across her lips. He couldn't resist kissing them, and whispering how much he loved her. And she smiled again and returned the lovely words.

The moment came when slow and easy wasn't enough. But Pierce saw that moment right in KC's eyes, and with a growl of possession he raised her hips and took control. The bed rocked with a faster tempo and who was pleasuring whom didn't matter anymore. Making love with a woman he loved and who loved him was the ultimate high, he thought somewhere in the feverish recesses of his brain. There was that one small deception between them, but it hadn't been anything wounding or hurting, and it had worked. It had brought them together; it had given KC the insight to allow them both to admit their feelings.

The ecstasy of fulfillment was wild enough to bathe them both in perspiration and drain them of even the ability to speak coherently, and they lay for long, satisfied minutes regaining strength and cooling down.

KC's thoughts drifted, encompassing all that had happened in Harmony. Falling deeply in love was the most meaningful event, without question. Certainly she couldn't have visualized giving her heart to a Montanan before meeting Pierce, and she had even fought against it *after* meeting him. Of course, that had been because of his stubborn defense of Dallas.

Pierce was curled around her; he was drowsy and as contented as he'd ever been in his life. "Can you stay the night, love?"

"All night?" KC stirred, her feet tangling with his legs. "No, I don't think I should stay all night. Granddad..."

"He'd understand. He knows how much I care about you."

Why, yes, that was true. She'd momentarily forgotten, but Dallas was ostensibly the first person to hear that Pierce had serious feelings for her. KC's heart began a nervous tattoo. Should she confess now? Explain how she'd had to know what happened with Kyle, and that overhearing Pierce's and Dallas's confidential exchange afterward had been purely accidental?

"I was thinking, honey. You could move in with me until we decide on a wedding date."

"I beg your pardon?"

"Move in here. Why not? It will be your home eventually, anyway. What do you say?"

KC squirmed out of his arms and sat up. "Pierce, you're rushing things. We hardly know each other."

Pierce wasn't alarmed; he completely agreed that they needed a little time to explore this wonderful new relationship. "Sure, but what's wrong with getting to know each other under the same roof?"

"No," KC said, with some caution, not thrilled to be presented with an opportunity to cross swords so quickly. "We love each other, I admit that freely. I admit that *happily*, Pierce. But living together? No, I'm afraid not."

The relaxed drowsiness that had made Pierce's eyelids heavy was fast disappearing. "What do you propose, then?"

KC scooted off the bed and began picking up her clothes. "I'll start looking for a job on Monday. When I find one, I'll look for an apartment."

"There aren't many apartments in Harmony."

"A house, then. Whatever."

Pierce hoisted himself to an elbow. "We could get married right away."

Yanking on her clothes, KC shot him a quick glance. "Please get up and take me back to town."

"You haven't given me an answer. Would you rather be married right away?"

Sighing, KC sat on the bed. "I don't know how you feel about marriage, which is one of our problems. Neither of us knows how the other feels about most things. But I view marriage very seriously. I'm convinced now that staying and giving what we feel for each other every chance is vitally important. But I'd like to wait a while before we talk about a wedding date."

"I guess that's sensible," Pierce agreed quietly. "How long? A month? Two months?"

Smiling, KC smoothed back the dark unruly lock of hair that was forever hanging down his forehead. "We'll know when the time is right. I'm glad you agree with me."

He caught her hand and pressed a kiss to her palm. "You're so important to me, KC. I hope you know that. And I hope you also know that I'll do everything I can to help you get established in Harmony."

"I do." Laughing happily, KC jumped to her feet. "Now, get your buns out of that bed and drive me back to town, Sheriff."

Thirteen

During the ride back to town, a warm glow kept a soft smile on KC's face. It seemed incredible to her how things had turned out in Harmony, and she couldn't stop looking at Pierce. She loved him, and it was beautiful to know it and wonderfully satisfying to be able to admit it openly.

Only one thing kept her from total contentment: what she had done earlier tonight. Every time she thought about sneaking around and purposely listening to a private conversation, a wash of guilt struck her. It was an internal discomfort, known only to her. But it was much too strong to ignore.

KC had always valued integrity, and one thought kept nagging her: this was no way to begin the most important relationship of her life. Secrets, especially guilty secrets, were insidious, destructive things, and Pierce deserved more than that from her.

He'd been reciting facts about the various businesses around Harmony that she might contact about employment. When KC didn't comment for some miles, he gave her a questioning glance and picked up a sense of weighty circumspection from her. "Something wrong, honey?"

Praying that a confession wouldn't damage the closeness they'd achieved tonight, KC nodded. "I have something to tell you."

Pierce's hands clenched around the steering wheel as understanding hit him. In all that plotting today he'd overlooked how KC might feel after the charade was over. It had seemed innocent enough in the planning stage, and, in all honesty, KC had had every right to be in on the final session with Kyle. She probably would have been invited to sit in if so many other factors hadn't been involved. Now she saw herself as a sneak, and Pierce realized she was too forthright a person to remain silent on something she considered duplicitous.

It was a trait he admired and certainly an asset in a woman he loved and pictured as his future wife. But it was too soon for confessions. Their relationship needed time to solidify and strengthen before it could withstand what complete candor about tonight might unleash.

"Honey..."

KC hurried past the objection she heard in his voice. "No, Pierce. I won't be put off this time. I've wanted to tell you all evening."

An uncomfortable weakness stole over Pierce. If KC confessed, could he do less?

"Tonight..." KC hesitated. It wasn't a simple matter to tell the man she loved that she was far from the perfect woman he'd labeled her. But she had to. The longer one put off something like this, the worse it became.

KC took a nervous breath. "I was in the storage room tonight," she blurted.

Pierce's insides suddenly felt heavier, as though pulled downward by too much gravity. A lot rested on what response he made. His options were false surprise or candor, and he didn't much like either of them. He sensed KC's startled curiosity that he hadn't immediately commented.

"Pierce? Did you hear what I said?"

His voice contained tension. "I heard."

KC's spirit dropped. He was upset. She closed her eyes while her stomach roiled. "I only wanted to hear what happened with Kyle," she whispered raggedly.

He couldn't let her suffer, Pierce realized. The whole thing had gone far enough. Whatever came out of both of them laying their cards on the table, he at least knew she was in love with him. Somehow, he would make things right.

Pierce cleared his throat. "We knew you were there."

At first the simple statement didn't make sense, and KC uttered a small, muted, "Pardon?"

They were nearing town and Harmony's streetlights were just ahead. Pierce slowed the van down at the first reduced speed sign. He forced a laugh, as if a note of humor would alleviate the seriousness of the admission. "Dallas and I knew you were in the storage room."

KC went stiff with disbelief. "How did you know? Did you hear me? Pierce, if you heard me, why...?" It still didn't make sense. If they knew she was listening, why had they talked about her?

"KC..." Pierce heard the anguish in his own voice. Her deception was so trivial compared to his. Why hadn't he thought how it would look to her? This moment had been bound to come, sooner or later. It was just a lot sooner than he'd anticipated. "I can explain everything," he said.

His tone had pleaded for understanding, which gave KC a start. She'd expected disappointment, maybe censure, possibly anger. She hadn't expected what she was getting. It actually seemed like Pierce was taking the blame, and why should he? "Perhaps you *should* explain," she said thinly, and saw him uneasily run his fingers through his hair.

"I had to do something," he said anxiously.

"*Do* something?"

"You weren't listening to either Dallas or me, honey."

And then it hit her. "Are you saying you *planned* tonight?" In utter weakness, KC sat back. "Oh, Pierce," she whispered, shaken to the core of her soul.

The van had reached the opposite end of Harmony, passing the two houses preceding the final curve in the road, beyond which lay the motel.

"It's not as bad as it sounds," Pierce cautioned.

KC stared blindly out the window, unable to muster up the strength to debate the point. She'd been so happy a few minutes ago in spite of her underlying guilt, and now the world was suddenly topsy-turvy again. She heard Pierce saying something about loving her and being afraid she'd leave without giving him a chance, and something else about Dallas. KC barely absorbed the words, and certainly not their meaning.

She wanted to see Dallas, she realized with sudden urgency. She wanted to hear, from her grandfather, what had really taken place tonight. So much had been a sham. All evening she and Pierce had dodged and darted around the truth, playing a game that looked rather cruel now. When he'd come to her motel earlier, he'd known she had heard everything. Because she'd had something to conceal, she had played right into his hands. She felt like an utter fool.

The van pulled into the motel parking lot and stopped. "Talk to me, KC," Pierce pleaded.

She looked at him, a brief glance of humiliation. "Maybe . . . maybe tomorrow. Right now I need to be alone."

"No! KC, please. Let me explain."

KC's gaze went to Dallas's dark motel unit. Dare she wake him, she wondered. Oddly, as disoriented as she felt, there wasn't a sign of tears. This was too big, too staggering, to weep about. KC almost wished she could weep, remembering with wryness how she'd had no trouble shedding buckets most of the day. And now, with newly-found gladness all but deserting her, there wasn't a tear anywhere within her.

She needed to think. She was embarrassed and strangely numb. She needed to talk to Dallas. "Not tonight," she declared with an emotionless-sounding firmness. Grasping the door handle, KC pressed it, swung the door open and got out of the van.

Pierce said nothing, and with a dull ache in his heart and a frozen expression, watched her walk to her motel unit. When she was inside and a light came on, he slowly put the van in gear and eased it out of the parking lot.

Within the confines of the small room, KC sat on the bed. She'd all but sent Pierce away, rejecting his explanation. In actuality, she'd barely heard it. The most difficult to accept aspect of what she'd learned was Dallas's part in it. It didn't seem possible that he would have consented to something that would only result in this sullied, degraded feeling for her.

The entire episode had been planned. *Planned!* She'd crept into the storage room, only needing to hear what happened with Kyle. And they'd known she was there. Pierce and Dallas had known!

KC covered her face with her hands. And while she sat there, burning with humiliation, anger began knotting her stomach.

How could they, the two people she loved most in the world, have done something so low and despicable?

For some reason, Dallas's deceit looked worse than Pierce's. KC couldn't stop thinking about her grandfather's role in the ghastly affair. Not that she was ready to forgive Pierce. But the need to talk to Dallas was growing by leaps and bounds, and the fact that it was nearing midnight was quickly losing import.

After another few minutes of painful, heart-rending thoughts, KC stood up and walked to the door. If Dallas was upset at getting awakened, she was past caring.

On the short journey from her unit to Dallas's, KC realized what she was hoping for: something from her grandfather that would completely absolve him of any complicity. He'd changed a great deal, but she didn't want to believe he'd become heartless enough to knowingly take part in tonight's fiasco.

KC pounded on his door, waited for a moment and did it again. Then from within she heard, "Hold your horses! I'm coming."

The door opened a crack and Dallas peered out. Without his glasses on, he blinked and squinted in surprise. "KC?"

"I need to talk to you, Granddad."

"Now? What time is it?" His expression changed. "Something wrong?"

"There's no emergency, but yes, something's wrong. May I come in?"

Frowning, Dallas gave it a moment's consideration. "Let me get my pants on."

"Certainly." KC waited until a light came on and Dallas swung the door open wider. He was putting on his glasses, sending her strange little glances. She leaned against the closed door with her arms behind her.

"It's late, KC."

"I know. I'm sorry I had to wake you. I was with Pierce tonight. He brought me home a few minutes ago."

Dallas cleared his throat, and KC's heart sank at his uneasiness. She didn't want Pierce's story to be true. She wanted Dallas to ask crustily, "Why in heaven's name couldn't this, whatever it is, have waited till morning?" He wasn't asking because he *knew* why she was there.

Heaving an unhappy sigh, KC left the door and perched on a chair. "You know what I want to talk about, don't you,

Granddad?'' she said sadly, and then jumped as someone knocked on the door. Right behind that came, "Dallas?"

It was Pierce! KC noted the tremendous relief on her grandfather's face and how eagerly he opened the door. Clearly, Dallas looked on Pierce's intrusion as reinforcements arriving. KC looked on it as darned nervy! She stood up with a vivid glare.

The two men exchanged a hearty greeting, as though this weren't the middle of the night. "I saw your light," Pierce said. "Everything okay?"

KC butted in, answering sharply. "You know darned well everything isn't okay! What do you think I'm doing here?"

"KC just got here," Dallas said with a weak grin.

"Oh. Well, I left, but turned around and came back. KC, why don't you and I go back to your room and talk? Dallas shouldn't be in the middle of this."

"You're right!" Dallas vigorously agreed. "This is between you two."

KC sent Pierce a withering look. "I'm not sure there's *any-thing* between the sheriff and me." Pierce's resulting wince gave her a pang, but she turned back to Dallas. "Why, Granddad? Why would you do something like that to me?"

Dallas's chin came up, and KC got a slight shock. The elderly man was uneasy about this confrontation, but he wasn't the least bit ashamed! "We did it for you, KC," he declared. "You were way down in the dumps, and we were worried about you."

KC looked from one man to the other. They were united in thought and spirit. She felt strangely out of it, she realized, on the outside of masculine collaboration. Anger at the both of them swelled within her, and humiliation and a desire to get away quickly followed.

Feeling choked, she darted around both men, yanked the door open and dashed out into the night. She ran all the way back to her own unit and rushed inside. Shaking from head to foot, she grabbed a suitcase and brought it to the bed.

KC started emptying drawers, dumping clothes into the suitcase willy-nilly, breathing hard, racing around the room.

"Is running away the answer?"

Pierce was standing just inside the door. KC gave him a wild look. "I thought I locked that door!"

He held up a key. "There's more than one key to these rooms."

"Why would I question anything you might do?" Her sarcastic tone tinged with anger, KC dropped an armful of underclothes on top of the growing pile in the suitcase.

He stayed near the door, watching KC's erratic lunges with a dark, sober expression. "Would an apology help?"

"I don't want an apology."

"I see," Pierce said quietly. "Is there anything you do want? I mean, I thought you wanted me. Apparently that was a premature conclusion. I also thought you wanted to be near Dallas, but here you are, packing to leave. Do you even know what you want?"

KC's cheeks burned with a hot flush. "I *don't* want to be hassled!"

"Is that what I'm doing, hassling you? Don't you think I might have a right to be just a little upset? We talked about marriage tonight. What kind of game would you call discussing marriage with a man, then leaving town?"

"Don't you dare mention games to me! Not after what you pulled—" Breaking off, KC raised her chin belligerently. "I don't want to discuss it." Bending over the suitcase, her shaking hands attempted to straighten the carelessly strewn clothing.

Pierce frowned. "Just like that? You don't want to discuss it, so that's the end of it?"

KC shot him a cold look. "I don't want any long drawn-out explanation of something I find repugnant and humiliating. You're not going to talk me into suddenly thinking I've misjudged you!"

Pierce stood stock still for a moment, then paced a small circle. He stopped again. "All right. No long explanations. But how about, I love you, I want you to be my wife, and I never pretended to be perfect."

KC squeezed her eyes tightly shut.

"If you can name me one person who doesn't make mistakes, one perfect individual, I'll walk out that door and leave you be."

Terribly bogged down, KC opened her eyes and stared at the mess she'd made of her clothing.

"KC?"

Anger suddenly exploded within her. "Don't ask the impossible! No one's perfect, and I know that as well as you. I'm just sick and tired of this whole damned mess. I never should have come here, I never should have bothered Granddad, and I never should have met you!" There was nowhere to run to, but KC lunged away, blindly, heading for the door.

Pierce caught her, and she came at him with clawing fingernails. "Leave me alone!" she screamed. Pierce grabbed her wrists and held them while he battled his own anger.

"I won't put up with a damned tantrum," he finally yelled when she wouldn't stop screaming and struggling.

"I'm getting out of here! I hate Montana. I hate Harmony. I hate *you*!"

That stopped the both of them. KC ceased struggling, shocked at her own fury, and Pierce slowly dropped his hands from her wrists. They stared at each other, then KC whispered raggedly, "I'm sorry. I don't know why I said that. I don't hate you."

Drawing a deeply troubled breath, Pierce walked away. He stopped at the dresser and leaned against it. "You might not hate me, but you don't like me very much right now, do you?"

She couldn't meet his eyes. "I'm disappointed, I guess."

"Because I manipulated you into something."

"Yes."

"Would you have believed the things you heard tonight if either Dallas or me had said them straight out?"

Would she have? Recapturing the day's despondency wasn't difficult; she was very close to it again, anyway. But its indirection? Its indecisiveness? Those elements were a little harder to grasp now. But in KC's mind, whether or not she'd been in any condition to listen to either Dallas or Pierce wasn't the issue. They'd gone too far, and she felt like such a complete fool, she might never get over it.

Her expression remained unrelenting. "We'll never know that, will we?"

"I know, and I think you do, too. Deep down, anyway. You were in no frame of mind to believe anyone. I tried to talk to you out by the river, and all you did was run away. Just like you're intending to do now. KC, running away never solved a damned thing."

"You ran away once."

"When I was sixteen years old. Good Lord, you're certainly not comparing the panic a boy feels over something he can't handle to what an adult might do under the same circumstances. Do you think I would run from an abusive father today? KC, I'd stand and fight, just like you should be doing."

"Fight for what?" she whispered tearily. "For what, Pierce? You and Granddad treated me like a child. Like someone with no sense at all. I was hurting today, but I was finding my way. You just couldn't stand back and give me a little room to digest everything, could you?"

Pierce rubbed the back of his neck, a weary gesture. "I was afraid you were going to leave without giving us a chance. I didn't understand what was going on with you. I realized that tonight at my house. The saddest part of this, KC, is that you really are a fighter, but you actually believe there's nothing left to fight for."

He pushed away from the dresser and moved closer. "I've got a few ideas about some of the things you might find worth fighting for. How about a home and a husband who loves you? And babies. And good friends, and a grandfather who thinks the sun rises and sets in your beautiful green eyes. KC..." Tears filled Pierce's eyes, and he looked away.

KC couldn't think for a moment. And then emotion swamped her in a sudden soul-searing rush. "Pierce?" she whispered, reaching out a hand to touch him. It landed on his shirt, and she felt his strong, steady heartbeat against her palm. "Are you crying?"

He gave her a ghost of a smile. "Men don't cry."

But men did cry, and those were tears in his eyes. "Oh, Pierce," she said on a sob. "I can't bear anymore unhappiness."

He moved then, swiftly, and pulled her close, wrapping his arms around her so tightly, she became part of him. "Then let's be happy," he said fiercely. "KC, let's be happy. We have so much. We have everything that's important in this world."

Like a row of dominoes, emotions began toppling within her, pain, frustration, anger. Where had she gotten the idea that life should be a rose garden? Everyone made mistakes, and Pierce's, like hers, had only been with the best of intentions.

An image suddenly flashed through KC's mind—a small girl with long, flaxen pigtails, lost and frightened, Dallas holding her on his lap and explaining that she would be living with him and Grandma Harriet now, that she would be their little girl now.

The image jumped—to holidays, to birthdays, to ordinary days with the little girl following her granddad around, holding his hand, and then to the unquestionable love that little girl had grown up with.

That was the kind of love Pierce was offering. And she'd been running away from it?

KC tilted her head back to see his face, and he didn't even try to hide his tears now. His voice was strangled, thick with misery. "If you leave, I'll follow you. I swear it."

She reached up and brushed a tear from his cheek, her soul strangely peaceful. "I'm not leaving. I love you," she whispered. "I love you with my heart, with my body, with my mind. I told you earlier tonight that Granddad had lost his way for a few years. I lost my way for a while, too. You did nothing worse than I did."

Hope was shining in Pierce's eyes, and he drew her back to him with a shuddering breath. "Neither Dallas or I meant to hurt you."

"Would you have ever told me about it if I hadn't started things tonight?" she whispered, really wanting to know.

Pierce was silent for a long moment. Then he raised his head and looked down at her. KC saw that his eyes were dark and serious. "The answer to that question is yes. But I won't be dishonest about it. Not now. I wasn't going to say anything about it for a long time."

"I see," she replied softly. "Pierce, I'm glad it came out tonight. I don't want to begin our relationship with a secret between us. That's why I had to confess what I'd done." She surprised Pierce by slipping from his arms and going over to the door. Opening it, she looked down the line to Dallas's unit. "It's dark," she sighed, sorry that she'd have to wait until morning to apologize. "Granddad must have gone back to bed."

Pierce came up behind her and wrapped his arms around her. "It's late. That's where we should be, too, in bed," he murmured, relaying through touch and tone every intention of spending what remained of the night in her bed.

KC hesitated a moment, then turned around with a teasing little smile. "Are you prepared to face Granddad in the morning when he sees your van parked outside my door?"

Pierce grinned. "I think he knows the facts of life, honey."

She couldn't resist one slightly barbed observation. "I think you and Granddad are a lot alike, Sheriff. That's probably why you two hit it off so well."

Pierce's grin only broadened. "Honey, I consider that a compliment!"

Epilogue

—

Dallas and Mary stood hand in hand and smiled a greeting when KC walked up and joined the small crowd at the length of wire fencing. "They're about to bulldoze 'er down," Dallas announced, loud enough to be heard above the noise of the heavy equipment working within the fenced off area.

This was everyone's last glimpse of the Harmony Saloon and Motel. Today it was going to be razed, and quite a few people had come to watch. KC squeezed her grandfather's free hand as the mammoth bulldozer moved into position. It chugged and belched smoke and moved slowly forward, and its enormous blade tore through the front wall of the old building as if it were made of paper.

KC sighed softly as the saloon came down, crumpling into splinters and dust. The motel units gave as easily, and within a very few minutes, the dozer began shoving the debris into one big pile.

The crowd began dispersing, returning to their cars. KC had wondered if seeing the physical destruction of his former business might be traumatic for Dallas, but he seemed remarkably unperturbed about the whole thing. "How's the job?" he asked as they strolled away from the fence.

"Just fine. We've been working on an exciting campaign for this coming spring." KC had found a surprisingly good job. With the plans for the new highway well underway, the local merchants had decided to band together and promote tourism in the Harmony area. The group had been quite enthusiastic about hiring someone with advertising know-how, and KC had been employed for five weeks.

"Well, Mary and I have some news," Dallas declared with that familiar twinkle in his eye.

Mary was every bit as nice as KC had hoped she'd be. Dallas and Mary had put on their little show one weekend, driving off together, supposedly to get married. They had returned to Harmony with matching gold rings and broad smiles, and then several dozen good friends had given them a big reception.

"What's your news, Granddad?" KC asked teasingly, knowing that nothing Dallas might come up with would surprise her anymore. He'd accepted the state's offer for his property without even a murmur, and KC had recently suspected he was getting antsy again.

"We're opening a Laundromat," Mary announced proudly. "This grandfather of yours just won't sit still. He's one of a kind, KC."

"He most certainly is," KC agreed softly, and threw her arms around Dallas's neck for a big hug. Her eyes were misty when she stepped back, but so were Dallas's. While he blew his nose, KC hugged Mary. "I love you both."

Then, smiling, KC started for her car. "See you later."

"Here comes Pierce," Dallas called, and KC stopped with her hand on the door handle of her little sedan. She watched the brown sheriff's car pull up and stop and Pierce uncoil from behind the wheel. Dallas and Mary got into their white pickup, honked the horn and drove off. A quick glance around told KC that everyone else had gone, too.

Her heart hammered as it always did around Pierce. He looked so handsome, so tall and strong and clean and handsome, that her knees felt mushy. He was wearing his dark glasses, and that lock of unruly, dark hair was down on his forehead. She would smooth it back, she thought breathlessly, just as soon as he got close enough.

"Hi," he said. "Is the excitement all over?"

"It was...until you got here."

"Oh? Are you excited, sweetheart?"

"Always, when you're around."

He kissed her, a slow, drugging kiss that went right through her. Then he looked regretfully back at the equipment and men working on the other side of the fence. There was no chance of anything intimate here. Smiling ruefully, he put his arm around KC's shoulder, and they began walking over to the fence. "The old place is gone," he said quietly.

"Yes. I thought it would bother Granddad to see it demolished, but he never even flinched. He and Mary are going to put in a Laundromat."

Grinning, Pierce shook his head in amazement. "What a guy." His gaze sobered on the activity beyond the fence. "I know it was necessary, but I kind of hate to see this, honey. Without the saloon and motel, you and I might never have met."

"Heartbreak Hotel," KC murmured, then smiled up at Pierce's questioning look. "Well it was heartbreaking. For a while."

He studied her with love and understanding and the desire she always kindled in him. "After I dropped you off last night and drove home, I laid awake for a long time. I think we've waited long enough, sweetheart. Let's set a date, KC."

"To get married?" she asked, though she knew full well what he'd meant.

"Yes. We've slept alone long enough. If you would have been with me last night, I would have made love to you every hour on the hour. It was one of those nights when I couldn't think of anything but you."

"You're insatiable," she teased. They had spent the evening at Pierce's house, and making love was a part of every date they had. She hadn't moved in with him or anyone else; that was something she couldn't do. But her little apartment in the upstairs of a family home in town wasn't all that private, and they went to Pierce's place when they needed to be alone.

Arm and arm they started back to their cars. "You don't have any more doubts about us, do you?" Pierce questioned.

She was so much in love with this man she couldn't see straight. Doubts? To be totally truthful, it was difficult to even remember the doubts and problems that had given her so much distress. She'd learned so much about Pierce. Beneath his rugged exterior beat a heart of gold. He was basically strong and stubborn, but he also had a wonderful gentle streak. The people of Harmony respected and liked him, and she'd met dozens of his closer friends. As a community, Harmony was a pleasant little town, and she hadn't had even one regret about the permanent move. "No doubts," she stated with a small smile, and reached up and gently brushed that magnetic lock of hair from his forehead.

"None for me either, honey. We've laughed and cried together. We've discussed and debated every topic either of us can think of, and we've spent most of our free time together. I think we're ready for the big step, don't you?"

With their gazes locked, she nodded soberly. "I think we are."

Pierce sucked in a quick breath. "When?"

They had already decided that neither wanted a big wedding. "This coming weekend?"

He grabbed her into a smothering embrace. "Oh, God, I love you! Next weekend we'll drive to Missoula or Helena for the ceremony. We'll take Rose and Dallas and Mary with us." His kiss was so ardent, KC couldn't catch her breath. Soon, very soon, they would be together permanently and wouldn't have to sneak kisses like this.

"Be patient, darling," she whispered.

"Until tonight," he returned with a wicked grin.

On tiptoe, she pressed another kiss to his lips, then slid from his arms apologetically. "Gotta go. See you tonight."

Pierce was halfway to his car when he spun around and came back to KC's. She was inside, and he bent over to peer through the open window. "I got another letter from the bank examiners this morning. They've completely absolved Kyle of any wrongdoing. They couldn't find anything incriminating when they were here, and they've closed the book on the case."

"Really?"

Pierce grinned wryly. "I guess Rudman was more clever than a hick sheriff, after all. I know he illegally borrowed bank money, but somehow he managed to put it all back and cover it up."

"Well, he's gone now," KC said soothingly. "And the people of Harmony are better off without him."

"That's for certain. I've got one small satisfaction to fall back on, sweetheart. Without Dallas's property, Kyle didn't have the clout to hold the state up for a ridiculous sum of money. He made a profit, all right, but it was relatively reasonable.''

He stuck his head in the window for a kiss. ''Do you realize that next week at this time we'll have been married four whole days?''

KC drove away smiling, envisioning a long, contented future with Pierce as her husband. Heartbreak Hotel? No, the saloon and motel could never be so cruelly categorized. The memory of the old rundown buildings would forever inhabit a special place in her thoughts. Dallas was happy and well cared for by a loving ''wife,'' and she, KC, had found Pierce. And it was all due to the Harmony Saloon and Motel!

*   *   *   *   *

SILHOUETTE® *Desire*™

COMING NEXT MONTH

#553 HEAT WAVE—Jennifer Greene
Kat Bryant had always been cool to neighbor Mick Larson, but when she was forced to confront him about neglecting his motherless daughters sparks flew and the neighborhood really heated up!

#554 PRIVATE PRACTICE—Leslie Davis Guccione
Another Branigan-O'Connor union? According to Matthew Branigan and Bridget O'Connor—never! But when Bridget caught a glimpse of Matt's bedside manner, her knees got weak and her temperature started rising....

#555 MATCHMAKER, MATCHMAKER—Donna Carlisle
Old-fashioned chauvinist Shane Bartlett needed a wife and it was Cassie's job to find him one—an impossible task! But the search was surprisingly easy. These two opposites were the perfect match.

#556 MONTANA MAN—Jessica Barkley
He thought she was a spoiled socialite. She thought he was a jerk. Could Montana man Brock Jacoby ever tame a frisky filly like Jamaica McKenzie?

#557 THE PASSIONATE ACCOUNTANT—Sally Goldenbaum
Accountant Jane Barnett didn't like things she couldn't control—things like relationships—but Max Harris was proof that an emotional investment could yield a high return in love and happiness!

#558 RULE BREAKER—Barbara Boswell
Women never said no to rebel blue blood Rand Marshall, March's *Man of the Month*—but Jamie Saraceni did. One rejection from her and this rule breaker's bachelor days were numbered.

AVAILABLE NOW:

At long last, the books you've been waiting for by one of America's top romance authors!

DIANA PALMER
DUETS

Ten years ago Diana Palmer published her very first romances. Powerful and dramatic, these gripping tales of love are everything you have come to expect from Diana Palmer.

In March, some of these titles will be available again in **DIANA PALMER DUETS**—a special three-book collection. Each book will have two wonderful stories plus an introduction by the author. You won't want to miss them!

 *Silhouette Books*

DP-1